TSUNAMI

Titles by the Author

The Opportunist

Tsunami

The DNA Murders - forthcoming

TSUNAMI

John Clark Wagner

Long Branch Cabin
Press LLC
11414 N. 109th Avenue, Sun City, AZ 85351

ISBN: 0996907009
ISBN 13: 9780996907002
Library of Congress Control Number: 2015920744
Long Branch Cabin Press, LLC, Sun City, AZ

For Jewell, Kimberly, Robin, and Devon

CHAPTER ONE

They had sailed up the coast from Rio to Fortaleza and from there had struck out across the Atlantic bound for Lisbon. The 45-foot yacht was well equipped for solo ocean sailing and Carlos was a skilled and experienced sailor. He had made the crossing from Lisbon to Rio alone earlier in the year. Now he returned home with Linda, his future bride whom he had met at Ipanema Beach and with whom he had spent a most enjoyable summer. They had crossed the equator and were back in the Northern Hemisphere and it was spring again.

After midnight, with the yacht on autopilot, they sailed a starboard tack close to the wind, with a steady wind and a favorable sea. They lounged lazily on a blanket on the foredeck, sipping wine, laughing, gossiping about their friends in Rio.

The man glanced at his wristwatch, rose from the blanket and took the helm. "We're close, now," he said, studying the horizon to starboard where the canopy of stars melded with the sea.

Suddenly the girl said, "Carlos, there ... I see a light."

He glanced at her then followed her gaze.

"There … there," she pointed.

"Ah, yes, there it is, La Palma," he said. "I can just make out the mountains against the stars. We are right on time. How is that for navigation, my Darling?"

"Very impressive; my compliments, Captain."

He adjusted the heading, trimmed the sails, and rejoined her on the blanket. They sailed another hour, keeping the feeble light, now joined by others, off the starboard quarter, noting their barely perceptible creep toward the stern of the boat as they bore on toward Lisbon.

Suddenly an enormous rolling wall of noise swept over them, a prolonged, terrible, rumbling thunder, which shook the air and trembled the very ocean. The girl leaped startled to her feet.

"What is that?" she cried out.

"I don't know," Carlos muttered, as he snatched up binoculars and swept the horizon toward the islands. "I don't see the shore lights … the islands … something is obstructing my view."

"What's happening Carlos, I'm frightened?" Linda stood close to him, clutching his arm.

Suddenly he cried out, "Oh, my god! It is a mountain of water! Coming at us! Quickly, get into your vest; we must abandon ship!"

Their life preservers lay at their feet on the blanket. When they were on deck, either they were wearing their vests or they were immediately available.

The mountain of water was visible now in the moonlight, nearly upon them, moving at awesome speed.

"Jump for it! Jump!"

Roy Hofstadter woke to the sound of labored breathing and snores in the big dark room in the flophouse on the lower east side of Manhattan.

"Noisy bastards," he muttered. He was about to protest loudly— *to hold someone accountable!* —when he became aware of a commotion on the street outside the window. Through the gap between the drapes, he could see that it was still dark outside yet, the noise sounded like mid-morning traffic. He tossed aside the blanket and set his feet down upon the linoleum. He was fully dressed in faded khaki shirt and trousers. His shoes and socks shared the cot with him, the laces tied together, the socks stuffed inside the shoes. A canvas backpack also shared his cot.

He glared about the room, seeing only shapes in the darkness. He considered the threat to the security of his possessions should he leave them unattended while he investigated the racket outside the window. Curiosity overcame his concern for his property, and he crept to the window, and pulled a drape gently to the side so as not to stir up the dust. He peered down on the street from his vantage point on the second floor.

"Too much traffic out there," he said. He continued watching, his brow furrowed, as moments later a low, undulating siren from somewhere far across the city added to the street noise, becoming shriller as it got up to speed.

"Uh oh, something's up, for sure," he mumbled, and raised the crud-encrusted window enough to lean out onto the sill. A man hurried along the sidewalk. Roy called out imperiously: "You, there. Yes, you; what's going on out there?"

The man glanced back over his shoulder and, without slowing his pace, yelled, "Big wave coming this way."

"What? What do you mean, "big wave?" he called after the man, who was walking away rapidly toward uptown."

"Hey, turn on your TV," the man responded. "It's on the news."

Roy pulled himself back inside and lowered the window.

"Television," he muttered, with a disapproving scowl. "degenerate propaganda garbage." (Roy did not watch television.)

He crawled back under the blanket. "Big wave coming, big wave coming," continued as a rhythmic chant in his mind.

He drew the blanket up to his chin and clutched his backpack to his chest, both for security (What the man said had alarmed him.), and to keep it from falling out of the cot onto the floor, *where the scavengers and thieves can have at it!*

Roy's attention span was unreliable, as was his memory. His mind tended to wander, seldom resting for very long on any one thing. His mood was volatile as well. Sometimes he was silent, gloomy, and introspective. Other time he was gay, bold, and even frivolous. Now, he was feeling feisty and defiant.

Once, he had been a well-respected sociologist, a tenured university professor, until he had experienced a breakdown, which required institutionalization; *or so they said.* He had disagreed, but had been overruled. "It's political," he said. "They want me out. I am tenured. I am not crazy! *You can't do this to me!*"

However, they could and did. They subjected him to various treatments including shock treatments of one kind or another. They kept him doped up on antidepressants and tranquilizers for months, and counseled with him until he could see the appropriate number of fingers. *Hah!* Finally, they had thrust him back out into society, weak and timorous, with his brain scrambled and with a tenuous hold on reality. *Whatever that is.* Consequently, his attention span came and went for no immediately discernible reason. In any event, another thought now leapt into his consciousness, supplanting the current one. The new thought had to do with something he had planned to do tomorrow.

"But wait, was it … tomorrow?" he asked himself in a low confidential voice, "or was it today?" He glanced at the clock over the doorway to the hallway to verify that it was well past midnight. "Yes, it was today, because I thought of it yesterday, and yesterday is now today. No, wait … tomorrow is now today. Oh, whatever. What did I plan to do today? It was something very important … to do with my research … yes, something to do with my research."

They institutionalized him for the better part of two years. *They would not even let me shave myself! The lousy bastards!* Then seven years ago, they decided that he was not a danger to himself or others, so they let him go. Since his discharged, he has been engaged in a protracted research projected. The research has to do with the observation of human absurdity, which addresses the question, "What will the fools do next?" In the beginning, because his research was so revealing of the shortcomings of his subjects (all of humanity), others were skeptical of it. *The Fools!* Therefore, he had elected to self-fund his project himself rather that to accept funding from institutions or the government—especially not the government. He drew disability payments from the government. *He-he. They have to pay to keep me alive.* In addition, he received occasional modest royalties from two sociology textbooks published twelve years ago.

After a while, Roy remembered the "big wave coming," still not having resolved the issue of what he planned to do tomorrow. He poked his head out from under the cover and unzipped the flap of his pack a few inches, stuck in his hand and brought out a small radio. He slipped the earpiece into his ear, pushed the power button, and turned the dial to a clear station where he heard an excited male voice. "… unconfirmed report … earthquake … ocean floor … northwest coast of Africa." He instantly perked up and focused, as best he could, sensing a possible absurdity in the making.

"… tsunami, moving at high speed toward the east coast of the Americas."

"The east coast of America," Roy snorted, "of course it's the east coast. It wouldn't be the west coast."

Even though certain of Roy's mental faculties were impaired intermittently (for whatever reason), his vast store of knowledge, acquired over a lifetime of study and observation, and his ability to reason, were intact and accessible much of the time.

"Nothing is certain," the excited voice continued. "We are seeking confirmation."

Roy clicked off the radio and mulled over what he remembered about tsunami caused by undersea earthquakes, recalling that such waves seldom were more than fifteen or twenty feet high, usually less. Still, the idea of a twenty-foot wave lapping up down at the Battery and splashing uptown, both thrilled and pleased him. "I really must observe this. I must record the reaction of the people." He pulled the blanket up to his chin again and glanced about furtively.

"Did you take your medicine?" A clear, authoritative voice reverberated inside his skull."

"What? Go away!" he shouted, and his shouting elicited stirrings from around the big, dark room. He lowered his voice to a whisper. "Leave me alone."

"I asked you a question. Did you take your medicine?"

"Yes, I took my medicine."

"No, you didn't."

"Well, I don't want it. It makes me—

"You didn't take it the day before yesterday either, did you?"

"Yes I did, I took it yesterday and the day before."

"Don't lie to me. You did not take it yesterday, nor the day before, either. When you lie to me, you lie to yourself. Get up and take your medicine, right now."

"No. I don't need it. I don't want it. I am better now. I am getting better, everyday—

"Uh, huh."

"Look! Look at the clock. It is tomorrow already. It's time to get up, Demon."

"Suit yourself, but I'm not leaving until you take your medicine. If you were trustworthy, I wouldn't have to bother with you."

"Roy snarled. "I don't have to take that from you!"

Silence.

With a sigh of resignation Roy unzipped his pack, stuck in his hand, and brought out pill bottles." I need water," he grumbled.

"Well, go get it and be quick about it, and get those prescriptions refilled, you're almost out."

Clearly, Roy had mixed feelings about the powerful, mind-altering medicine he had been taking for years. He believed the medicine made him ill rather than cured him, that if he could only go without it for long enough he would be well again. He had never been able to go long enough to test his hypothesis.

With a sigh, he shuffled down the hall to the bathroom clutching the pill bottles in his hand muttering to himself. When he returned he got into bed without a word and popped the earpiece back into his ear. Dance music was playing on the station. He switched to another station. Two men were talking about sports. A third station was also playing music.

"What's going on here?" he snapped. "Don't these fools know there's a big wave coming?" He peered suspiciously around the room. "Is someone playing a joke on me? Is this a hoax, huh? Is that it? It's a hoax!" He cackled. "It's a joke! That's very funny."

A voice from across the room said, "Shut up over there, you crazy bastard. People are trying to sleep here."

Roy did not answer. He switched back to the first station and heard, "… caused by an undersea earthquake. State and local governments are sounding the alarm in the coastal areas urging people, as a precautionary measure, to vacate low-lying areas along the shore."

"I understand about tsunami," Roy said. "I know all about them."

His thoughts swung back to earlier times. His face clouded, remembering. A chill ran through his body. "Before everything went to hell!" he shouted angrily.

"You want to get hold of yourself Professor Hofstadter. This is what happens when you don't take your medicine."

"I thought you were gone. What do you want now? You said you would leave me alone if I took the pills."

"Actually that was not what I said. I said I would not leave *until* you took your medicine, not that I *would* leave if you did take it. You see the difference don't you, Roy; you do understand, don't you?"

"Yeah, yeah, I understand—a cheap trick; and don't patronize me. And don't call me Roy; I'm Professor Hofstadter to you."

"What's come over you, Professor? Do you want to go back to the way it was?"

Roy cowered, remembering. "No." he said, cringing.

"I thought not. I'll leave you alone now; try to get some more rest."

"Yeah, yeah," Roy grunted. "Goodbye and good riddance." He pouted for a while and then returned to his contemplations. "People don't even know what a tsunami is," he mumbled. "...know jive and jazz and boogie-woogie and rock and roll and hip-hop and soul and sports and drugs and sex and basketball," he cackled, loudly.

Several people in the other beds only mouthed low grumbling curses, as if in acknowledgement of the futility of real protest when Roy was experiencing one of his relapses. Others were aware of his, always futile, attempts to get off the medication.

Roy leaped up and returned to the window, and, on his knees, his elbows on the sill, watched the activity on the street. He thought about a twenty-foot ocean wave coming through The Narrows into the bay. "Won't be much left of it by the time it reaches the Battery," he said, "a little splashing, maybe some flooded basements here and there."

"Hey, you nut case," the same angry voice shouted, "you better shut up. I'm asking you nice, now, and then I'm coming over there and smash your face in."

"You shut up, yourself!" Roy shouted back.

A loud curse and abrupt movements, like rusty bedsprings flexing under unaccustomed duress, and bare feet slapping the linoleum, spurred Roy to action. He grabbed up his shoes and backpack and scurried across the room, out the door, and down the hall, and outside to the sidewalk. He sat on the stoop, looked around to make sure that his would-be assailant had given up the chase. Then he took stock of the street, confirming that there were more vehicles and walkers than usual. He donned his socks and shoes, checked over his backpack, slung it on his back, connected the strap across his chest, and took off walking uptown, his thoughts on the Empire State Building. "Get me a good seat to watch the show," he said.

"If I were you, I would try the upper observation deck." The voice said.

"Oh?"

"Yes. It's two hundred feet higher than the lower one, with a much better view."

"I know that. I've been there before."

"Sure you have, several times, in fact. You always think about jumping, too, don't you, Roy?"

"I think about a lot of things. You don't know everything about me."

"No?"

"No."

"I know plenty."

"Oh yeah? I have nothing to hide. You got something to say, say it."

"Why do you always think about jumping?"

"How long are you going to hound me, Demon, anyway?"

"That's up to you."

"Up to me? Then what if I sent you packing?" Roy snapped."

"If you think you can handle it on your own just say the word, pal, and I'm out of here, permanently."

"Hey, don't get so huffy."

People scurried by Roy in both directions, some no doubt noticing that, although alone, he seemed to be engaged in a heated conversation with someone. They paid him no mind; they were accustomed to seeing, gruff, disheveled old men talking to themselves. Most of them were harmless. A man hurrying toward him jostled him in passing. Roy lost his balance and would have fallen on his face in the gutter had he not rather deftly stepped into the street and done a little twisting dance to regain his balance.

"Bastard!" Roy shouted. The man glanced back and gave him the finger.

Roy made a ceremony of righting himself and of adjusting his pack, while glancing about indignantly. Still, nobody paid any attention to him. He mounted the curb and proceeded on his way, dipping and dodging to avoid further collisions.

Two blocks from the Empire State Building, he came upon an all-night diner, a small, narrow place behind a plate-glass window, with barely enough room inside for a long counter and stools. It seemed to him that it was business as usual inside since there were four customers sitting at the counter casually munching.

"Maybe they haven't heard about the 'big wave coming,'" he said. He looked around the street. There was no evidence of panic or even concern. "Hmm, well then, I have time for breakfast." he observed, and went inside the diner and took a stool near the door, depositing his pack on the floor between his feet to keep tactile guard over it. The waiter was a plump young woman wearing a hairnet over brown, mousy hair. She moved back and forth behind the counter attending to her customers. When she finished refilling coffee cups she stayed at the other end of the counter leaning against it, chatting with the short-order cook, smiling and giggling. He grinned back at her while he scraped the greasy grill with his spatula.

"Hey." Roy shouted at her, "how about a little service over here."

She ambled over, her eyes crawling over his wrinkled army surplus kakis, which he obviously slept in and over his stubble of facial hair, and his hair in need of a trim, and jutting out from under a nondescript baseball cap in all directions.

"Kin I hep you?" she said, her voice nasal and unsympathetic.

Roy had a barely controllable urge to give her a good tongue-lashing for her impertinent manner. He could easily say something to her that would put her in her place, inflict emotional pain. *Ah, but what is the point, she is too vulnerable.*

"I'll have two eggs over easy, madam, bacon, toast, orange juice, and black coffee." He spoke rapidly, his tone imperious. "And hurry it up please; I have to get up to the observation deck of the Empire State Building."

She scribbled on her pad. "That'll be five-fifty."

It took Roy an instant to realize that she was asking for payment in advance. "I'll pay when I finish eating," he said gruffly.

"You'll pay *now*."

"What? I don't pay in advance, lady."

"Suit yourself." She walked away.

"Wait!"

She turned. "I need to see your money, pops," she said.

"Pops? I'm not your daddy; don't call me pops." *Hmm, maybe she isn't so vulnerable, after all.*

She glared at him. "Pardon me, sir, but we don't serve no bums in here, 'less we see their cash up front. No charity cases, see? This is a 'cash and a carry' business, understand, pops?"

Roy scowled at her. "Bums? Charity cases? I'll have you know, madam, that I am Professor Royal Menken Hofstadter, Doctor of Philosophy, late of the University of Illinois."

"Say, Roy, don't pay any attention to her," the voice in his head said. "She's only doing her job. Just show her your money, if you want your breakfast, that is; or better still, go ahead and pay for it."

"I'll be damned if I will!"

"Easy, now, easy, remember you're a professional man."

"Yes, but she … she …"

"I know, Roy, I know … nevertheless, they obviously get a lot of deadbeats in here."

The waiteress's eyes widened. "Who you talkin' to, mister?"

"It's come to this has it? That I, Professor Royal Hofstadter, Doctor of Sociology, am begging for my breakfast in this…this—

"Greasy spoon? Yes, it is sad, Professor Hofstadter. However, have you checked yourself out in the mirror lately? I have to agree with the young woman, you do look rather like a bum. Perhaps you need to have your medication adjusted again, the dosage strengthened. Of course, that won't do any good if you don't take it."

Roy ignored the voice, surveyed the other customers, who were looking on in amusement. "Did you require these people to pay in advance, madam?" he asked her, a little less imperious than before. She scowled at him impatiently and turned to the grinning grill-man, who had stopped scraping the grill, and held his spatula suspended at port arms.

"Get Luigi out here," she said to him.

Almost immediately, a burly Luigi emerged from a door beside the grill, wiping his hands on his apron. "Wat-sah-da problem?"

"This crazy bum, is sittin' here talking' to hisself, and he ain't got no money, 'parently, and he wants breakfast."

"Hey, I got money!" Roy shouted.

"You. Out." Luigi said, pointing first at Roy then at the door. "No bums allowed."

"Wait a minute!" Roy fumbled in his pockets, came out with a bill, and waved it in front of the woman's face. "See? I have money."

"Beat it fellow, we don'a want your money," Luigi said.

Furious, Roy grabbed up his pack and headed for the door while Luigi and the woman smirked at him.

"By the way," Roy said, turning back, his hand resting on the door opener, "do you cretins know a tsunami is coming this way? If I were you, I would be thinking about higher ground—the second floor, perhaps, or the third."

Luigi looked at the waitress, who shrugged.

"A what?" Luigi asked.

"A tsunami, a big wave, you moron."

"Luigi's never closes; twelve years, I never locka the doors. Now, get out, you bum, ana you don't come back no more."

Roy angrily slammed out the door, looked around for something hard, like a brick, to throw through the window, but finding nothing handy he hurried off toward the Empire State Building.

The lobby of the Empire State Building was like recess at the schoolyard, with the kiddies all hurrying out to play, all jolly, and gay. Night workers from the offices, maintenance and cleaning people, happy to leave early, not worried, not afraid, glad to be going home. Tsunami? What is that? What, me worry?

The up elevators stood empty, waiting. Roy took one. When he got to the observation deck a few people were there ahead of him. He ambled around checking them out. "Tourists," he said, contemptuously. "Expecting a show, are we?"

The sky was low, gray, and hazy, delaying the dawn; the lights of the city reflected off the underside of the haze. He dug into a pocket, and withdrew an old wristwatch without a band. The gold plating was peeling away at the edges from age and hard use. The corrosion of the underlying copper alloy produced a brilliant, interesting shade of green. He read 5:32 a.m. He leaned into the protective barrier for a glimpse of the street below, but could distinguish nothing except the lights of the slow moving traffic. He considered jumping again as he always did, but discarded the idea.

He took his radio out of his pack and plugged in the earpiece. He held the little radio fondly in front of his eyes as he adjusted the dials. As battered as the old watch, the radio was a birthday gift from his wife from long ago. He found a place against the wall and sat down on the floor. "Where are you, demon?" he whispered, suddenly apprehensive, without knowing why. There was no answer. He heard on the radio: "...civil defense authorities have dispatched a supersonic military reconnaissance jet from Myrtle Beach Air Force Base in South Carolina. The plane is equipped with a sensitive radar altimeter. The mission is to intercept the wave in mid-ocean, measure its height, and estimate its time of arrival here on the coast. We await the pilot's report. Meanwhile, Mr. Cleaves, perhaps you can tell us what we should expect to hear from the pilot."

"Yes, of course, Mike. As you know, tsunamis resulting from undersea earthquakes are seldom higher than ten to twenty feet. Nevertheless, the tsunami that struck Indonesia a few decades ago, which was less than twenty feet in height, did enormous damage, killed over a hundred thousand people—

"Yes, that was because of the low elevation of the densely populated land along the coasts."

Roy clicked off the radio. He was the only person sitting; the others loomed over him. Their number had increased since his arrival. They were of all ages and ethnicities, laughing, chattering, pointing, and gesticulating, as they stepped over and around him.

Roy pretended to ignore them. "I don't need your approval," he snapped, at nobody in particular.

People in a nearby cluster stopped talking and turned their gazes downward into his rheumy eyes. "Are you all right, old chap?" one asked.

Roy looked away, and busied himself fiddling with the dials on his radio, as if he were tuning it, and had not heard what the party had said to him. *Old chap!* He knew what they were up to. He sat back against the wall, and turned the radio on again. The radio announcer's voice was even more excited that before. "Ladies and gentlemen, we have the pilot of the reconnaissance aircraft on hookup. Let's listen."

The tinny voice of the pilot came on: "The wave is presently four hundred and eighty nautical miles from the coast. As expected, it is less than twenty feet in height, and is moving about five-hundred miles an hour. I'll have to hurry to beat it back to the coast." He laughed at his own wit.

"Cleaver fellow," said the announcer. He played the voice back several times. "The wave will no doubt do some damage to the beaches and low-lying coastal areas from Florida to Maine, but Homeland Security has *finally* gotten the word out to those areas, and, we are told, now, that horns and sirens are blaring in every little town and village all along the coast. So what do you think, Mr. Cleaves?"

"Well, the good news is that there will be hardly any serious damage to the major population centers, only a little mess and inconvenience, perhaps."

"That *is* good news," the announcer agreed, "but its little consolation for the poor souls in those very low-lying regions, and those who don't get the word—there's got to be some out there."

"Yes, well, there will most likely be some incidental loss of life, and property damage. That's always the case."

"Yeah," Roy mumbled, "the lowlanders always get it in the neck, always in the path of every disaster."

He switched through the stations. The discussions were pretty much the same, now. Every announcer seemed to have a visiting expert, and he heard the tinny voice of the pilot until he was sick of it. One announcer identified the pilot by name, rank, and military unit, and with much ado, thanked him for his service.

"Phony bastards," Roy said. His medication was kicking in and curbing his belligerence to some extent. However, he was becoming somewhat excited anyway; even if the height of the tsunami was disappointing, he still had work to do, observations to record. After all, that was what he did; he was a sociologist, a man of science; he was, Royal Menken Hofstadter, Ph. D., and he was engaged in important research.

He pulled a small, worn, spiral-bound notebook, with a red cover, from the breast pocket of his khaki shirt, slipped a yellow number two pencil stub from the wire spiral, flipped open the notebook to the place marked by a paper clip, and began scribbling, his lips working to the cadence of his scribbling. People took notice of him once again, sitting alone on the floor, writing in a little notebook and talking to himself. Roy sneered at them, "Sports fans!" He yelled, eliciting a few smiles and chuckles.

Some of the people milling around him had radios of their own pressed against their ears, or they had tiny earpieces, like his, in their ears. They chatted excitedly with each other, about the news from the pilot, and, Roy imagined, congratulated themselves that while the tsunami might kill a few unfortunate lowlanders, and destroy their possessions, it would not discommode the sports fans in the slightest, but would provide them briefly with entertainment. *After all, those lowlanders live in the lowlands by choice.* "They are volunteers!" He screeched aloud, "Just like our modern army."

Roy focused his attention as well as he could, on the people who shared the observation deck with him, studying their behavior, their appearances, their clothing, and their gestures. Something about them had caught his trained eye. It was something beyond the 'sports fan' syndrome, the anticipation, the excitement, the gaiety. His eyes brightened. Ah, he thought, I have it. It is hunger, perverse hunger—and fear, too. "Why, it's the Roman Coliseum!" he shouted gleefully. "Bring on the lions! Bring on the Christians!"

"You're afraid." The voice interrupted his glee. "You don't fool anyone with your false bravado and clamoring."

"Me Afraid? No, they are afraid, not me. Why should I be afraid?"

"Why, indeed. You considered jumping again, didn't you? Why didn't you jump?"

"Why?"

"Yes, why?"

"Because … I want to see what happens … I want to watch the show."

"What show, a tiny little wave lapping at the shore? Is that the extent of it? Some show."

"Well, you just answered your own question. Why would I be afraid of that?"

"It was what the pilot said, Professor, that's what you are afraid of."

Roy felt a stab of discomfort. "What did the pilot say?"

"He said 480 miles out to sea, and that's well beyond the continental shelf, huh, Professor? And he said five-hundred miles per hour, and he said twenty feet high."

Roy furrowed his brow in thought, with a growing sense of foreboding. He played the pilot's tinny announcement over in his mind. "It's on the tip of my tongue. It's … it's … it's something awful."

"You know the answer, just say it."

Roy began speaking, slowly and quietly at first: "The Japanese word, tsunami, means, harbor wave, because the typical wave is barely noticeable on the surface until it encounters the upslope and nears the shore. The massive 'body' of a tsunami is below the surface. When it encounters the upslope of the continental shelf, the friction of the ocean bottom slows it down, while the top surges forward and upward. The fact that this particular wave measured twenty feet high in mid oceans means—

"oh my Lord!" he shouted at the top of his voice while leaping to his feet. "We're all doomed! The city is Doomed! We're all going to die!"

The people near him drew back, startled.

"What's the bum yelling about?"

"Who knows?"

"Who cares?"

"He talks to himself."

"He's nuts."

"Damn winos, can't get away from 'em. They are everywhere. Get a job, fella."

"He's on drugs."

An old woman drew away from him, clutching her bosom, as if Roy were about to have his way with her. "He's obviously mentally ill," she shrieked."

"No, no." Roy said, making his voice as calm as he could manage. "We've got to get away from here. There's not a moment to lose." He tugged at a man's coat sleeve. "You don't understand the wave will be huge! Huge!"

"He's delusional. Get away from me."

The man pulled Roy's hand from his coat sleeve and gave him a slight shove. Roy tripped over his own feet and fell to the deck again, banging his head slightly against the wall, just enough to daze him. He lay there, gasping, quivering with fear, expecting an angry foot to his groin, or to his head. It did not come; the "sports fans," had already turned away.

"You didn't have to kill the old boy."

"Oh, he's all right. I didn't hurt him."

"Roy struggled to get hold of his emotions, ashamed of having lost his composure, but nevertheless gripped with terror, the strongest emotion he had felt in years. Fear of what was coming puffed away, like an unexpected breeze, much of the haze in which he spent his days.

Dawn was breaking; a dim diffused light illuminated the cloud layer to the east and visibility increased quickly. He scooted up into a sitting position against the wall, clutched his pack to his chest, uncertain as to what to do. Suddenly he no longer had any difficulty remaining focused on the moment; suddenly a few precious moments may very well be all that he had left.

A man with a radio to his ear yelled, "Listen to this, everybody!" He increased the volume so everyone could hear. The voice on the radio blared, "...a scientist with the Swiss Academy.

I repeat: Cambria Diego is a volcano on the island of La Palma in the Spanish Canary Islands off the northwest coast of Africa. Sometime last night, the western flank of the island of La Palma slid into the Atlantic Ocean. The land mass that slid into the ocean was thirty kilometers long, and estimated to weigh somewhere between one-half and one trillion tons. It created a wave, a mega-tsunami, 800 meters high, and with a wavelength of thirty to forty kilometers. It is traveling at 720 km per hour, and has caused terrible destruction to the islands in its path. It will strike the coast of the Americas within the hour. The tsunami, when it strikes the coastline of America, could be hundreds of feet high!"

A woman screamed. She stood at the rail looking south toward the bay. All heads turned toward her. "The bay is draining away!" She screamed. "The Ocean is disappearing!"

Everyone ran to the rail, crowding and pushing. It was true, the ocean was receding, the bay was dropping, tumultuous and swirling, with massive eddies and whirlpools.

"Eeeiiii!" a woman shrieked. "It's the end of the world! Oh, Jesus, save me!"

As if of one mind, the people rushed headlong toward the elevators, pushing and screaming. Some fell, and others trampled over them, unmindful of their cries.

"Fools!" Roy shouted after them, wild-eyed, laughing hysterically, "Wildebeests."

Soon he was alone on the observation deck, trembling with morbid anticipation and dread, still unsure of what to do. The fear-filled voice of the announcer rang in his ears, "… hundreds of feet high! …will be upon us at any moment!"

Even as he quaked with fear, Roy sensed that he was feeding on the excitement—*it was 1937, Orson Wells, The War of the World!*

Overhead, the sky magically filling with helicopters. He sprang to his feet and ran to the railing to watch them. They landed atop the high buildings, gorged themselves with people, and lifted up and away. The activity became desperate and frenzied as the minutes clicked by. Two helicopters collided in a fiery ball, raining burning bodies, fuel, and hot metal down upon the people below; another helicopter overloaded and unable to get airborne, tumbled over the edge of a building, its rotors hacking away chunks of concrete and glass as it slid down the side of the building. Bedlam erupted everywhere with the screams of engines, the blare of horns, and sirens, shrill and wailing.

"Oh, my god, it *is* the end of the world!" Roy screamed. His belligerence and animosity burned away then, as he witnessed the suffering and the dying, as he contemplated the scale of the destruction. Those who had shared the observation deck with him had run in panic, as if there were sanctuary below, but he knew that there was none.

He paced back and forth, sweat running down his face. "There can't be much time left," he snarled through clinched teeth. "How high am I? Will I be above it? The announcer had said, 'eight hundred feet'...no, no...he said meters! Did he say meters? Jesus, that's ..." Roy tried to do the math in his head. "That can't be right; that ridiculous!" he screamed.

Emotionally exhausted, Roy slumped against the wall again, clutched his pack to his chest and squeezed his eyes together to shut out the horror. His bitterness and animosity returned and overshadowed his moment of humanity, as the thought of the helicopters rescuing the "big shots" triggered a surge of intense hatred. His mind raged with indignation ... with injustice .... "Where's my helicopter?" he screamed. "Why don't I have a helicopter?"

At that moment, he realized that he was no different from the rest. He wanted to live, too, at any cost. That was why he didn't jump. He snatched up his pack from the deck and ran wildly toward the stairs.

CHAPTER TWO

Trans Global flight 373, in route from Tehran to New York City, was minutes out of New York, and letting down to traffic pattern altitude. On board, in the first class section, Joe Conway, Director of Intergovernmental Affairs for the Middle East for the United States National Security Agency, heard the ding, and glanced up to see the "fasten seatbelt" sign. He handed his glass to a passing attendant and fastened his seat belt. He was tired, and still had a long way to go to get to his Georgetown townhouse outside of Washington, D.C. He reflected wearily on his trip to Iran, a weeklong conference on Middle East stability. Many of the same old animosities still plagued the region of the Middle East. The giant Boeing 747 broke through a thin overcast. In the distance and to the right was the shoreline of Long Island, and beyond that, the skyline of New York City.

He peered sleepily out the window as the airliner began a long straight-in approach to Kennedy International Airport. The landing gear came down with a clunk, and as it did, Conway experienced a bizarre and frightening sensation. It was as if the plane were falling toward the ocean, yet his body experienced none of the tactile sensations one might expect from so abrupt a change in flight attitude. Nevertheless, out the window, the sea rushed up under the belly of the airplane, which his senses told him was impossible.

Someone screamed, the plane surged forward and began climbing.

"What's going on?" he asked, looked around the cabin dumbfounded. People were straining to look out the windows. The captain's voice came over the speakers filled with alarm and emotion. "Ladies and gentlemen you're not going to believe this. A wave, a giant ocean wave, has swept over Kennedy Airport. It is completely underwater! And New York City … holy shit, will you look at that!"

While Roy was taking stairs three at a time, and Conway was in an airliner over New York in an advanced state of shock, far to the west in Indiana, U. S. Assistant Secretary of Agriculture, Charles McGruder and his wife Mildred were asleep in the upstairs bedroom of his parent's farmhouse outside of Martinsville. They were in the bedroom that had first been his nursery and then his room thereafter until he left home in order to attend Indiana University.

Charles, Mildred, and their two children were home to discuss important family matters with his parents. Neither McGruder nor Mildred enjoyed the rat race in Washington, so he was seriously considering resigning his position in the Winston administration in order to return home and take over the management of the family's eighteen-hundred-acre farm. "Dad wants to retire," he told Mildred, "and I like the idea of managing the farm." Mildred liked the idea too, so they were home to work out the details.

Around four-thirty in the morning, local time, Charles' father, Walter McGruder, shook him awake. "Charles, wake up," he whispered, something terrible has happened."

They left Mildred still sleeping, and joined his mother, Martha, in the den. She was sitting on the arm of the couch, staring at the television, the volume low. She handed him a cup of coffee as he entered. "It's awful, Charley," she said, "just awful."

⇥ ⇤

Roy was lucky he had not broken his neck, running at full gallop down the stairs. He made it down to the thirty-seventh floor before the twenty-four-mile-long slug of ocean smashed into Manhattan, and his building and all the others shuttered, swayed, vibrated, and played dominoes. Roy bounced off the walls of the stairwell and then went soaring over the handrail toward certain death, but his flailing arms caught the top rung of the handrail and held on until he could wrap a leg around a railing post. He dropped his backpack in the process and it tumbled into the void. The building vibrated, shuttered, and swayed, with grinds and shrieks. He pulled himself back to the landing, where he lay flat, still holding on to the railing post, as the building continued its terrible gyrations, and the noise outside was defining and indescribable.

"Where are you, Demon?" he screamed. There was no answer.

"God!" he said, his voice shaking uncontrollably, I realize I have been derelict in the religion department for the last several decades—actually, since I was a child in parochial school. His chattering teeth and his shaking made it difficult to talk and he decided to *think* his communication with God, since God could read his thoughts, anyway: *I am kind of in a bind here, God, and, uh, you, uh...you know that I am not a believer, don't you...but I'm sincere. You can see that. You have to respect that ... right? There is no use of me trying to kid anybody, but, hey, the nuns and the priests always told me to pretend that I had faith, and faith would be granted unto me. So I am pretending—*

His thoughts trailed off, hollow and pathetic inside his skull. He wanted to say to himself, "come on, Roy, be a man, take your medicine," but he was too afraid. It was just as well, because nobody answered, anyway, not the voice, not God, not anybody.

Suddenly the whole building snapped with a deafening sound, as if something massive had slammed into it, and it swung violently in an arch, like a released bent sapling. The movement was so abrupt and violent that it threw Roy onto the next landing below, knocking him unconscious.

Quiet and stillness had returned when he revived; there was only the sound of water, like steady rain, draining through the innards of the building and splashing when it struck somewhere below. Roy hurt everywhere but more so in his right hip, which seemed to be out of joint. He tried to stand but went over sideways from the pain. He became aware that the floor was no longer level and that the building was no longer plumb. He dragged himself across the concrete floor of the stairwell to the fire door, wrestled it open, and then crawled through, encountering an open bay of office cubicles whose contents were broken and busted and lay helter-skelter all over the floor: furniture, computers, papers, and all manner of things. To crawl through it dragging his bum hip was an agonizing feat. He made it to a window, peered out and immediately drew back in horror. He curled up in the fetal position on the floor amid the trash, and passed out again.

Day two of his ordeal, Roy could hardly move. He spent the morning on the floor convinced he was dying and quite reconciled to it, if it would only be quick. Horrible visions flashed endlessly through his mind, terrifying him. To add to his misery, he was suffering withdrawal pains from the powerful medications he had been on for over seven years. In the past four or five days, he had only had the one daily dose of his medication back at the shelter.

The next day, in the throes of withdrawal, he experienced delirium, with periods of intense agitation, confusion, hallucinations, and profuse sweating. Semi-conscious, he thrashed about wildly amid the wreckage of the building contents. At times he experienced uncontrollable trembling, and loss of awareness of his surroundings. In the process of all this thrashing about he apparently popped his dislocated hip back into place. The pain, though initially intense, gradually melded with his otherwise miserable state.

When he finally became rational enough he realized that he was parched with thirst and ravenously hungry. Once again he tried to stand but could not. He crawled, laboriously and carefully, through the rubble searching for a source of water. He came upon a break room with the floor littered with food and drink from busted vending machines laying all about. He two bottles of water and ate a can of beef stew and a can of pork and beans, and two bags of chips.

The following day, with very little rest during the night, the effects of withdrawal from his powerful medications were much worse, and his hold on reality was tenuous.

⊶✠⊷

The low elevations of the coastal lands around Chesapeake Bay and the Potomac River Estuary conspired with the unheard of magnitude of the tsunami to wreak a terrible toll on the cities, towns, and villages, including the nation's capital, Washington. Many people died in their sleep, many over their first cup of coffee, or driving early to work.

Within minutes of the initial wave, the traffic copter of TV station WQAF, which was already airborne in anticipation of another heavy traffic day on the interstates and bypasses, was approaching downtown DC, or more accurately, where downtown DC was minutes before. In normal times the strict airspace prohibitions would not have permitted its presence there without the risk of encountering fighter interceptors. Today all the rules vanished along with much of the city and the people. The helicopter pilot and the camera operator achieved a measure of fame that morning as networks around the world picked up the feed of their on-the-spot coverage of the disaster; they would each later receive a prize for TV journalism and video photography.

Clarence White, Associate Justice of the Supreme Court, lived outside of Washington with sufficient distance and elevation to be out of the path of the flood. An early riser, he awoke peacefully unaware of the drama unfolding scant miles away. He got the coffee maker going and while he waited, he flicked on the little TV on the kitchen counter to catch the news and traffic information in anticipation of his drive to the court. The first thing he saw was chaos in the TV newsroom itself, complete bedlam. It took him a few startled moments to get his bearing and glean what was happening. Reports coming in from the helicopter played continually with dramatic live footage. Everyone in the station seemed to be talking at the same time, yelling, cutting in on each other, breathless, frantic, and hysterical. Justice White, mesmerized, could only stare at the screen in shock and amazement.

A reporter wailed: "The capitol is gone! Washington, D.C., is in ruins!"

"Justice White could only exclaim, "Oh my God!"

It was then that sirens began sounding, more than one, muffled and far away.

His wife of fifty years, Helen, ran down the stairs. "What's all the racket, Clarence?"

"Unbelievable Helen, terrible. Take a deep breath and prepare yourself before you look at the television."

Justice White and Helen continued watching for almost an hour, during which time White attempted several times to make telephones calls to government officials, but each time the line was either dead, or busy, or out of order. The same was true of his cell phone. As the situation continued to develop he concluded that most everybody in the city proper and surrounding lowlands was probably dead, drowned, crushed and swept away.

The TV station reported that military personnel from Fort Meade had flown by helicopters to what was left of the White House, and were searching for survivors. They found none. They were attempting to gain access to the elaborate underground facilities beneath the White House, but so far had not succeeded. The fear was that no timely warning was received by the occupants, and that the underground facilities went unused. The fate of the Vice President and his family and staff at their residence on the grounds of the National Observatory was not yet known."

"Helen," Justice White said, "Do you realize that the country may be leaderless, that the President, the vice President…all of them may be dead? Everybody was here; the congress was in session … If so, the United States is vulnerable to enemy attack at this very moment. Moreover, we are vulnerable to public panic, which could be just as bad. Why have there been no announcements over the Emergency Broadcast System? Has that been knocked out too?" He switched through the television stations. Most of them were off the air. He found none with the Emergency Broadcast going, just station and network news coverage from outlying stations.

"Where is my radio, Helen, the little red one with the hand crank? It has an emergency broadcast band."

"Calm down, Clarence, or you'll have another heart attack. Try to relax. I'll make you some breakfast."

"I couldn't eat a bite now, Dear, and there's no time, anyway. I have to get dressed and get down to that television station."

He tried the telephones again before leaving; they were still inoperative. He drove the few miles to the television station through heavy traffic. The parking garage and lot at the TV station were packed. He found a space on the street a block away, and hurried back to the station, moving fast for a man of 75, with his white hair bouncing and blowing in a slight breeze.

People milled about outside the building in animated conversation, but inside in the lobby, even though crowded, things were now more orderly and subdued, as if the people waited for some solemn pronouncement that they dreaded to receive. White presented his Supreme Court identification to the woman at the desk. "I urgently need to speak to the Station Manager," he said. "It's very important."

The woman examined his identification. "One moment, sir." she said. She punched buttons on the intercom and spoke into it. "Mr. Trevor will be right here, sir."

Moments later, Mr. Trevor burst through double swinging doors, beside which stood a uniformed, armed security guard. Trevor was a beefy man of perhaps forty, in shirtsleeves, his tie was open and askance. He charged over to the receptionist. She nodded in White's direction. The man turned and approached Justice White, and said, "Yes sir, what can I do for you?"

"May I speak with you in private, Mr. Trevor?"

"Come with me," Trevor said, without hesitation. He led the way through the swinging doors down the hall and into a vacant office. He offered White a chair, and sat opposite him, waiting expectantly for him to speak.

"It appears that the nation's capital has been destroyed. I have tried all morning but have been unable to reach any officials of the government. The fate of our leaders is unknown. There is a good possibility that they are all dead. If so, the country is extraordinarily vulnerable just now."

"I understand, sir, go on."

It is essential that we do our best to maintain government continuity during this tragedy, or at least the appearance of it, so as not to tempt our potential enemies, as well as to reassure our own citizens that someone is in charge. I want to try to contact government officials over your television station and, if successful, meet up with them somewhere nearby. Will you help me?"

"Yes, of course I will help you, it is an honor to do so. You can make your announcements from a studio in the back. The government officials can call into the station. I will dedicate telephone lines. We can set it up quickly. Just say the word."

"Excellent! Let's do it then, right now."

"Come with me."

They hurried down the hall to a darkened studio. Trevor switched on the lights. "You sit there at the desk," he said, "while I round up some people to get this thing on the road". He flipped out his cell phone, and made three calls in quick succession. Almost immediately, people began pouring into the room, turning on equipment, pushing the caster-mounted cameras about. Trevor called from across the room. "Whenever you're ready Justice White, do you want to make a practice run?"

"No, let's go for it."

The cameras and the soundman got into position, the lighting was adjusted, a man with a clipboard said, "I'll count down from five." The man began to count. At the count of one, he dropped his hand and pointed his finger at White:

"Good morning, fellow citizens of the United States, I am Clarence White, Associate Justice of the United States Supreme

Court. By now, you probably know that this morning our nation experiencing an extraordinary destructive act of nature. A giant tsunami wave has wreaked destruction upon the eastern coastal region of our nation, with great loss of life and destruction of property. The nation's capital, Washington, D. C, and environs, have not escaped this destruction.

"We do not know the fate of all of our nation's leaders at this moment, but it is imperative for those of us in government who survived to come together quickly to maintain the continuity of government during this emergency. I take it upon myself to speak on behalf of the Government of the United States, and the Office of the President. I ask all government officials within the sound of my voice, especially those who live and work in or near Washington, D. C., to call this television studio and report your name, position, agency, and your current location and telephone number."

A young woman ran up close to the desk out of camera range holding up a hastily constructed cue card to Justice White displaying the telephone number to call.

White read the number three times, and closed by saying, "May God preserve and protect the United States of America. Good luck to us all."

"Judge White, you can stay right where you are," Trevor said. "You can have the use of this studio all day if you need it, or longer. I will set up more phones and get some people in here to answer them. Is there anything else your need?"

"Coffee and doughnuts would be nice, if you can swing it, sir."

"Coming right up."

The station repeated the message at fifteen-minute intervals for the next hour and hourly thereafter. The response was brisk, and kept White and his helpers hustling. Calls came in not just from the immediate area, but also from around the nation and the world. Most of the callers, however, were lower level workers or middle managers, with no cabinet level officials or top policy makers, people who could take over and run the government. The highest-ranking respondents in the area were Dillard Beaumont, Senator from New Mexico, Thomas Langford, senator from South Dakota, and General Theodore Bradford, Chairman of the Joint Chiefs of Staff, who was returning by car from a fishing trip when the wave struck. He saw the announcement on TV when he stopped for gasoline.

White explained to the three men what he was doing, and asked them to come to the station immediately. They all agreed to do so, arriving within the hour. It was still only eight-thirty in the morning. The four men gathered around a table, while the phones continued to ring.

"Gentlemen," Justice White began, "it is hard to believe that we four very well may be the only top tier federal government officials left in the D. C. area. Perhaps others will show up later. Nevertheless, we have an existential crisis on our hands, and we cannot wait. We do not know the fate of the President, or Vice-President, nor the cabinet members. The search for survivors continues. If there are others out there who outrank us, God bless them and let them come forward, let them step up and assume command. Do you follow me?"

"The other three men nodded."

"Then, I suggest that we form a committee and assume command of the Government of the United States on an emergency basis, and announce the same over this television station—inform the people and the world what we are doing. To do otherwise would be to place the survival of our nation in jeopardy. I think that we should immediately declare martial law in the affected areas, and that you, General, as the Chairman of the Joint Chiefs, should take over direct operational command of the Armed Forces of the United States, subject to the authority of this committee as a whole, and do what needs to be done out there. You know what that is better than we do."

White paused, and looked at the faces of the three men.

"Do you think we are possibly jumping the gun?" Senator Beaumont said.

"Maybe so," White said, but I'm willing to take that chance."

"Then, so am I."

The others nodded agreement.

General Bradford spoke: "Justice White, you are to be commended for your initiative and foresight. I am all with you. However, in order to maintain civilian control over the military, I suggest the three of you constitute a committee, a tribunal, if you will, and that I take my orders as commander of the military directly from you. Then, I will get at my duties immediately, and dispatch troops to maintain order, and engineering units to clear roads and look for survivors. I suggest that your first priority is to verify the fate of the president, if at all possible, and if he is dead, as we believe he is, find and install his successor, without delay."

"I agree," said Langford, and I nominate Justice White to be the Chairman of the Committee. I propose that we decide things by majority vote. What say you?"

They nodded agreement.

"Then," Langford continued, "Hearing no objection, I will assume the duties of Recording Secretary.

The three civilians thus designated themselves a tribunal to head the government until the restoration of appropriate civil authority. Their first action, by unanimous vote, was to designate General Bradford Commander of all military forces, and to direct him to place all defensive and strategic military bases and units on red alert, and to prepare for anything, up to and including nuclear retaliation.

Justice White announced their actions over the air, being as truthful and complete as possible, while being circumspect with respect to the fate of the President and Vice-President until more certain information became available. He announced Martial

Law in the impacted areas, as the general had recommended, and authorized him to assume direct command of all troops, to dispatch engineering units with heavy equipment to the impacted areas to clear roads and search for survivors. By noon of the first day, a makeshift rump government was in place and things were moving.

"General Bradford," Justice White asked, "can you find us a place to set up temporary shop, a military base, perhaps? Unfortunately, our costal facilities were wiped out the same as the cities; we'll need to move to a base inland, one large enough to provide good logistical support. I am thinking perhaps, Wright-Patterson Air Force Base. What do you think General?

"My first impression is that Wright-Pat would be well suited for the new "Pentagon," but for the government offices, I don't know. Let me think about it."

General Bradford set about establishing communications links with key military facilities, and ordered Federal troops to strategic locations all along the coastal areas adjacent to large centers of population to maintain order and lend assistance to civilian authorities. Word traveled quickly, and by nightfall, he had designated military bases from Maine to Florida as survivor processing centers, and military helicopters as well as civilian were searching for survivors. The Governors of each of the impacted states activated National Guard units and placed them under the command of General Bradford, if needed. Otherwise, they functioned under the command of the Governors, who used them to restore ground transportation corridors, and to develop alternate routes around and through the devastated areas. United States officials, on junkets or special assignments overseas, continued to call the designated telephone numbers.

On the morning of the second day, a gossamer Federal/State Command structures existed, tied in to the governors of the affected states, and to embassies and military bases worldwide. The

Committee was moving at incredible speed, improvising, shooting from the hip, and, even though all of this was taking place without constitutional authority, nobody questioned the authority of the Committee, or of General Bradford.

Once things were in place, the Committee sent General Bradford to Wright-Patterson to explore the base as the possible interim seat of the Federal Government, not knowing what needed to be done nor how long it might take. The people who were calling in from all over the nation and the world needed a place to go, and there was a pressing need to get quickly back to the business of government.

The broadcast continued at regular intervals during the day and through the night over the Emergency Broadcast System as well as commercial radio and television to the nation and the world for all senior federal officials of the cabinet, congress, court, and administrative agencies, to report to the nearest military base or embassy and make their presence knows. Twenty-five additional Congressmen were located, and one cabinet secretary, Dwayne Blander, Secretary of Agriculture. He was the only call-in so far to be in the line of succession, though far down the line.

"I suggest we will wait until morning." White said. "Other may yet call in. Ok gentlemen?"

Ok with me."

"Me too."

"Then, if no one of higher rank has called in by then, he is our man."

Morning came and no one of higher rank than Dwayne Blander had called in, and the constitutional line of succession produced a new president. Blander was far down the chain, ninth in order of succession. He was a man most people had never heard of—a farmer from Kansas. The Administrative Committee commandeered a C-23 transport aircraft from the Air Force, and they all flew out to

Kansas to fetch him. Because of security reasons, the committee did not inform Blander of his good fortune until he was safely on board the aircraft. Once they were well on their way back east, the four of them clustered around him grinning like Cheshire cats as Justice White told him he was in line for the Presidency. "After three day of broadcasting to the entire world, you are the only surviving Cabinet Officer. You may decline the honor, if you wish, but I hope you do not. Christ, I don't know what we would do then."

Blander turned white, and sat back in his seat. "Say that again, Judge, I'm not sure I'm hearing you right."

"You heard me right, Secretary Blander; you're next in line to be President of the United States."

"The President, the Vice President, the Speaker, the President Pro Tem, the Secretary of State...?" Blander recited.

"All dead, apparently, and more; you are ninth in line, sir, in the constitutional line of succession."

"Then, of course ... I will accept ... It's my duty. I'll do my duty."

"Excellent! Excellent!" General Bradford said. "Justice White is prepared to swear you in!"

"What? You mean now?"

"Of course now, sir, right now." Bradford said. "The country is leaderless—has been for days. We're damn lucky, gentlemen, damn lucky."

Blander searched their faces; from one to the other, perhaps to see if anyone broke into a laugh, and shouter, "April Fool!"—or perhaps for someone to save him from his fate. "So say you all?" he asked.

Everyone nodded.

"Very well, gentlemen, God help us."

"If you would stand sir, in the isle, and raise your right hand," Justice White said, rising from his seat. The others scrambled up and stood at attention as Justice White administered the oath.

"You're sure this is all legal ..." Blander began, but trailed off.

35

"I'm only sure of one thing, Mr. President," Justice White said. "Never before in American history have decisions of such sweeping import been made in such haste. If any man should question their legitimacy, let him take the matter to court. I'll be waiting for him."

"Then my first official act is to keep together your Administrative Committee as my Presidential staff until further notice, until I can assemble a proper staff, and replace the dead Cabinet Secretaries."

"Your Assistant Secretary, Charles McGruder, survived, Sir. I suggest that you immediately designate him your successor. He's standing by in Indiana."

"Consider it done. Someone let him know. General Bradford, dispatch a military aircraft to Indiana to fetch McGruder."

"Mr. President," General Bradford said, "we don't yet have a place to bring him. We were considering using Wright-Patterson Air Force Base as the temporary seat of government, because of its location and logistics. What do you think?"

"I think Wright-Pat is an excellent choice for temporary Military Headquarters, General," President Blander said, "now that the Pentagon is no more, but I think the government offices should not be on a military base. We don't want to create the appearance of a military dictatorship, a takeover, a coup, do we?" I like the idea of using Philadelphia, if possible for the temporary seat of government. Why? The city is large enough, close to the action, and was, after all, the birthplace of the nation—our first seat of government. Did Philadelphia experience very much damage from the tsunami?"

"Very little, I understand. Some damage along the river, but the city is intact."

Then, do you suppose you could come up with suitable temporary facilities there, and in a hurry, that would accommodate the administrative offices, the congress and the court?

"I don't know, Mr. President. Give me a few hours to explore it."

"Fine," Blander said. "Now, why don't we deviate from our course, and swing by and take a quick preliminary look at Wright-Pat?

Then, what the hell, just go on over to Indianapolis and pick up my assistant, Charles McGruder, and give him the news that he is now the Secretary of Agriculture, and get him going? Don't put off until tomorrow what you can do today, that's what I always say. An hour or two won't hurt anything, will it?"

"Not at all; that's a good idea, Mr. President."

"Fine. Now, if you men don't mind, your new president would like to take a little nap; this is turning into a very stressful day. Wake me on final approach to Wright Pat, or whenever, if we need to confer."

"You got it Mr. President."

About an hour later, the big transport plane was about to enter the traffic pattern for Wright-Patterson Air Force Base, and General Bradford called out, "We better wake up the president."

"I'll do it," said Langford.

Langford walked up the isle to where President Blanton had moved up the middle armrest and made himself a little nest with a bunch of cushions. Langford clasped his shoulder and shook him gently, and said, "Mr. President." Blander did not respond. Langford went through the ritual two more times. He felt Blander's pulse at his wrist, then at his throat. He turned and walked back down the aisle, his face white, drained of blood, to where the others were, and said, "President Blander is dead."

Charles McGruder and his family, clustered around the console television in his parent's family room, transfixed by the flow of events. Aircraft flying over coastal cities transmitted images of unparalleled devastation leaving viewers numb and awestruck, early in the morning, Justice White came on the television and made his first announcement. All ears listened transfixed as he explained the situation. Then he described the committee,

named the members, and called for all federal officials and em-
ployee to report in and give their locations and circumstances.

Charles and his assembled family expressed a collective sigh of
relief, just knowing that *someone* was in charge. Immediately he dialed the telephone number shown on the screen, and even though
the TV station allocated a whole bank of numbers for the purpose,
the line was busy. He tried a dozen times more throughout the morning before getting through. He supplied the requested information,
put down the phone and said, "I'm to stay put until further notice."

"Well, Charles, I expect we'll have to put off your taking over
the farm for a while," Mr. McGruder said. "How do you feel about
it now?"

"You're right, Dad, It'll have to wait. Sorry. Yesterday I was all
set to tender my letter of resignation to Secretary Blander, but I
cannot leave now. What do you say, Mildred?"

"I agree Charles. It looks like we are stuck where we are for a
while longer, that is, if the country survives. If it doesn't, then all
this doesn't matter."

"You think the country might go under?" Mrs. McGruder asked.

"No, no." Charles said. "Everything will work out, somehow, you'll
see. We mustn't get morbid." Secretly, he was not nearly as optimistic
about the country's future as he wished to appear to his family.

The telephone jangled. Charles sprang to his feet. "I guess this
is it, he said, certain it was the anticipated call from the Committee?
He was wrong; it was his life-long friend, Gregg Barton.

"Hi, there, buddy. Heard you were in town. Thank God for
that."

"Thanks, Gregg. You know, I had planned to call you this morning, but then—

"Yeah, terrible. Can you get away for an hour or so, to talk and
maybe have a beer? I can swing by and pick you up."

"Sounds great, give me twenty minutes."

"You got it."

Mildred walked into the room. "I heard the phone. Was that the government people?"

"No, that was Gregg. He wants me to have a beer with him. I can't sit here all day waiting for the phone to ring. If they call before I get back, take a message, or if they must talk to me immediately, give them my cell phone number."

Charles and Gregg were on their third beer, and deep into a conversation about old times, as well as current events, when Charles's cell phone began vibrating. "Hello," he said, expecting Mildred's voice.

"Secretary McGruder, this is General Bradford, Chairman of the Joint Chiefs of Staff. How are you today, sir?"

"I'm fine General; just having a beer with an old friend, and waiting for someone to call and tell me what to do.

"Good, glad to hear it. How far are you from the Indianapolis airport right now, sir?

"Why, uh, about an hour's drive."

"I'm sorry to spring this on you this way, but we need you right away. In fact, the Committee and I are on a Military transport plane inbound to Weir Cook Airport. If possible, we want you there to meet us. We will have a quick turnaround. There is no time for explanations right now."

"What about my family?"

"They'll have to stay where they are for now, Mr. Secretary. Can you make the plane?"

"Yes sir, I can make it, but let me respectfully correct you—I am only Assistant Secretary of Agriculture."

"No, let me correct you, sir. This morning, when your boss assumed new duties, you were elevated to Secretary. Congratulations. We'll explain it all when we see you."

They talked a minute more about logistics—the military aircraft would come to the Air National Guard ramp, and so on— while Gregg sipped his beer, and waited.

"Believe it or not, Gregg, that was General Bradford, Chairman of the Joint Chiefs of Staff of the United States. He just told me that Blander has been given some sort of promotion, and that I'm now Secretary of Agriculture!"

"Wow! Congratulations. You're coming up in the world, sport."

"I don't know about that, but he says there's a plane inbound to Weir Cook airport to pick me up right now. Can you drive me?"

"You're not even going back to the farm to pack?"

"There's no time. I'll explain to Mildred and the folks on the phone in route to the airport."

"Okay, let's go."

The big transport plane was already on the ramp, with the rear cargo doors open and the loading ramp extended, and a jeep waiting to take him out to the aircraft. McGruder said goodbye to his friend Gregg and hopped in the jeep, and the driver drove out to the plane and right up the ramp to the inside. The big cargo ramp started retracting and the doors closing as the driver escorted McGruder to the passenger section of the plane where General Bradford and the Committee greeted him. The greeting was cordial, if a bit hurried, and as they settled into comfortable seats, the engines began to whir and soon they were airborne.

White began: "I hope you will forgive us for the cloak and dagger business, Secretary McGruder. I will be brief and to the point. General Bradford told you that you about your promotion to Secretary of Agriculture.

"Yes sir."

"Well, the reason for your promotion was that your boss, Wayne Blander, was elevated to the Presidency."

"Pardon me for saying so, Judge White, but it appears to me that this hasty search for prospective presidents is liable to miss somebody. You could end up with two or more people, each thinking he should be president."

"We're being very careful and very thorough with our search, and our verifying procedures, but if that should happen, we will deal with it. Now, back to you, Mr. McGruder, there have been additional developments, concerning you and President Blander. You see, we just flew out to Kansas this morning and got President Blander and swore him in as president a little while later here on the airplane. Then we headed for Wright-Patterson Air Force Base in Dayton to look the place over. President Blander was taking a nap, back there in the back seats, and he had said to wake him when we were in the traffic pattern to Wright Pat. Well, when we went back to wake him, Blander was dead."

"Dead!"

"Yes, dead, apparently from a heart attack. I guess it was too much of a shock for him. That makes you next in line for the presidency."

CHAPTER THREE

R oy was having a bad time with the withdrawal. He had delirium tremens, hot flashes, and very scary and confused
thoughts. He needed the medicine a little longer. This was not
the time to go cold turkey. In desperation, he set out limping and
listing down the stairs at a slow and careful pace to search for his
backpack, which contained not only his medicine, but also his radio, and his assortment of necessities. He found it on a landing
far below on the tenth floor soaked through, with his medicine
ruined. He took up residence there on the tenth floor, searched
for and found new vending machines, and hunkered down to try
and survive, with occasional and randomly occurring episodes of
screaming, flashes of paranoia, wildly fluctuating mood shifts, and
out-of-body experiences.

He experienced two more day of hellish suffering until the pain
subsided somewhat and his mind began to clear. He wanted to get
away from there as quickly as possible. He went outside the building through a third floor window onto the rubble to check the conditions. The mud in some places was still soft and treacherous. He

wore a handkerchief over his mouth and nose—the stench of rotting corpses was overpowering; bodies were in plain view, broken and mangled in the mud and wreckage. Animals had devoured some bodies, and blowflies covered and buzzed around them. Maggots feasted democratically on the best, the brightest, and the near-do-wells alike.

He entered two nearby building remnants through third and fourth floor windows, and worked his way up and down thru filthy and obstructed stairways into what remained of stores, occasionally finding something that would have been useful under other circumstances, but contributed nothing to his present situation.

He abandoned his exploration and headed back toward his familiar surroundings to ponder his escape from the ruined city. On the way, as he wove and threaded through the mess, giving as wide a birth to the rotting corpses as possible, an unexpected noise startled him. He stopped and listened for a recurrence of the sound, but heard nothing. He continued on his way but his curious got the better of him and he retraced his steps, thinking some poor animal, a dog, perhaps, was in extremis. If he could not save it, he would put it out of its misery. Arriving once again at the spot, he stood listening, and heard a weak thrashing about in the muck followed by a moan. It sounded human. He clawed his way through the trash, tossing things aside, until he saw a motion from an amorphous mass of dark mud and crud. It moaned again and moved. Coming closer he saw it was a woman. He saw her naked mud-covered breasts and her matted hair. He bent down. An eye opened slightly in the black ooze. She emitted a weak, choked, muffled scream, and weekly thrashed about, as if desperately trying to squirm away. He pulled her from the mire. She wore no clothes at all. The fear and exertion must have sapped her last bit of strength for she became still. He scooped her up in his arms and carried her out into the sunlight. Laying her down gently, he wiped her face with his handkerchief, removing the mud from her eyes, mouth, and nostrils. He carried her back to the building, and up the stairs—no easy feat—threading his way over, under, and around obstructions, slipping and sliding, stopping frequently to rest, bracing himself against the wall, holding her in his arms. Near exhaustion, he put the naked, unconscious, mud-covered woman over his shoulder like a sack of potatoes and, heaving with exertion and covered with crud and sweat, he made it to the tenth floor where he had established his base camp. He placed her on a couch in a nice office and covered her with a window drape.

From the janitor room, he retrieved a bucket of water drained from the building piping, which he warmed with a tiny Sterno camp stove from his recovered backpack. He ran his hands gently over her entire body searching for wounds and broken bones. He found no apparent fractures, but found cuts and abrasions and swollen areas. He opened a bottle of water from the vending machines and got a few drops between her lips.

Cleaning her was a long and arduous task. He exposed small cuts and abrasions, which, if they were not already infected, would be soon enough. He applied alcohol and iodine from his first aid kit. Her hair was hopelessly matted and tangled. He cut it to a length of two inches, combed out the remaining tangles, and washed it. It was black.

She opened her eyes only once during the process and looked at him through fearful slits, but was quickly gone again. He bundled her up when he finished, in clean towels from washroom and covered her with a window drape. He heated soup, but could not arouse her.

It had been years since Roy had been responsible for another human being, indeed, for any living thing other than himself, but his parental instincts kicked in and he pulled a chair close in front of the couch and sat in the chair holding her hand to comfort her should she awaken and be frightened. He fell asleep. Her shrill cry woke him. It was night, and in the dim moonlight, he saw her bolt across the room, screaming, toward a window. She struggled to open it, banged her hands against the glass. He dashed after her, grabbed her, held her, and got her flailing arms restrained. She stopped screaming, and began to weep. He pulled her to him gently, held her in his arms and allowed her to sob. She whispered, hoarsely, "water."

He led her back to the couch, covered her, and held the bottle of water for her to drink, whispering gently to her, as he stroked her hair, "It's all right, you're safe now." She clutched at him. He lay beside her, and cradled her in his arms. She went to sleep again, and eventually, so did he.

The following morning the woman moaned and cried and drifted in and out of consciousness but managed to drink some of the warm soup that he reheated on the camp stove.

"Who are you?" He asked her, during a moment of consciousness. She did not respond; she did not speak at all that day.

It became clear to him that some of her injuries, though they would not be serious under normal circumstances, were likely to keep her ill and weak. There were ominous deep-red borders around even the tiniest cuts that were tell-tell sign of possible infection. Collectively they could be life threatening, could overwhelm her immune system in her weakened state. He knew that she needed antibiotics to fight the infection, but his pack had done all it could do.

Carlos opened his eyes to his own screaming. Linda hovered over him. He was not at the helm of his yacht as he had dreamed, he was lying on his back on a listing deck, on a large bench cushion. Close overhead a makeshift canvas canopy flapped in the breeze, and provided shelter from the sun. He tried to move, and screamed again.

"Don't try to move just yet, Dear," Linda whispered. She held a cup of water to his lips. He gulped it down.

"More," he said, his voice week and raspy, nearly inaudible; his hands trembling.

"A little later, Darling," she whispered. "Too much might make your ill."

Linda stroked him gently and tried to arrange him more comfortably by slipping a folded jacket under his head. Presently, he seemed to revive. He saw the bandaged splint on his left leg below the knee.

"You broke your leg," Linda said, anticipating him. "And you struck your head on something in the water. I don't know what. I was not close enough to see. It knocked you unconscious."

"How did you get me on the boat? How did you—

"I saw the boat, that it was still afloat. The mast was gone, the rigging trailed in the sea, and it was down in the water at a bad angle, but it wasn't that far away, so I towed you to it."

"How long did it take you?"

"I don't know, a couple of hours, maybe."

Carlos viewed the girl with astonishment mixed with admiration, which made her blush.

She bent to him and gently kissed him. "I was scared of sharks, so I hurried."

"I still don't understand," he said. "How did you get me aboard?"

"I used the starboard winch to crank you in; and a length of rope ... sheet ... and a piece of sail to make a sling. I put it around your body, underneath your arms."

Even with all his discomfort, Carlos could not suppress a smile. "What about my leg? It's broken, you say?"

"Yes, I set it while you were unconscious. I knew the pain would be bad if I waited."

"How in the name of heaven did you set my leg?"

"I used the winch again; that's a handy gadget."

Carlos grimaced at the effort to suppress a tiny chuckle, at this remarkable woman he had chosen for his wife. "How about you, are you hurt?"

"No, I'm fine," she said, "considering."

"How long have we been drifting?"

"Two and a half days; it's mid-afternoon, now." She handed him a second cup of water. He took the water eagerly, wincing at the pain of movement, and drank it down."

"You need to lie still, now," she said. "I'll get you something to eat. Some of the stores are still usable. There is cold soup. I'll get it for you." She leaned over and kissed him once more gently on the cheek.

"Wait, what's the condition of the boat? We are on deck, so the cabin must be flooded."

"Yes; it is up to here on me." She indicated her shoulders. "I salvaged what I could and brought it on deck, and lashed it to the high rail—canned foods, water containers, whatever I could find. I don't think the boat will sink. We only have to hold out until someone rescues us."

"The hull is obviously breeched, but the flotation is working," he said. "It's doing its job. Yes, you are right, we can hold out until help arrives. Did you find the flares? Were they intact?"

"I found no flares."

With great effort and pain, Carlos raised himself on one elbow and looked toward the stern of the vessel. "There, in that compartment beneath the bench. That is where I had them."

The girl scooted along the tilted deck, while holding on to the high rail. "It's empty, Carlos," she said, "I'm sorry."

"No matter, ships will come along, or search aircraft. You have done marvelously well—saved our lives. We will be all right. Now, help me to my feet"

"Are you sure you should try?"

"Yes, I must." he said.

It was no use. He fell back helpless.

"There's no hurry," she said. "Try and rest, your strength will return."

⊨⊰⊹⊱⊨

The only order that President Blander gave during his brief presidency was that General Bradford look into setting up temporary quarters for the Federal government in Philadelphia, the birthplace of the nation. Bradford liked the idea, the symbolism of it, so he negotiated the acquisition of the Empire Hotel and auxiliary buildings for that purpose. Workers, toiling around the clock, quickly fitted out the buildings with security and communications equipment, with cables running over the floor, along the baseboard of walls, above false ceilings, through holes punched in walls, anyway at all to get the building in operation quickly. In the absence of physical security, large numbers of armed soldiers guarded every inch of the twenty-four story building. Surviving federal employees began arriving by military transport, by commercial flights, by trains and private autos. It was a remarkable spectacle to watch.

Outpourings of good will and offers of assistance flowed into the new offices, surpassing even 9-11, when the nations of the world had rallied around America; or Pearl Harbor, which had propelled America into World War II. Now, once again, it seems most nations were able to set aside their grievances and bitterness at the conduct of the United States during the years after nine-eleven, and to think again of what America once was, and what it might become again someday—a shining beacon on a hill.

A few staunch allies of the United States, principally Britain, Poland, and a handful of nondescript Pacific island kingdoms, proclaimed a national time of mourning and announced loudly, "We are all Americans!" Meanwhile the bloated corpses of hundreds of thousands of Americans floated up on the beaches all along the Eastern

Seaboard. Notwithstanding all the flowery sentiments, General Bradford announced to the world, to any potential enemy who might think the moment propitious: "As a precautionary measure, the US is on high military alert, defcon 3, the bomber are on standby, and the nuclear missiles, thousands of them, are armed and poised and ready!"

As the frantic efforts continued to reestablish the government, and to provide aid and assistance to survivors, radio and television evangelists proclaimed that God had wrought His wrath upon America for her sins.

Roy sat at a tenth floor window with the glass missing, keeping watch over the nightmare world outside. Planes and helicopters were a regular feature now. He frequently heard gunfire somewhere to the south, he estimated it to be from the banking section of the city, though it was hard to tell anymore, and saw military helicopters converging on the area. Smoke wafted up from numerous points on the landscape. "Damn, I need my radio," he said. The radio lay at his feet, banged up and inoperative from its terrible fall and days long soaking in filthy seawater. He had rinsed it off and dried it out, but it would not play, despite his best efforts to revive it.

The air flowing through the broken-out window somewhat refreshed the room, and dissipated the stink of death, which otherwise wafted up both from outside and from the lower floors where many rotting bodies lay piled up like disarrayed cordwood at the exits, where panicked people's last minute attempts to save themselves had failed.

In frustration, he took up the radio once more, tried again to repair it. He removed the back with his penknife, jiggled all the wires and connections, held it close before his eyes and searched for damage. He had found new batteries in a wall clock. He put in a new set.

His mind was still not right, and frustration wreaked havoc on him. He was not out of danger mentally or emotionally; his hands still shook like palsy from his days without his medication, frustrating his efforts, bringing on bursts of rage. He screamed and threw the radio across the room, bouncing it off the wall. It began playing a lively show tune. He thought he heard a startled giggle from the woman, but when he whirled around, she was still and silent. He ran across the room, gathered up the radio, gingerly carried it back to his seat at the window and replaced the back. As he tuned through the stations, the first thing he heard was a Tele-Evangelist describing the wrath of God, re: the tsunami. Roy scowled his disapproval. "Bloodsucking charlatans!" he yelled, and quickly moved the dial. Hungry for news, he searched for public service announcements from the Emergency Broadcast System hoping to find something about rescue efforts. He found none but came across a program discussing the tsunami. A man was talking:

"...once the cause of the destructive wave became knows, partisans and pundits demanded to know why the U.S. government had not anticipated the landslide on the island of La Palma, as obvious as the danger was."

Already the blame-game had started, even before the mass graves, all up and down the coast, had been properly filled and covered and words spoken over the dear departed.

An astute listener had called into one such talk show, and pointed out that scientists had done extensive studies of the island of La Palma as a potential source of tsunami; not only had this information been widely published, it had even been made into a documentary for Public Television, which had been shown on stations all over the world. The narrator of that Public Television program, a scientist himself, had stated emphatically that it was only a matter of time until the west side of the island slid into the ocean, resulting in a devastating tsunami, which would then pose a massive threat the east coast of the Americas. Apparently, people had paid little attention, had view that program, if they saw it at all, with the same frame of mind and cognitive awareness as they watched stories of UFOs and haunted houses, or of the weapons of mass destruction in Iraq. The simple truth was that nobody could have done anything about it anyway."

Roy switched off the radio to preserve his batteries and sat thinking. For the first time in years, he wished he had a television set. He would like to see some of the goings-on on the tube. He would like to see that show about La Palma Island. He agreed with what the man had just said. Nobody could have predicted the tsunami closer than a few thousand years, and even if someone could have, nobody would have paid any attention to him.

Roy was still sitting in the chair looking out his tenth floor window, and thinking about the predictability of the tsunami, when suddenly a chill went up his spire. He whirled around to find the woman's half-lidded eyes fixed upon him. She had said nothing since he rescued her, and hardly moved, except when he helped her to the bathroom. The eyes now seemed alive—interested.

"Are you feeling better, this morning, madam?" he asked?"

She looked directly at him, and then closed her eyes again, without speaking.

"Hey, don't go to sleep on me again; how about a little soup? It's already warm. It's chicken noodle, today."

He leaped up and ran to his Sterno stove. The pot was still sitting on it even though he had extinguished the flame to save his fuel. "You just wait, I'll have you some good, hot soup in a jiffy."

He turned the radio back on, thinking that might loosen her up some more, and while he spoon-fed her chicken noodle soup, the man on the radio continued talking about La Palma Island:

"In 1971, during the last minor eruption of the volcano, a rift appeared along the western face of the mountains approximately three meters wide, and the side of the island actually slid downward toward the sea by three meters, as well. Geologist did extensive studies to determine the cause and learned that volcanic lava seepage had heated up trapped water, forming steam. What is puzzling to the government officials and scientists is the apparent absence of any volcanic activity prior to the current slide. All the seismographic charts for the time-period leading up to the event show no tremor activity. Our government officials have appointed a committee to study this mystery."

The woman stopped taking the soup and closed her eyes once again. "Had enough?" Roy asked, and she nodded weakly. Roy turned off the radio again, but continued to sit beside her. He took her hand in his, and stroked her hair. He felt her forehead; it felt normal to him. He had not left her alone since he found her. She was still a sick puppy, but he figured she was over the hump. She seemed to have lost her fear of him; she no longer drew back when he approached her.

Suddenly she said in a weak and raspy voice, "What's your name?"

Surprised, Roy said, "Why, I'm Roy, what's your name?"

"I don't know," she whispered. He saw a tear form in the corner of her eye. "I don't know who I am. I remember waking up cold, with you hovering over me, washing me. I thought I was dead. She looked toward the window. "What happened out there? Is that the way it is—the way it has always been? I can't remember."

"Giant ocean waves destroyed New York City. It's gone."

"New York?"

"Don't worry about any of that for now, you've had a bad time of it, you need to take it easy. It will all come back to you. You will have to give it time. In another day or two, when you're stronger, we'll signal a helicopter and they will take us out of here."

"Helicopter?" she said, seeming more confused.

"Just rest and we'll talk later. Drink some more soup and build up your strength, okay? We'll talk later."

Roy had her dressed in his extra underwear and shirt, which he had washed out thoroughly in a big janitor's sink, and hung to dry in the sun and fresh air. Now he gave her his extra pants as well. Later in the day, he got her up on her feet for a few minutes. After a couple of assisted circuits of the room, she collapsed back onto the couch.

"You should sit up as much as you can, but don't try to walk by yourself. You might fall. Ask me to help you."

"All right…Roy."

━━◁┼ ┼▷━━

An airplane flew over dropping leaflets. Roy left the woman and hurried down to the third floor, where he exited through a window to retrieve one. It contained the information he had sought concerning rescue operations. The catastrophe was so extensive that personnel and helicopters were in short supply, so the military had established pickup points at regular intervals and flew survivors by helicopter from the pickup points to rescue centers. Survivors had to get to the pickup points on their own. There was a map on the backside of the leaflet showing the location of pickup points in Manhattan.

While Roy busied himself studying the leaflet, the woman said, "Could I have a bath?"

"A bath?"

"Yes. I feel so…awful."

"We can arrange that," he said. "There's a bathtub on the next floor up, and clean water trapped in the building pipes. I would not drink it, you understand, unless I boiled it, but it is okay for bathing. Are you up to walking a little way, do you think?"

"Yes, yes."

Roy grabbed up his pack, led her by the arm, and they proceeded slowly to the stairwell, up the stairs, and to the bathroom.

He opened the taps, and water poured out of the faucet into the tub. "It's a little on the cool side," he said. "We can't risk building a fire to heat that much water. It would take a long time, and there would be smoke, and—

"I understand," she said, as she stuck her hand in the water. "It isn't cold." She left the water running, filling the tub half full, and as he started to leave the bathroom, she stopped him. "Please don't leave, I need your help." She slipped out of her clothing and stood naked, and motioned for him to help her into the tub. She stepped in and sat down in the water. "Burr," she said. "Hurry; wash my back, quickly, it's colder than I thought."

Roy picked up soap and a cloth and washed her, being careful of her cuts and abrasions. She allowed him complete liberty, and coaxed him when he hesitated. He bathed her with the same dispatch and dispassion as when he used to bathe his dog, Prince. She stepped out of the tub and Roy patted her dry. She slipped back into Roy's clothing.

"Sorry we don't have proper clothing for you."

"I like wearing your underwear," she said, with a gleam in her eye. "My hair is so uneven. Do you think you could trim it for me?"

"Sure I could," he said smiling, thinking that the emergence of female vanity was a good sign. He was not about to tell her that he had messed up her hair in the first place. "I have comb and scissors in my pack."

It was as if the near comatose woman of the past few days had suddenly become vibrant with life. Soon the snipped hair encircled her on the floor.

"Thank you, Roy, I feel so much better." She looked him over. "You could use a bath yourself, Roy. If you don't mind my saying so. Run some clean water. I will wash your back for you. Turnabout is fair play."

"Oh, no thank you, ma'am."

"Oh, come on, Roy, I won't hurt you."

"No," he said again, firmly.

"Well, what if I wait for you outside, and you do it yourself. I didn't want to say this, Roy, but you stink."

"I stink?"

"Yes, Roy, something fierce."

"Okay, you wait for me outside the door, now, and don't go wandering off."

"I won't."

When Roy finished bathing, he felt much better. He called to the woman, "Do you suppose you could give me a haircut, too?"

"Sure."

He sat on the edge of the bathtub with a towel around his waist and the woman trimmed his hair and combed it neatly. "There," she said, "you look like a new man."

Roy examined himself in the mirror over the sink. "You're right," he said. He dug in his pack for his safety razor and a small can of shaving crème. "I have everything in this pack," he said. As he brought it forth and shaved, while the woman waited patiently watching him.

The following day the woman felt strong enough to accompany Roy on a search of the two adjacent floors for batteries for his radio. They found a few more wall clocks. The woman was tired after their adventure and quickly fell asleep on her couch.

Roy noticed that the woman appeared more feminine and attractive now that she had come out of her stupor. He guessed she must be in her mid-thirties, but he was not about to ask her. She impressed him by her visible efforts to gain strength and to bring her emotions under control. He knew it was an effort for her. She still had episodes of apparent stark terror, when her eyes would fill with panic, her body would stiffer, and she would emit a muffled moan, or cry out. A moment of embarrassment always followed the episodes, as her big, brown eyes, searched his face for understanding. He always gave it. At such times, he took her in his arms, squeezed her gently, kissed her cheek, stroked her hair, and whispered to her that she was safe, that everything was all right. Comforting her gave him a boost as well.

"What do you feel when that comes over you," he asked her, his curiosity getting the better of him.

"Fear that something is about to get me, and I don't know what."

"Well, it will pass, you'll see."

There were times when his own panic would rise, and he would have to turn away from her and suppress his urge to scream or break something. He would swallow hard, and choke back the scream.

They were quite a pair.

The radio helped him. He worked out an itinerary of radio programs where the news was the freshest, tartest, and most volatile. He listened with a range of emotions from awestruck fascination to vitriolic indignation and hateful anger at what was transpiring in America: politically, socially, and economically. "They never learn, he screamed aloud," startling the woman. In spite of his effort at self-control for her sake, his anger and his acting out were cathartic, and the louder and angrier the better.

He could not bring himself to grieve for New York City. To him, its destruction was like the flushing of a giant sewer. Over the years, since the second great depression, and the country's loss of Super-Power status, he had spent most of his summers there, and he had filled several notebooks. He kept his observations to himself, though; he did not go around bad-mouthing the city, not while he was there, anyway. He was afraid of what it would do to him. Those who were powerful were dangerous maniacs, in his view; and those who had been powerful, but who had lost their power, were bitterly vindictive and vengeful

"What? What did you say?" Roy looked around, startled.

"I only said your name, the woman said. "You looked so … strange."

"Strange? How strange? What do you mean, strange?"

You were sitting so still, staring off into space for a long time. It frightened me."

Roy realized he had been "levitating," drifting in the fog. "We have to get out of here," he said. "I think you're well enough to travel, don't you?"

"How will we get out of here?"

"We'll signal a helicopter. You heard on the radio about the gangs out there robbing and killing people, and about the fighting at the Gold Reserve and in the diamond district. We will have to be smart and careful. We will get ready today, and I will signal a helicopter early in the morning just outside the building. Then if anything goes wrong we can come back inside."

Roy heard a rustling behind him…then the lights went.

CHAPTER FOUR

Roy came to himself—heard strange noises—laughter and sobbing comingled. He realized he was lying on the floor, his eyes closed, and his head throbbing. How did he get on the floor? He opened his eyes. The heard the woman; she was sobbing and pleading. He raised his head a few inches and turned it toward the source of her voice. She was on her back on the couch; a man was atop her; they were struggling. The man was laughing. He was raping her, and the more she sobbed and screamed, the rougher the man handled her. Rage and fear surged through him, bringing him fully awake. He trembled as he suppressed the urge to spring at the man. Instead, he inched his way across the floor toward a chair, unnoticed by the man, who was absorbed in his crime. Roy pulled himself up and stood wobbly behind the man. He picked up the chair and brought it down with all his might on the man's back and head. The man collapsed without a sound on top of the woman. She screamed, "Get him off of me! Get him off of me!" Roy dragged the man off her, and slung him violently across the floor. Screaming and crying, he kicked the man violently and repeatedly in the head, until there was no sign of life. "Roy, stop!" The woman screamed. "Enough!"

Roy panted for breath, his body convulsed. He slumped to the floor. The woman pulled down her T-shirt, leaped up from the couch and came to him, knelt, and embraced his quivering body.

"There are two others Roy; they will be back," she whispered.

"Two more?" He gasped.

"Yes," she said, "they went looking for money. I heard them say that when they returned they would force you to tell them where your money is hidden."

"What money?"

"They said you have money. I told them you had no money but they did not believe me. One of them laughed. He said it was a good thing he didn't believe me, or they would have killed you then, you and me both. He said he didn't believe it because of all the bodies. What did he mean by that, Roy?"

"I don't know. Now, listen, there is not much time. We have to get ready for them. Tell me how they were armed. Did they have guns?"

"Yes, they all had guns; that man's gun is there, against the wall." She pointed, by the door. Roy had not seen the rifle. He dragged the body out of sight behind the couch, crossed the room, picked up the gun, and turned it over in his hands. "It's a semiautomatic. I'm no gun expert, but I can handle this thing." He worked the breach mechanism and verified that a live round was in the chamber, and that the clip was full, then turned back to the woman. "We have to catch them by surprise. We will have only one chance to get it right. Lie down on the couch, as you were before; pull up your shirt to distract them. I am sorry, but I must ask you—

"I understand. I'm ready."

Roy stopped talking and froze. "Shush," he said. "I hear something." They both were quiet. The noise outside in the hallway grew louder."

"They're coming back."

The woman resumed her position on the couch, as if she were asleep, or dead, her shirt up, as Roy had asked.

"Good," Roy breathed. He slipped behind the door. The men entered the room, laughing, saw the woman sprawled on the couch. They stopped dead in their tracks. "Wow! Look at that." They glanced around the room. "Where's Fred?"

"He must a got all he wanted. I hope he didn't slop it up too messy, because I'm next."

The man moved over toward the couch, unbuckling his belt as he went. Roy pushed the door aside. The two men turned at the sound, he opened up with the semiautomatic rifle, cutting them in half. Blood and guts splattered over everything, including the woman. She shrieked and scrambled up, and ran around the room like a wild woman, screaming. Roy threw down the rifle and ran to her, "Everything is all right, now," he said. "We 're safe. Let me get that shirt off you and get you cleaned up." Her sobs and shaking subsided, as she tore off the bloody undershirt and grabbed up the drape from the couch.

"Roy led her to the utility room, on the same floor, rather than going up to the bathroom. At the big janitor's sink, he drained water into a bucket. "Keep your eyes closed, lean against the wall while I douse you good. You've been through enough hell for a lifetime," he whispered, "and you've been marvelous. I am proud of you. It's just about over."

"Do you promise, Roy?" She sobbed.

"Yes."

The woman stood limp and passive with her head tilted slightly back, her eyes closed, while Roy poured the water over her, several buckets, cleaned the blood and gore from her body, and out of her hair. Then he wrapped her up once more and led her back. They entered the adjacent room. "Don't go back in there," he said. "I have to go in and take care of things, and get our belongings. You lie down and rest. I won't be long."

Roy returned to the scene of the carnage. He went through the pockets of the three men he had killed. He found a bundle containing jewelry and wads of money tied up in a cashmere scarf.

He set it aside and examined their wallets, removing identifying documents.

When he finished he drug their bodies to the window, and tossed them out and watched them tumble the ten stories to the ground. He collected his backpack and supplies, took one of the rifles, a knife, and a pistol, and joined the woman in the other room.

"I heard on the radio this morning that the scavengers are shooting at helicopters now," he said. "Seems they are waging all-out war. We will leave the building in the morning at first light, or as soon as the helicopters appear. We will hide ourselves one more night in this building."

They busied themselves with preparations for their early morning departure, preparing food, and finding another hiding place. After they had eaten, and before darkness fell, Roy sketched in the day's events in his notebook, until his eyelids sagged to slits, and his mind wandered into the fog, into the semiconscious dream state to which his mind often retreated, though not so much now as before.

Roy's notebooks came in other colors besides red; there were blue, green, yellow, and purple, though he never bought he purple ones. He did not like purple; he did not even like the *word* 'purple.' When he bought the notebooks, he always got an assortment of other colors. Roy liked to alternate them. He had never been able to decide which was his favorite, though he had given it much thought; today it was red; tomorrow it would be yellow. What is one to do?

The woman sat down beside him. "You are so quiet, Roy, what are you thinking?"

Roy looked at her, a distant look. "What?"

"I asked you what you were thinking."

Roy glanced at her, then at the red notebook in his hand, and the yellow pencil stub, and realized that he had been drifting disembodied again. He inserted his notebook carefully in its place in his left breast pocket. "Nothing important," he said.

"You were wonderful today, Roy. You saved my life again." Her eyes misted up. She moved close, leaned her head on his shoulder, and kissed him tenderly on the cheek. "How can I ever repay you?"

"You just did, Darling," he said.

The morning of their departure from the Big Apple, Roy and the woman stood on a mound of hardened mud atop the mountain of debris that rose to the third floor level of the Empire State Building. The mound was too small and the surroundings too jagged and dangerous for a helicopter to land. Roy built a small, smoky fire close to the building in case they needed to make a run for cover back inside. He carried the rifle slung over his shoulder, and the pistol at his waist. While keeping close watch on their surroundings, they waited with their bundles for someone in the sky to notice them. Presently, one of the helicopters approached. It was a small two-man type with a bubble over the cockpit, and with the Plexiglas doors removed. Two men were inside. The pilot hovered fifty feet above the wreckage, off to the side, and the other man called to them through a bullhorn. "Can you travel?" the man asked.

Roy nodded his head vigorously.

Again the bullhorn sounded. "How many of you?"

Roy pointed to himself and the woman.

"Do you need anything—food, water?"

Roy shook his head. The helicopter continued hovering. Then the bullhorn sounded again. "We have no helicopters available now to fly you out. We're tossing you directions to the nearest pick-up point; it's about a mile in that direction." The man pointed. "I've drawn the best route on the map. We have been patrolling the route already this morning and it should be safe, but keep an eye out for gangs, anyway. Okay, now, watch out for the downdraft."

The helicopter moved slightly closer, and the man tossed out an object, trailing a red ribbon. It fell at their feet. Roy picked it up and examined it. It was a map, showing their current location and another location marked with a red "X." "Go to that pickup point, day or night. Someone is always there. Be careful and good luck to you."

Roy nodded his head and waved to them. The helicopter pulled up and swirled away.

Roy listened to the local civil defense station one last time before they set out. He heard that fighting continued downtown at the Federal Reserve Bank between a unit of Marines and a gang bent on breaking into the underground vault where vast quantities of gold bullion were supposedly stored. He clicked off the radio, surveyed their immediate area once more. He selected several reference points to establish his bearing, and then he and the woman set out in the direction of their pickup point, picking their way carefully through the debris.

Less than a mile, the man had said. It was hard for Roy to believe that help was that close. It would likely be a rough mile, though, fraught with peril. Instructions on the back of the map admonished them to avoid contact with other people, and contact with objects in the environment that might be contaminated. Disease was a mortal danger.

Going was slow. At places, the stench was terrible. They encountered no bandits, and by midmorning, had arrived on the edge of a clearing that seemed to be a gigantic parking lot. Large yellow earth-moving machines had cleared the area and now sat idle around the periphery. Mounds of trash, garbage, destroyed building components and automobiles formed a perimeter twenty or thirty feet high, like the walls of a fortress. Across the way, they saw a large tent with a red cross on the side. There were armed soldiers, and people near the tent, standing, sitting, and moving around. Parked nearby was a large olive drab camouflaged military helicopter.

"It's the Red Cross. You can have someone look at your wounds properly," Roy said.

"No, I don't want to see a doctor. I am fine now. You did a wonderful job. My cuts are all healing nicely."

"Nonsense, you must go to the first-aid, immediately."

"No, Roy, they will ask me my name, and I don't know my name. What would I tell them?"

"Tell them the truth, and they'll see to your treatment and help you locate your family. Your amnesia may be from a blow to the head, or something serious. You need to see to it immediately, don't you see?"

"I'm afraid of what they'll do to me."

"They won't do anything to you. They'll help you."

"How can they help me if they don't know who I am? They will lock me up somewhere; that's what they will do. They'll put me away somewhere in an asylum, or a prison."

"Oh, no they won't; these people aren't monsters—any more than anyone else these days. They are ordinary people. The monsters aren't running this show, not at this level anyway."

For the first time since he come across the woman, Roy was peeved at her, and his tone and demeanor showed it. She began weeping. "You go on," she whispered hoarsely. "I'm not going. I'm going back."

"Back? Back where? Don't be silly, there's nothing to go back to. You'll die in that cesspool quick enough."

The woman puffed up at him. "What business is that of yours? You should have left me where you found me. Leave me alone, please."

All of a sudden, Roy realized that the woman was not as well as he had thought. She really might have brain damage—a concussion, perhaps. He would need to be careful with her and avoid upsetting her. While the woman sobbed, Roy sat on a chunk of broken concrete, and motioned for her to sit beside him. She hesitated. They were still some distance from the tent and nobody bothered with them.

"Okay," he said, "we'll tell them you're my wife, or my sister, if you prefer. How does Mary sound to you for your name?"

"Mary is fine."

She stopped crying, and sat down on the curb beside him, sniffing. "Promise me you won't leave me alone until I find out who I am."

He put his arm around her shoulders and pulled her toward him. "Well, it's not that I don't enjoy your company, Darling, especially the bathing part, but we don't know how long that might take—

"Oh, all right, then! Just forget it. Go away and leave me alone. I don't need you. I need to think what to do for myself."

"Oh, dear God," Roy mumbled. They continued sitting there, side by side, their bodies touching. It was as if she needed the warmth of his body to sustain her, even as she struggled to take responsibility for herself. Neither spoke for a while.

"Okay," Roy said. "I promise I won't leave you until you find out who you are. We won't tell them about your amnesia."

"Do you mean it, Roy?"

"Of course I mean it, provided you get a physical checkup as soon as possible."

"I promise I will. I'll get the checkup."

"One other thing…"

"What's that?" Mary said, cautiously.

"We best not tell them anything about the men who attacked us, you know, the ones I killed. They might not understand."

"Absolutely not," she said. "Do we have a deal, then?"

"We have a deal."

Mary smiled slyly while snuggling up closely to him as they continued sitting on the curb. "You don't mind terribly, do you, Roy?" She asked, in a quiet enduring voice, which melted his heart; and while at that particular moment, he would have liked nothing better than to be free of her, he was suddenly helpless as a puppy. "I have too much time and energy invested in you to quit now," he murmured. "I'll stay with you until you find your way back to the world, if you don't take too long about it."

Mary accepted his answer. "What's my last name, then?"

"Smith, Jones, take your pick."

"Come on now, Roy, what's the big deal; tell me your name, so we don't get tripped up."

"Oh, all right! It's Hofstadter, okay?"

"What are you angry about?"

"I don't know. It is just that I haven't given anyone my last name for a long time... except that cow-faced serving girl in that greasy spoon."

She smiled, "It's a nice name. I'll be your wife then, Mary Hofstadter, if that's all right with you."

"I could do worse, I figure."

They got up from the curb and walked on toward the tent and the helicopter, with Roy thinking that he had known the woman for only a few days, and already she was telling him what to do. He didn't like anyone telling him what to do.

"Where will they take us?" Mary asked, sweetly.

"Your guess is as good as mine."

A few men and women in military uniform, and a few sad and retched civilians were outside the tent as they went inside. A uniformed man sat behind a table. Without preamble, he said, "Good morning. May I have your names, please?"

"Roy and Mary Hofstadter," Roy said quickly.

"Spell that last name for me."

"Roy spelled the name."

"Address?"

"We were from here, Manhattan. It's gone, now," Roy said rather clumsily.

"Well, what was your address when it was here? The soldier said, without missing a stroke on his keyboard."

Roy gave him the address of the flophouse in the Bowery. What difference did it make, now? Who was going to verify it?

"Where have you been for the last twelve days?"

"Mary, my wife, was shook up pretty badly," he said, "we've been holed up in a building until she was able to travel through that mess out there."

The man typed rapidly while Roy spoke.

"Are many people coming here?" Mary asked. "Are there many survivors?"

"Yes, quite a few. But the number has fallen of in the last couple of days."

"Where are you sending us?" Roy asked.

"We'll fly you in that helicopter out there to an Army Reserve base, Camp Lamar. It is about an hour's flight from here. You're lucky, it has the best facilities."

"Are there a lot of places like that?"

"Dozens of them, all up and down the coast, from Florida to Maine, the soldier said. "We were sending people to an Air Force Reserve station near Yonkers until yesterday. Fortunately for you it's all filled up, because it's not as well equipped as Camp Lamar."

"Do we have to go in the helicopter? Can't we go some other way?" Mary's face showed lines of concern. "Can't we go by bus or car?"

"Afraid not, ma'am; that transport chopper out there will be leaving here in about twenty minutes. We'll have you out of this hellhole before you know it."

"I don't suppose you have a listing of survivors from New York City." Mary asked.

"Nothing like that here, ma'am, they can help you with all that at the base where you're going. Everything is there, food, clothing, lodging, medical assistance…." He trailed off to nothing, perhaps bored with repeating the same phrases. "You folks help yourselves to the coffee and sandwiches on the tables back there while you wait." He motioned to a couple of folding tables in the back of the large tent. The latrines are outside. Oh, and you'll have to turn in your weapons before you get on the helicopter."

"Thank you, sir." Roy said. He handed the soldier the rifle and the pistol from his belt. "Hear that Mary, hot coffee and sandwiches."

"Oh, dear, a helicopter," she said. Her face whitened and she seemed genuinely apprehensive.

"You afraid of a helicopter, Mary?" It felt strange and unnatural calling her "Mary" after a week of thinking of her as "the woman".

"Well, yes, I am."

"You've had a bad experience flying, then?"

"I don't know. I can't explain it. I don't remember anything. I only know I'm afraid."

"Try to relax. I won't let anything happen to you. Didn't I tell you that?"

That statement seemed to ease her tension. They ate from the table at the rear of the tent and later took a turn at the row of portable latrines outside. Soon, as the soldier had promised, they loaded onto the big chopper, and the engines started with a shrill scream and blowing dust. Eight other people, six adults and two children, all haggard and cadaverous, shared the machine with them. They sat side by side on benches along either side of the cabin, each with a seat belt and harnesses. Mary sat at Roy's side, pressed up close to him, and clasped his hand tightly.

When they gained altitude so that Roy could see out the windows he was startled by the devastation. There was a gray band along the coastline in both directions: rubble, ships, buildings, forests, splintered things, from the edge of the sea to miles inland, as far as the eye could see. All along that vast stretch, both north and south, there were many fires burning; columns of smoke rose high into the air, whipped around by the changing winds at the different altitudes. It was how Roy might have imagined Hell. Mary placed her head on his chest and closed her eyes and did not open them again until the helicopter landed.

On the twelfth day after the mountains slid into the sea, Joe Conway, of the National Security Agency, Director of Intergovernmental Affairs for the Middle East, stood on the bow of the battleship USS Amarillo, looking through powerful field glasses at the devastated island of La Palma. Behind him, a Marine Corps chopper warmed up on, and three men stood together nearby. They each had satchels, and camera cases slung over their shoulders. All of the men were dressed in civilian clothing, and on the left breast of their identical dark blue windbreakers, was a colorful seal of the NSA. They were about to be transported by helicopter to the face of the devastated volcanic mountains for a cursory aerial examination, then landed at a vantage point near the peak of the volcano, where they could see up close the aftermath of the slide. Conway had selected the three men because of their imminence in their respective fields. Simon Gilbert was a geologist with the National Geological Survey; Rafael Iglesias was one of the foremost volcanologists in the world; and Frederick Gorman, was a Chemical Engineer of extraordinary acumen, with extensive expertise in explosives. Conway approached them and called above the noise of the helicopter, "Ready gentlemen?"

They nodded.

"All right then, let's do it."

They climbed into the chopper and it lifted off the ship and moved swiftly toward the island. The spring sky was clear, and the air was brisk and refreshing. By afternoon, the sun and the warm ocean currents would most likely fill the sky with cumulous clouds.

The chopper flew along the faulted area of the mountains as close as the pilots dared, to allow the men to look for obvious anomalies, for anything which might relate to causation. Given the absence of volcanic activity prior to the event, causation was still a mystery. It was natural for people to wonder at the cause, and easy enough for some group to claim responsibility, as Al Qaida reputedly had done, according to communiqués from field agents in Europe and the Middle East.

Conway and his men took photographs from many vantage points as the chopper moved over the awesome twenty or thirty-mile-long amputation on the face of the volcanic mountains. With special cameras, they took infrared photos to identify differences in temperature, to identify any heat sources, and they took polarized light photos by which they hoped to identify residual pressure lines in the rocks. Then they landed near the peak, close to the edge of the slide.

When they were finished, the pilot flew around the island to the opposite side and landed on a pad in a complex of buildings on the outskirts of the town of Santa Cruz de La Palma. The pilots stayed with the chopper, while the men were loaded into an SUV and driven into the basement-parking garage of a building near the beach, where they took an elevator to a large conference room on the fourth floor. The room contained an enormous walnut conference table around which sat a dozen somber-aced men. A large picture window provided a breathtaking, panoramic view of the ocean and the shore, with only a few intervening rows of tiled rooftops.

"Come in gentlemen." said the man at the head of the table, as he arose and walked to meet them. "I am Gregory Mendes, Assistant Minister of Interior Affairs.

"Good morning, Minister, I am Joe Conway. Thank you for agreeing to meet with us today."

"My pleasure, I assure you, Mr. Conway. My government is happy to share with you the results of our preliminary inquiries into this enormous tragedy, and to cooperate in your independent inquiries. We are sensitive to the possible ramifications of the situation; given the incredible destruction your nation has experienced."

"Thank you. The president wished for me to extend to you his personal appreciation for your understanding and cooperation in this delicate matter, and he sends his condolences for your own losses here on the islands."

"Thank you," said the minister, thoughtfully. "And I want to further assure you that the gentlemen assembled here have top security clearances, and have been apprised fully of your country's concerns. I have conveyed to them that the United States in no way holds Spain accountable for this tragedy, which we believe to be an acts of God, and nature. However, we all wish to satisfy ourselves that no human intervention occurred, as the rumors suggest. So, let us begin with introductions all around."

After introductions, a pudgy, nearly bald man named Parza, who had identified himself as the Director of the Spanish National Laboratory, spoke first. "Scientists under my direction," he said, in a wheezing voice, but with flawless British English, "have explored the vast slide area, repelling where necessary, searching for any anomaly, but particularly attuned to the presence of any evidence of explosives, such as cordite, M2, and all the common military explosives. We found nothing. However, let me acknowledge that the area is huge, it is steep, and it is treacherous. We still have a long way to go before we are prepared to state definitively that no human beings played a role in this extraordinary disaster."

"Did you check for abnormal levels of radioactivity?" Conway asked.

"Radioactivity? Why, no, surely you don't suspect a nuclear detonation."

'We rule out nothing at this time, Doctor Parza. But, why are you incredulous of that possibility?" Conway asked.

"It is because the mountain slid into the sea, sir; it wasn't blown into the sea. Had a nuclear device exploded, even a small one, it would have hurled rock and debris out in a wide pattern, for miles around. There is no evidence of that at all."

"But you said you searched for evidence of an explosion. How is a conventional explosion different from a nuclear explosion, in that regard?"

"Very simply, because certain types of low level explosives such as those used in quarry and mining operations conceivably might have been used to jar the unstable mountain without dispersing the debris over a wide area. We searched for evidence of that, too, and found none; additionally, I think it highly unlikely that conventional explosives could have been employed in sufficient quantity to destabilize the mountain without a great many people knowing about it."

"Why is that?"

"So much work would have had to be accomplished in preparation for the blast, drilling mainly, over a long period of time, and such huge quantities of explosives would have had to be used, that it would surely have been noticed and become widely known."

Conway glanced at Frederick Gorman, his explosive expert, who nodded his agreement.

"I'm okay with it, then," Conway said. "Then how do you account for the landslide, Dr. Parza?"

"My best theory is that the schism that occurred in 1971—I assume you are familiar with that situation, Senor, where the mountains slid three meters toward the sea. That event destabilized the substrate, so that it was simply a matter of time until the mountains gave way—time and chance. There was no way to predict when that might occur. Scientists who studied the mountains subsequent to the 1971 event shared this belief. There is no significance attaching, in my opinion, to the time of the occurrence. It is my further opinion that the rumors and insinuations that terrorists somehow caused this disaster are the works of pranksters, merely yanking our chains."

"Thank you, Doctor. Who's next?"

"I agree with my learned colleague in great part," said a man with a Van Gogh beard, one Victor Leone, of the Sorbonne, who was there at the invitation of the Spanish Government, "however, I would like to add something. I certainly agree that the incident that occurred in 1971, in which the western slope of the island slid three meters toward the sea, did indeed predispose the huge mass to further degradation, but I disagree that it would likely have broken away without further perturbation."

"What sort of, uh, perturbation, sir?" Conway asked.

"Well, the '71' incident was occasioned by a volcanic eruption, a mild one to be sure, but in that instance, superheated water from lava incursions deep within the mountains was the cause. I know what you are going to say, that we had no eruptions this time. That is apparently true, but the fissures that developed during the previous eruption surely remained down there, and there could have been lava infiltration indiscernible on the surface. Yet such a lava incursion could have been sufficient to heat the water over time to trigger another reaction."

"Interesting," said Simon Gilbert, Conway's geologist. "Then, shouldn't there be smoke or steam vents, Professor, even now?"

"Smoking vents? Perhaps, but perhaps not; I can't say that they would necessarily be present."

"But surely," Gilbert persisted, "now that the mountain has slid into the sea, now that a trillion tons of rock cover is gone, surely, there would be smoking or steaming vents, from the infiltrating lava, or from the superheated water. Does anyone agree with me?"

A general discussion ensued on this point and others. Conway listened intently to the exchange of views, attuned to any nuance, any revealing subtly of language, which might indicate insight, knowledge, hidden meaning, anything beyond mere speculation. Around noon, the room fell silent.

"I think we are finished, gentlemen," Conway said, thank you for your insights. Mr. Mendes, that about wraps it up as far as I'm concerned."

"Not so fast, Doctor Conway, we have a luncheon prepared for you, which features our excellent Canary Island cuisine. I'm sure you and your colleagues will be pleased."

"Wonderful, sir, thank you for your hospitality. May we include our flight crew? Conway said. "They remained with the helicopter?"

"By all means, I'll send a car for them," Mendes said, "and assign sentries to guard your aircraft."

When Conway and his associates returned to the destroyer, he placed an encoded radio call to the temporary headquarters of the NSA in Philadelphia. Afterwards, he telephoned his secretary, who along with her husband and children had been on vacation during the tsunami, and hence escaped the fate of so many in the Federal Government.

"Jasmine, I need you here. I need to play the tourist. Can you meet me at the American Embassy in Madrid two days from now, and be prepared to be away from home for a week, maybe two? I will explain everything when I see you."

"When have I ever said no?"

Conway's secretary was Jasmine Jones. She was thirty-two, married, and the mother of twin boys, age four. She had worked at the NSA for nine years. In fact, she had already been there for five years when Conway first came to work. Management assigned her as his secretary because she was Persian, and spoke Farsi, as well as Arabic,

French, and a little Russian. Between the two of them, they were fluent in seven languages, and conversant in three more. Jasmine was married to a tall muscular, redheaded Georgian, named Sam Jones, hence, Jasmine Jones. Her maiden name was Pahlavi. Sam was in internal security, and had been a friend, confident and something of a father figure to Conway when he first came to the agency out of graduate school. He was ten years Conway's senior. Conway had been best man at Sam's and Jasmine's wedding, and the godfather to their twins. On occasion, when Conway needed compatible cover for a sensitive mission, he asked Jasmine to accompany him and pose as his wife or fiancé. This was one of those times. Jasmine was delighted at the prospect, simply because of the adventure, and the opportunity to travel to exotic places. She did worry about leaving the twins, though, and about leaving Sam unattended. During previous absences, which typically lasted for no more than a week or two, the agency had footed the bill for a professional live-in nanny to care for the twins, and a maid to take care of Sam. Sam did not oppose the idea of his wife traveling with Conway. He had addressed the issue this way: "Joe, you son-of-a-bitch, you mess with my woman and I'll kill you. Understand?"

Conway understood, and said so, and they shook hands on it.

Jasmine was on a flight the next day to Madrid.

In spite of the flotation material installed in the yacht's hull, it continued to ride lower in the water with each passing day. A third of the tilted deck was now awash, and there was danger that the craft could capsize or sink. Fortunately, the sea was calm. A squall had come up two nights before, and had further stressed the vessel, but, more disastrously, the squall had swept away the last remaining water container which Linda had so valiantly salvaged from the flooded cabin.

It was near midday and the sun was blazing. Carlos lay secured by a section of rope to the rail beneath the remnants of sail rigged to serve as protection from the sun. His bare feet were only inches higher than the lapping sea. He was in a delirious sleep. Linda lay five feet away, also lashed by rope to the vessel. She too was asleep. Her skin showed the effects of harsh sea and sun. Her hair was matted and course. Her breathing labored. Carlos woke and grimaced with pain. He placed the finger of his right hand on his neck to gauge his pulse; it was racing. Even that small effort exhausted him. His hand plopped down on the deck and he sighed piteously. His condition had deteriorated so badly that now he could barely move his body. He struggled to focus his thoughts, as his mind faded in and out of delirium. He could not understand why help had not arrived. His parched, cracked, bleeding lips and swollen tongue prevented him from speaking, from calling out to her, had he been so inclined. His utter helplessness drove him to a level of despair beyond all imagining. During lucid moments, he struggled to recall how long they had been adrift. He could not remember. Their food and water were gone. He knew he was done for, but the girl might have a chance, if only it would rain, and if she did not have to devote so much of her energy to keeping him alive.

Poor Linda, he thought desperately…so young and beautiful … and now … it is my fault … I should not have brought her on such a perilous journey. My pride drove me; I wanted to show off for her, to impress her. Now look where my vanity has gotten us … I have killed us both … but maybe not.

He moved his head as much as he could to survey the horizon, but there was no hope in his gaze. A tiny tear materialized at the corner of his eye. Without him, she might still miraculously survive. He would have liked to say goodbye to the woman he loved, but no, he must hurry; she would have none of it if she were awake. He slipped the cross and chain from around his neck, and with the corner of the cross he struggled to scratch a message of farewell on the deck, but the corners of the cross were smooth and rounded, and he was unable to do so. He hung the cross on a cleat, and with his last remaining strength, undid the knot that secured him to the dead craft and slid down the sloping deck into the sea. Linda stirred, but continued her exhausted sleep.

CHAPTER FIVE

As soon as Roy and Mary stepped off the helicopter, which transported them from New York City to Camp Lamar, they were ushered from the landing pad into a capacious hall in a large one-story building where many other people were standing, obviously brought in from other helicopters or perhaps by other modes of transportation as well.

"Attention everyone," a uniformed woman said. "I'm Sergeant Hilton. Welcome to Camp Lamar. We will get you checked in shortly, but before we begin, does anyone need immediate medical attention?" She looked around the hall. "Anyone who needs immediate medical attention, please raise your hand. We will take you to sick bay first, then finish processing you later."

Several hands went up, including Roy's on behalf of the woman.

"What are you doing?" She asked.

"I want to get you examined, as we agreed."

"No. Put your hand down. I'll do it later."

The other people who had held up their hands followed a young soldier out of the hall. The remaining people lined up before three folding tables with women in military uniforms and the processing began.

They answered the questions, and Roy provided a brief statement describing their circumstances. They received nametags to wear while at the center, and file folders containing their preliminary information to carry with them through the remainder of the processing. Roy leafed quickly through the folder and found a sheet of informational material and a map of the camp, with streets, buildings, and facilities indicated.

Another soldier guided them to the mess hall in an adjacent part of the same large building. There, they had lunch, consisting of soup, sandwiches, coffee, and fruit, cafeteria style. "This is where you will take your meals while you are here at the base," the solder said. "Present your ID to the cashier; there will be no charge. You will find reading, game, television, and restrooms out the entrance and down the hall. You may use all these facilities freely during your stay. Free telephones booths are along the walls in the main hall. Everything is shown on the back of your instruction sheet."

After the meal, the soldier took them to the hospital two buildings over for physical examinations and debriefing. Along the way there he pointed out the housing office where those who were unable to make immediate connections with family or friends, or who were able to go their own way unaided, would sign in later to obtain a bed for the night. At the hospital, he turned them over to the care of an orderly in the waiting area. "Have a pleasant visit," he said as he departed. They presented their folders to the orderly and sat in the waiting area until called.

Roy did not care for the military, not since the Zionist Neocons had come to power forty years before, launching four decades of perpetual war for International Zionism, and the New World Order, as it made its ultimate push for world domination. He opposed the regime, was an outspoken critic of it, and he, along with many others, paid dearly for it. He was loath to say, think, or feel anything positive about the military after the horrors of that tragic epoch, which had set humanity and civilization back a hundred years. Yet he grudgingly acknowledged that in the present instance, the military had so far done a decent job of rescuing the woman and himself, and attending to their needs. He realized deep down that it was unfair to equate the military to the loathsome monsters who directed their activities then, but it was difficult always to be fair. He sat quietly awaiting his turn, while Mary perused the map of the base; then she examined the list of instructions given them. "What's this debriefing about," she asked.

Roy glanced at the last item on the list. "Oh, I imagine some clerk will ask us some questions. You know, like, 'where were you when the wave hit?' or, 'how did you manage to survive?'"

"I don't want to answer questions. I'm afraid they'll find out about me."

Oh, my, he thought, here we go again. "Suppose they do, that's what you need. Tell them, let them help you find yourself, locate your family."

"They'll put me in a hospital. You promised you would help me, Roy, if you aren't going to keep your word, just say so."

"Look, I'm trying to do what's best for you. You are obviously not thinking clearly. You should tell them about your problem."

Mary stared off into space as if she no longer saw him or knew he was there.

"Mary?"

She did not answer.

"Oh, all right. What's it to me. If you want to take the risk of serious complications, it's your choice."

"Well, I'm not telling them anything, and that's that."

Her adamancy surprised him, as well as disturbed and aggravated him. He did not welcome the stress. Stress had long taken its toll on him. He yearned to be through with it, to be away from the press of people, and to drift into that comforting fog, that strange defensive mechanism which he had experienced at particularly trying times, since his tribulations began. It had protected his mind from overload. He could not induce it; he could not control it. Something beyond his volition assume command, a defense mechanism of some sort. It compelled him to slow down, to disengage, and to drift into the soothing mist. Twice, early on, following his discharge from the hospital, he became aware that time had passed for which he could not account. It had not recurred since that second episode. Now, the extreme manifestation of his condition seemed to consist of a brief twilight state, a nitrogen peroxide laughing-gas state, with reduced sensitivity to pain, where he levitated, where he lifted off like a helium-filled balloon, and drifted placidly through the cool haze. For the last seven years, he had functioned at times in a near normal state and at other times in a neurotic state, ranging from a fearful paranoia, to giddy silliness. It had enabled him to cope with the absurdities of the world.

That was before the woman intruded into his life with her problems and demands and forced him to be nearly sane all the time! It was too much to ask!

Or was it? At least he believed he knew what he was doing these days, and why.

"All right, then." Roy said, with a sigh of resignation, "Don't tell the clerks anything. We'll just stick to our story."

Before Mary could answer, however, before they could work out the details of their planned deception, the attendant came and ushered Mary away. Mary looked back at him plaintively.

Roy had no actual injuries requiring treatment. He expected a quick examination. However, for reasons that defied his understanding, the clerk required him to fill out a medical history form, which he did grudgingly, omitting parts of his medical history that he did not wish to share or discuss with strangers, thank you very much. He went where the white clad medical types told him to go, allowed people to probe him and give him a cursory going over, including a hurried vision test, and a blood pressure test, and had him cough, and bend over. He provided blood and urine samples for them to analyze at their leisure. The process took about thirty-five minutes, counting the time spent waiting for the next phase. Then the attendant took him to another room, which he surmised must be the debriefing. The nameplate on the door said Major Leonard T. Freund, M.D. Psychiatrist. "A Psychiatrist!" he snarled "Is there any category of humanity that I hate with such ardor as these fellows?"

"What did you say, sir?" the orderly asked.

"What's the idea of a Psychiatrist?"

"Just a debriefing, sir, that's all, there's nothing to worry about. The interview is required to complete the processing, if you want assistance."

"What kind of assistance?"

"Food and lodging until you connect up, sir."

"Hmm, well—

"You're next for doctor Freund, sir, go right in."

He opened the door.

"Come in, and have a seat, please," a man at a desk said, barely glancing up.

Roy sat in the straight chair in front of the desk. As always, he placed his pack at his feet. Back at the hall, when he and Mary checked in, the soldiers offered him a place to store his things. He declined the offer. He did so this time for good reason; because the pack contained the money and jewelry he took from the bodies of the rapists he had killed. He was not about to let it out of his sight. He waited for what he figured was a sufficient amount of time for the man to finish his scribbling and pay some attention to him, and then his ire began to mount. *Arrogant self-important bastard!* It was all he could do to contain himself. He wanted to snatch up his bag from the floor and charge out of the room. Just then, the man looked up at him with a brief phony smile. "I'm Doctor Freund," he said. "What's your name, sir?"

"Roy took in a deep breath and said cautiously, "Roy.""

"Roy, what?"

"Yes," Roy said, his inner rage subsiding, replaced by a mischievous impulse.

"What is your last name?"

"That's correct."

"What's correct?"

"Yes, it is."

Major Freund stared at Roy across the desk. Then he said, "Oh, I get it, you're doing that Bud Abbot-Lou Costello routine, right? The 'who is on first' thing. That is very funny. He laughed."

"I glad you enjoyed it," Roy said, beginning to relax a little."

Freund continued looking him over. He said, "You look familiar to me. Have we met before?"

"I don't think so."

"Hmm, well, now that we have had our entertainment, suppose you give me your full name, that's a good fellow."

"It's Hofstadter. That's spelled H-o-f-s-t-a-d-t-e-r."

"Roy Hofstadter. All right, Roy, what is, or was, your address?"

"It's on the form, there, Doctor." Roy said pointing to the folder, he had placed open-faced on the front edge of the desk.

"Oh, excuse me." the doctor said, as he looked at the paper. "Hm, I see here you list your permanent address as Champaign, Illinois. However, you were in Manhattan when the tsunami hit. In the Bowery, it says here."

"That's right."

"That's a rough neighborhood isn't it—wasn't it?"

"Yeah, that's correct—rough neighborhood."

"Hmm, so, how did you manage to survive the tsunami?"

"I was in the stairwell of the Empire State Building at about the thirty-seventh floor level when the shit hit the fan."

"Did you have family living with you there in the Bowery?"

"No, I lived alone."

"Okay … let's see, uh … Roy, your street address there was…?"

While Dr. Freund read the address, Roy had a flash. He had forgotten about his arrangement with Mary; suddenly he remembered, and said, "except for my wife, Mary."

"Excuse me?" Freund said, glancing up from the papers, looking puzzled.

"I said, except for my wife Mary."

Dr. Freund gazed at him for several moments, silent and expressionless, and then he said, "I asked you if you had family living with you, and you said 'no' and then when I am in process of formulating my next question you say, 'except for my wife Mary.'"

"That's right, just me and my wife Mary; no kids, no dogs, no cats, no canary, just Mary and me. I'm sorry; I've forgotten your next question."

"I haven't asked it yet. What do you do for a living, Mr. Hofstadter?"

"I'm retired," Roy said, puffing up a bit, sensing that the dreaded probing into his private affairs was imminent.

Doctor Freund studied Roy's shabby appearance, the backpack on the floor at his feet, his disheveled hair and stubble beard.

"What was your profession before you retired, sir?"

"I was a Sociology Professor—a while ago."

"Indeed?" Freund said. He stroked his chin. "Hm," he said again, appearing puzzled. Then suddenly his face brightened, and he exclaimed, "Royal Menken Hofstadter? I thought I recognized that name. "Professor of Sociology, University of Illinois!"

Roy was startled out of his mischievousness. "You … you've heard of me?" He stammered.

"Heard of you? Why, I used your textbooks in college, in undergraduate school, in my sociology class. What was it? —*Man and the Crowd*. I even remember your photograph from the dust jacket, now that I think about it. That is why you looked so familiar to me when you sat down. And that name—how could one forget that name?"

"Well keep it to yourself, Doctor," Roy whispered. "I'm traveling incognito."

Freund ignored the comment and continued gushing. "My undergraduate major was psychology, with a sociology minor," Freund said, enthusiastically. "I took a Masters after that, before I went on to med school," he added, importantly. Then he leaped to his feet, and ran around the desk, his hand extended. "This is a great honor for me, Professor Hofstadter."

"For me, too," said Roy, sarcastically, unable to dispel his long-held dislike for psychiatrist on such short notice. He shook Freund's outstretched hand, limply.

"You're a long way from Illinois, Professor." His expression took on a serious air. "You say you've been living in the Bowery, in an area of flophouses and bordellos, if my memory serves? How can this be? —an important man of letters such as yourself, a man of stature?"

"Field research."

"Field research?"

"Yes,. I watch people. I watch them to see what they will do next. I keep notes in my journals, and when my journals are full, I mail them to Box 123, Champaign, Illinois."

"Why, that actually sounds like fun. So, you say you're retired, then you are unaffiliated, which means you are doing independent research ... another book in the works, huh, Professor?"

"One never knows, does one?"

"And how long have you been conducting this field research, Professor Hofstadter, if you don't mind my asking?"

"Not at all, seven years, come November 22."

"Seven years. Hmm, then you must have learned a great deal about human nature in all that time."

"You would think so, but surprisingly little. However, I have developed a few theories."

"I don't wonder. During those seven years, have you traveled extensively, or have you been in New York all that time?"

"Extensively across America, but New York is where the action is, as you know, so I usually spend a few months there each year during the summer. Then I usually go from there to Miami, or New Orleans, or Phoenix, to avoid the harsh winters."

"Your wife—Mary, did you say? —she accompanies you on your, uh, field research?"

When Mary came up in the conversation, Roy found himself faltering and struggling for something plausible to say. He realized he should have told the doctor the truth about Mary for her own good, but he had promised her, and a promise was a promise. Unfortunately, they had made their decision to lie to the doctor too late to get their story straight. It was too late now to worry about it. He thought it best to end his interview with Dr. Freund, saying as little as possible about Mary.

"Sometimes but not always," he said. "Speaking of my wife, she is waiting for me. This whole matter has been hard on her. I don't like to leave her alone for very long. How much longer will we be, Dr. Freund?"

"Oh, I'm sorry, just a bit longer, and I promise to be brief. I'll just familiarize you briefly with our operation. Our goal here at the center is to treat any injured brought in and to provide aid and shelter for the refugees until they can make other arrangements. In some cases, very little is required; in other cases, people are alone and without resources of any kind."

"I have to confess that so far I'm impressive with your center," Roy said. "The trains are running on time."

Freund seemed puzzled by that comment, but he smiled and continued. "There are telephones in the center adjacent to the hall where you processed in. The phones are free of charge, and available day and night to call anywhere in the country. In most cases that and a night's lodging are all that people need to get them on their way. Some, though, have serious injuries requiring hospitalization including mental or emotional needs."

"I don't wonder." Roy said. "What greater trauma has anyone experienced than seeing his city swept away?"

"Yes. Well, anyway, we do what we can here in our temporary hospital with our limited facilities. If we can't handle an issue, we send the patient to permanent medical facilities further inland."

"I see," said Roy, fidgeting in his seat.

"Did you have any injuries, Professor, or trauma requiring counseling?"

"I got tossed around and banged up in the stairwell of the Empire State Building, but I have recovered from that pretty well, I only have a little soreness left which nature is attending to, although I don't know about my mind yet."

Freund smiled. "Any medical condition requiring medication?"

Oh, oh, thought Roy, here we go! He would tell Freund nothing about this psychiatric history. "Not unless you can prescribe something to fix a limp dick, Doctor."

The doctor took a couple of seconds before he broke into laughter, and shook his head, as if at the antics of a precocious child. "You have quite a sense of humor, Professor."

"I'm not laughing, Doctor, I really can't get it up anymore, not that I have much occasion to use it in that capacity lately."

"I'm sorry. Poor Mary, how awful for her," the doctor said.

"Well, it's no picnic for me, either."

The doctor chuckled again. "Listen, if you like we can discuss it."

"They had a brief discussion about impotence and the causes and treatments for it. Freund asked a few more questions about their ordeal in New York. Finally, Roy got up to leave, shook hands with Freund, thanked him, retrieved his pack from the floor, and headed toward the door.

"One last question, Professor,"

Roy stopped and turned.

"I'm always wondered about that middle name of yours."

"Oh, it's just an old family name, that's all," Roy, said. "Goodbye, Doctor Freund."

As Roy resumed his seat in the waiting area to await the arrival of Mary, he considered that Freund was not such a bad sort for a psychiatrist. He leafed through a magazine for a few minutes, got up and got a cola from a machine, sipped the cola, and wandered down a hallway peeking into rooms. He came to a small lounge with stuffed chairs. There was no one in the room. A TV mounted on the wall played to its phantom audience, the volume low. A news special was playing. He went inside and sat in a stuffed chair to watch.

"...fighting in southern Arizona along the Mexico border between law enforcement personnel and an unidentified group, believed to be a drug cartel. According to a recent report, a news helicopter, dispatched to observe the fighting, has crashed. We are attempting to verify this report."

Roy leaned forward and listened. "Now what?" he said, and kept watching and listening for a few moments longer, then he returned to the reception area to wait for Mary.

A half-hour later, she arrived.

"Well, how did it go?" He asked.

"No permanent damage," she said, smiling. "In fact, I'm feeling much better. They cleaned and treated my cuts and dressed them and gave me antibiotics, and some pills for my nerves, and some to help me sleep." She showed him the pills. "Then a psychiatrist interviewed me; I couldn't get out of it. He asked me questions. You won't believe the story I made up for him."

"Oh my, what was his name?"

"Frond I think."

"Did you tell him you had amnesia?"

"Of course not; I did just what we agreed to do. I told him I was Mary Hofstadter and that you, my husband, was here with me. I had to make up an address for us in Manhattan, and I told him you were a stockbroker. I hope that's all right."

"Jesus, Mary! I talked to the same guy; they'll throw us in jail for sure for lying to the government."

"I was afraid of that. You told him something different?"

"Yes, of course I did. How could I do otherwise? We didn't get our stories together." Roy displayed a rare moment of anger toward Mary, unjustly, he realized immediately.

They'll have to catch us first," she said, apparently feeling the effects of the 'nerve' medicine. "They're too busy to notice us."

"I hope you're right. Are you ready to get something to eat before we find a place to sleep?"

"Yes."

They walked back toward the mess hall. "You know, Roy," Mary said, "it's the funniest thing; sometimes my real name seems right on the tip of my tongue. Like just now when that psychiatrist was asking me questions about myself, and I was making things up. I knew they were lies."

"Well, of course, you did, Darling—they were lies."

"Yes, I know they were lies; that's not what I mean. I *knew* they were lies, on a different level. I could feel they were lies."

"That's wonderful news, Mary, you're making remarkable progress." He said, as he patted her hand paternalistically and glanced at her askance.

She withdrew her hand. "You don't understand, do you?"

"Apparently not."

"Never mind, it's not important."

It was mid-afternoon and already there were several people in the cafeteria line. "I'm not very hungry," she said.

"Me neither. We'll eat light, and then go to the housing office and get us a bunk for the night." Roy said. He took the map of the base out of his pocket and verified the location of the housing office. He turned the map over and read the information printed on the back. "Says here they use this base to train reserve military units in the summer; must be why they have such good facilities."

"Good facilities?"

"Well, yeah, relatively speaking."

"Relative to what?"

"Say, you sure you're not Miss Amy Vanderbilt?"

"I'm not sure of anything."

"We should stay here for a few days, if we can," Roy said. "You might come out of it, and we could track down your relatives. It could happen any moment, you know."

"I don't have any money."

"I have money. What made you think of that?"

"I don't know—you've done so much. I just don't want to be a further burden to you."

She seemed to be genuinely concerned. It worried him how her moods changed so abruptly. She must be as fragile as a kitten inside.

"You don't have to worry about that," He thrust his hand into his pocket, and pulled out a roll of bills bound by a rubber band."

"Where did you get all that?"

"I didn't steal it if that's what you're thinking."

"It never occurred to me."

"I had some all along, and I found more it in the offices back there in our building." He didn't mention the loot he had taken off the hooligans. "No sense leaving it there for the looters, was there?"

"Of course not; it's lucky for us you didn't. How much is it?"

"I don't know; I didn't count it, but it's enough so that you don't have to worry about money. My net worth and my standard of living have improved greatly since I met you, my dear. You brought me luck."

"Some luck."

"I don't need much; I live close to the street," Roy intoned, boastfully. "I keep my possessions with me at all times. I can move fast when I need to, faster than a speeding bullet."

"And now you have that big roll of bills to slow you down. By the way, don't you get tired of carrying that pack around with you all the time?"

"Are you kidding? I would be naked without it. No, I like having it with me."

She looked at him skeptically. "I'll bet you wear aluminum foil in that baseball cap of yours to keep the space aliens away."

He feigned alarm. "How did you know?"

Mary laughed.

This woman was turning into a real talker, and a very smart one at that, he thought. She, who went from tears to smiles to tears again in an instant, was now suddenly the life of the party, joking, laughing. What did that doctor give her, anyway? She had such a pretty face when she laughed. She had come a long way since he pulled her from the rubble caked with mud. He regarded her recent displays of humor as a personal triumph—a prerequisite to her mental health and recovery. She was surely getting better; he was getting better, too. He had thought more than once that the disaster might actually have saved his life. Perhaps this woman with her extraordinary needs had provided him with a momentary reprieve, a reason to go on. However, he worried that when the shock finally wore off and she remembered her life, it might not be so pleasant; it might be too much for her to handle. Of late, he had decided he wanted to be there when she came back to the present from wherever she was now.

"No, it's true," he said, "having few possessions is a wonderfully liberating state of affairs. I can pick up and go wherever I please, whenever I please. In fact, I plan to head south soon. I had planned to go down to Miami and winter there. I always liked Miami—but there is no Miami, now."

"I knew it. I'm holding you back. You want to go south and I'm holding you back." Her face clouded.

"I'm in no hurry. I wouldn't miss all this excitement for the world, like seeing the Big Apple get its comeuppance."

"Take me with you," she said.

"What?"

"Take me with you" Her voice was pleading, imploring."

"You mean south?"

"Yes."

"You can't be serious."

"Oh, but I am serious, Roy. Please don't say, no." She cuddled up close to him and took his arm."

"Listen, lady, maybe you didn't hear what I said, I travel light. So light in fact, that some people might even consider me a bum."

"Well, as far as I know, I'm a bum too."

"Nonsense, you're a grand, cultivated lady, probably rich, too. Here, open your mouth and let me see your teeth."

"What?"

"Let me see your teeth. I can tell your social strata by looking at your dental work. Come on, nobody's looking."

"Don't be silly, I'm not a horse, I'm a person." She spoke under her breath and glanced about furtively. The people directly in front of them in line were paying no attention to Roy and Mary, who were still last in the serving line.

"You can inspect my teeth later, if you must," Mary whispered, "in the privacy of our room, if we get one."

Roy put his left arm around her neck, got her by the chin with his right fingers, and gently coaxed her to open her mouth. "Open up," he whispered.

"You are crazy," she mumbled, "you really are." She glanced around once more to see that no one was watching them.

She opened her mouth and he looked inside. "Ah, ha," he whispered in her ear. "Just as I thought, perfect teeth, not even a filling or a crown."

"Oh, yes there are. I have two crowns, one up, one down," she pointed.

"No kidding," he said, and looked carefully where she pointed. "How do you know that? You have amnesia, remember?"

They had been putting food dishes on their trays as they moved along in line and and carried on their bantering conversation, and now they arrived at the checkout counter where they displayed their nametags to the clerk. She rang up their tabs but did not charge them. They proceeded on to a table.

"So, how do you know that?" he persisted.

"I don't know, Roy, I just do. Stop changing the subject. When are we going south?"

"We'll go south when you get your memory back, if you still want to go then. Hurry up and eat, now."

They ate their food without further conversation. Roy was not sure if she was serious about going south with him. It was an absurd idea, of course, but in spite of himself, he actually began to consider it. That would certainly be a change.

No, that was not going to happen. He would say good-by to the woman as soon as possible. The only thing holding him back was that he had given her his word not to abandon her until she got her memory back, which probably was not such a smart move on his part. He could not remember if he had actually meant it or not when he said it. In any event, he now intended to keep his word, unless she turned into a real pain in the ass.

Conway was all too aware of the state of affairs in the nation as he waited for his audience with the President of the United States.

Conway and his secretary, Jasmine Jones, had made a quick visit to key cities in Europe and the Middle East. They met with embassy officials, and a few select other individuals of his acquaintance, and they listened and talking to ordinary people. The information they gleaned added to the information he and his team had garnered on La Palma. In the end, Conway had formed an opinion, which shortly he would impart to the new president, a man named Charles McGruder. It was not what he had expected to bring back from his inquiries abroad, and he was not looking forward to the meeting. He had already given his report to his boss at the National Security Agency, Admiral Stanfield. Stanfield had called him in later, discussed it with him, and directed him to go to the temporary White House and report directly to the President.

It was strange walking into the lobby of a luxury hotel in the heart of Philadelphia to see the President, even though the lobby and the outside were swarming with armed military personnel and contractors still working to get the building operational.

A snappily dressed middle-aged man who identified himself as Mr. Smithers, Presidential Aide, met him at what had been the front desk of the hotel and took him, by way of a secure elevator, to the previous penthouse suites now the Presidential offices. After emerging from the elevator, Conway followed Smithers through the main reception area crowded with desks and workers, down a hallway, past two armed guards, to whom the man nodded, past a second small cluster of secretaries, through a doorway and into a spacious office. The president was standing when they entered.

"Good morning, Doctor Conway, come in please. That will be all for now Smithers, please wait outside."

"Yes, sir."

Conway would not have recognized the man had he not recently seen his image on television. He had succeeded President Blander, who died of a heart attack after only a few hours in office. McGruder had been president for so brief a time and under such extreme circumstances, that there had not even been time to produce the obligatory photographs of the Chief Executive, which one traditionally sees in federal offices.

The President was in his shirtsleeves. He was a rather undistinguished man of medium height, a bit on the plump side, with thin sandy hair and brown eyes. He appeared to be in his mid-forties. Conway thought he looked more like the manager of a shoe store, or someone whom one might bump into at a Rotary Club meeting, rather than one of the most powerful men in the world.

The President extended his hand, "I'm about to have a diet cola, Dr. Conway, would you like one?"

Conway shook the President's hand. "Don't mind if I do, sir."

"Okay, have a seat right here and I'll fetch them."

The president crossed the room and opened a door, behind which was a refrigerator. He removed two cans, crossed the room again, smiled casually, handed one to Conway, and took a chair opposite him.

"This is not what I expected, Mr. President."

"Oh? What did you expect, a glass?"

"No, I mean I expected you would be in a room full of stern faced generals and bureaucrats."

The President smiled. "I hope you're not too disappointed."

"Not in the least."

"Admiral Stanfield gave me a copy of your report, Dr. Conway, but I wanted to hear it from you, personally. I understand you believe the landslide on the island of La Palma might not have been an act of nature, but the result of a deliberate, calculated act."

"Let me be clear. I found no evidence that. I only came to believe that it was possible, though improbable."

"All right then, tell me how you came to that opinion. Take me through it."

"As you know, sir, I was dispatched by Admiral Stanfield to inspect the slide area and meet with the locals. I had a team of some of the best scientist in the world with me, and the scientists we met with were no slouches, either. I asked them if they had found any evidence of explosives, and they assured me they had not, and further that perpetrators could not have used explosives without detection. They went on to sum up their collective views of what caused the landslide. The main theory was that the volcanic eruptions of 1971 weakened the island's substrate to the extent that the land finally simply gave way.

The mechanism for the 1971 incident was volcanic heating of trapped water inside the volcanoes. The water converted to steam, building up tremendous pressure, causing the mountain to slide about three meters toward the sea. There was no volcanic activity this time, and one of the scientists said rather casually that volcanic heating was the only way the trapped underground water could possibly heat up sufficiently to convert to steam, to build up the kind of pressure required. He made this statement as if it were a foregone conclusion, not subject to any question whatsoever. I am by nature suspicious of such assertions, so I thought about it a great deal. It occurred to me that one might heat the water with a nuclear reactor such as are used in nuclear submarines and ships, which are designed rather compactly, compared to their cousins in nuclear power plants."

"Back up a minute," the president said. "Why did you rule out the notion that volcanic activity could have caused it, since that appear to be the most plausible explanation?"

"My geologist pointed out at that there were no steam vents after the slide—no evidence of volcanic activity of any kind on the exposed surface."

"I see. Then you are thinking somebody transported a mobile reactor into the mountain, into the volcano? Frankly, Doctor Conway, that sounds far-fetched to me, for a whole lot of reasons."

"I know, sir, it does to me too, and, once again, I am not saying that someone actually did it, I am saying that I believe that it is possible that someone could do it that way. I am responding to what the scientist said that the only way heating could have occurred was through volcanic infiltration.

I believed it to be possible to use nuclear energy to heat that much water to steam. I consulted a professor of physics at MIT, a friend. His name is Gregg Cooper, whom I have known and been associated with for several years. He agreed with me that it was well within the range of possibility. If that is true, then the problem becomes one of how "they" could have gotten a functioning nuclear reactor inside the mountain without detection. I learned that there were tunnels already in existence far back into the base of the volcanic mountain. That's how they could have gained access."

"Okay, skip the details for now," the president said, "bottom line; you and your physics friend believe it is possible."

"Yes."

"If it's possible, then maybe someone did it, and maybe the rumors floating around are true. These rumors, these rumblings are giving impetus to the clamor for war from extremist elements within the United States. Such a war, I am convinced, would prove disastrous for the entire world. It would be the last straw. It must not happen. I understand that after your inspection of the island and your meeting with the officials, you and an associate traveling around the area, listening, observing, and talking to people. What did you learn from that? Terrorist usually like to claim credit for their deeds. Is anybody bragging, or claiming credit?

No, but that is understandable, they know what the Zionist are capable of."

"There are members of my cabinet that agree with the warmongers. They still want that definitive war between the Christian West and Islam. Trust me Dr. Conway this is not good news to me, and your opinion is not a welcome one to me. Some otherwise decent people are upset enough to nuke the hell out of somebody, playing into the hands of the conspirators."

Conway looked quizzically into the eyes of the new president. He marveled at how forthcoming the President was with him. Conway studied his face. He saw lines of worry that he had missed before.

"How could we determine, one way or the other, Doctor Conway, if that landslide was natural or man-made?" the President asked, switching back, once again, to the previous question.

"If there was a nuclear reactor in that mountain it should be down there on the ocean bottom. It might be in plain view, or under a mountain of rubble. We could go down and look for it, but if it was buried our search would be pointless, unless—

"Unless what?"

"Unless the reactor was giving off detectable radiation, something that instruments could detect."

"You mean like a Geiger counter?"

"Yes, but a very sensitive and sophisticated one, mounted on a small two-man submarine which could move slowly and close to the rubble on the ocean bottom. The rubble field extends for miles, approximately 26 miles along the coast line."

The president considered that for a few moments. "All right, Dr. Conway let's leave it there for now and go back a moment—forgive me for jumping around—you said earlier that they, meaning the terrorist, knew what the Neocons are capable of—what did you mean by that?"

"I was saying the Islamist might not come right out and tell the world what they did this time, because they are afraid of what the 'Mighty Satan' would do, like 'nuking them back to the Stone Age.' Besides that, if they are guilty, as long as the world believes it was a natural disaster it takes the heat off them, and they are free to plan their next move. I imagine that would be more important to them at the moment than bragging rights, although I'm sure they could use such a coup to good effect in motivating and recruiting others to join their cause."

"The way it looks, they don't need any more motivation," the President said, as he reached for a silver cigarette case. They are quite motivated as it is. Cigarette, Dr. Conway?"

"I don't smoke."

"Mind if I do?"

"No."

The President smiled apologetically. "I've taken up cigarettes again, temporarily, in the privacy of my office. I gave them up years ago. Can you believe that? Stupid, nasty habit...but frankly I never expected—

"I understand, sir."

"Thanks." The president lit up, drew deeply, and exhaled away from his guest. The air conditioning system sucked up the smoke and whiffed it away. "Back to this notion of nuking them, two questions come to mind, which my advisors and the Pentagon Generals seem to slough over. The first one is: who, in your opinion, is the 'them' we speak of these days?' Who are these people? As I am sure you know, from our years of fighting 'them,' that the terrorist are a fluid and elusive group. They have been around now for a long time, and our best efforts have proven ineffective in rooting them out. Every time we obliterate them somewhere, they soon crop up somewhere else. They come from many nations. They are not all Arabs, they are not even all Muslims, and they do not all come from the same country. There are Christians, Europeans, even Americans among them. There is really no place to nuke, even if we were crazy enough to do it. This is their greatest strength, that they have no single country for us to attack, and the fact that they do not fear death. If they fear we will nuke them, where is it they fear we will nuke?"

"To begin with, they fear that the 'Great Satan,' which, in their minds means Neocons, and that means Zionist, will generate any pretexts to attack and destroy Muslim nations to further Israel's territorial and hegemonic ambitions in particular, and in furtherance of their world agenda in general. They believe the United States is essentially a Zionist puppet state, and that Israel is really in charge. In their view, it is no problem for us to create a pretext and generate a ground swell of support within the US, given our controlled press and mindless, hedonistic populace."

"So they fear we will bomb their cities? The Islamic Federation covers a lot of territory."

"Mecca and Medina, sir, their holy cities in Saudi Arabia, would be my guess."

"That would never have occurred to me, or to anyone else in my government!"

"I wouldn't be so sure about that, sir. Are you forgetting Dresden? How about Hiroshima and Nagasaki? How about Bagdad, for that matter, Libya and Syria. If they are somehow responsible for the tsunami that's possibly the reason they're not openly bragging about it."

"Okay, you've made your point." The President frowned, fidgeted, and studied his hands, as if Conway's comments had triggered something weighty and distasteful.

"You realize, Doctor Conway, even if it is true, even if the hand of man brought down that mountain, rather than nature, and even if you could prove conclusively that these so-called radical 'Islamist' did it, we will drop no nuclear bombs on Mecca or Medina while I am president. However, I still need to know the truth as well as it can be determined in order to deal with these mad-dog Neocons and assorted nut-cases who still plague us after all these years, and to somehow put an end to the insanity of perpetual war. Do you understand that?"

"Yes, sir, I do understand it, and I agree with the sentiment."

"All right then, how did they do it, how did they pull it off?

"Back to those tunnels again, sir, those extensive existing tunnels into the mountain. On one pretext or another, agents could have transported reactor components into that mountain and reassembled them there. Then they could have drilled into the trapped water, piped into it—

"How long would this search with the submarine take?" The President interrupted.

"One, maybe two weeks at the most, once we are on site, if the Navy and others within the government cooperate fully and everything goes smoothly. If you give the word, we can start putting it together immediately, I mean today. I will need the assistance of my MIT physicist friend, Gregg Cooper. I have discussed the situation with him. He has a top secret clearance because of his work in the MIT labs."

"Could you do this secretly, without the mission becoming known?"

"I think so. I believe we could remain submerged throughout the entire investigation, by attaching the minisub to the port of a submarine—a nuclear submarine and remaining submerged the entire time"

"Could you direct the mission yourself?"

"Yes, sir."

The President considered it briefly. "All right, Doctor Conway, you have my approval—whatever you need. You will be working directly for me, now, but through Mr. Forester, My Chief of Staff. Smithers will take you to see him while you are here, as soon as our meeting is over. You will communicate and work through him and him alone, but you are in charge of the effort; tell him what you need. Politically, this is a highly important and sensitive matter, and I am giving it top priority and top-secret classification. Do you understand?"

"Yes, sir, I do."

"Further, you are to report your findings to me and to me alone, not to Forester, not to anyone else, unless you hear otherwise from me personally. Do you understand me?"

"Yes, sir, I understand."

"Do you accept that I will decide what use I will make of this information, not you, and not anyone else, whether you agree with me or not? Do you accept that premise?"

"Yes, sir, I accept it."

"All right, then." The President rose from his chair and crossed the room. "By the way," he said, in a less intense tone, "I understand you lost your home at Georgetown in the disaster."

"That's correct."

"Where do you live now?"

"I have a motel room in Gaithersburg, but I've been on the road so much it hasn't mattered."

"Then I want to house you nearby—if you have no objection."

"That's fine with me, sir."

"Okay, then, unless you have something else, go talk to Mr. Forester. Smithers will take you to his office. I will give Forester a call right now and tell him you are coming. I want you on this as soon as possible. And remember, keep it close to the vest—strictly 'need to know.'"

"Yes, sir."

The President took Conway's hand and escorted him to the door. "Thank you for your willingness to serve your country, Doctor Conway, and good luck," he said. He summoned Smithers and gave him his instructions.

After Conway left, President Charles McGruder walked to his desk, picked up the telephone receiver, dialed, and talked for several minutes, put down the phone, turned and walked to the window behind his desk. The window was tinted and covered with narrow strip Venetian blinds. He quietly studied the city below. Then he sat in his chair. Tiny beads of perspiration blanketed his upper lip and around the hairline at his temples. He turned his chair abruptly around to the desk, hit an intercom button, and said, "Winston, get Hadley and Barton in here—on the double."

"Yes, sir, right away."

"When they get here send them right in."

Hadley was Brad Hadley, ex-senator from Massachusetts, who was now McGruder's political advisor. While he waited for Hadley, the President slumped in his chair, massaging his right temple with his fingertips. "God, how did I get myself into this?"

It was obviously hard for some in the old power structure, to realize and accept the fact that he was legally and legitimately the president. He knew there were better qualified men for the job, by a long shot, but The Committee had been rigidly determined that they follow the line of succession to a tee, that they preserve the rule of law and constitutionality at all costs. It made perfect sense because once you step over the line everything goes and the nation becomes a nation of men and not of laws. The coastal area was already under martial law when he became president. He, like so many others, thought it nothing short of miraculous that the nation made it through these dark days without an attack from without or a coupe from within. But they and he knew it was too early to celebrate, to let down the guard. For his own part, he was thinking of that rabid bunch of warmongers previously in the pentagon, currently lounging comfortably at Wright-Pat, along with their allies in the congress, what was left of them. Fortunately, for the nation, many of those people were dead, thanks to the tsunami, but not nearly enough of them, as far as he was concerned. We have Associate Justice Clarence White and his committee of quick-thinking patriots to thank for saving our asses."

However, Justice White and the Committee had been compelled to negotiate with the various factions and power groups within the political establishment in appointing replacement members of the cabinet, the administration, and the congressional staffs. So all the people with whom the President had to deal were not sympathetic to his views, by any means.

He reflected that President Dwayne Blander's body was not even cold, and McGruder's plane had not even landed, from carrying him back from Indiana, before the Neocons were bending his ear. They wanted World War III, or maybe one should call it World War IV, since many considered that the last forty years of perpetual war was really World War III.

The warmongers, too, had heard the wafting speculations that somehow the hand of man had brought down the volcanic mountains. Instinctively and reflexively "radical Islam," which still opposed Israeli hegemony in the Middle East was their natural suspect; and barring actual proof, they would settle for any plausible pretext to attack them again. It would not do for the warmongers to get wind of young Doctor Conway's mission, whose findings could deprive them of that pretext. Admiral Stanfield, head of the NSA, was in the President's camp. He would look out for Cooper.

While the President waited for his aides, he took his handkerchief and dabbled at the perspiration on his face. He reflected further upon the incredible events of the last weeks, from that morning when his father had awakened him to tell him about the tsunami. He, like millions of others, watched in horror the unfolding events of the greatest natural disaster in human history, and its aftermath.

The buzzer interrupted the President's thoughts. The door opened and a man walked into the office. He was a slender, well-built man of about forty, with black crew-cut hair. He looked like a mid-western college basketball player from the 1950's era. McGruder watched him cross the room and take the chair in front of his desk.

"You heard, Gregg?" The President asked. Gregg Barton, his friend since childhood was his advisor on domestic affairs. The President had asked him to listen in on his conversation with Conway on the intercom.

"Yes."

"What do you think?" the President asked.

"Doctor Conway seems sincere, and competent."

"That's what I thought as well." McGruder paused, thoughtful, and then continued. "When Hadley gets here, we'll talk about this situation. Bart, I cannot begin to tell you what it means to me to have you here with me. I honestly don't think I could handle it alone."

"You won't be alone as soon as Mildred and the kids get here."

"Yes, it'll be great to have them here, but that's not the kind of aloneness I mean. I still cannot believe that I am actually the President of the United States of America—what is left of it. Do you realize I cannot even remember the names of all my cabinet members yet? I have to stop and think when I meet one of them in the hall, or sneak a peek at the list of names I carry in my pocket. I am having meetings with a room full of strangers. They are looking to me for answers, for leadership. A month ago, I had a comfortable, obscure office in the Department of Agriculture. Why, my being in President William's administration in the first place was a total fluke, you know that."

"Yeah, I know, Charles, but you have only yourself to blame. You should not have worked so hard back in Indiana to get Williams elected. But you're here now, pal, and you are the President, so get used to it, or you'll give yourself an ulcer."

"It's been a revelation to me, Gregg, the powerful people who have come out of the woodwork. They explained to me when my first impulse was to decline the honor that continuity of government was of paramount importance; that maintaining the line of succession in the face of the severest challenges and threats to the Republic would demonstrate resilience, would have a calming effect on our people, and would give our enemies pause. That's what I do, Gregg, contribute continuity. They know and I know that there are ten thousand people better qualified than I am to take the helm. So I don't think they expect much in the way of actual performance from me, just keep the seat warm, and stay out of the way."

"Well, fuck them, Charlie! Regardless of what they thought then or think now, the fact remains that you really are president, and you do not owe those bastards anything. Now, I have known you all your life, since we were kids together and went through school from kindergarten on. Hell, we played hooky together, went fishing together, even played on a statewide high school championship basketball team together. I know what you're made of, Charlie, and I don't have any doubts about you, and you need not have any either. You have a brain, Charlie. You just listen and learn, and you do the right thing. That's all there is to it. It's just like running a hardware store, or that farm you grew up on. A brain and a set of balls is all a man needs, no matter what the task."

"I didn't mean to get you so stirred up, Gregg, but you do make it sound simple."

"It is simple."

The president sat back in his chair, and clasped his hands behind his head; a smile crept across his face. "Now, you know why I want you here with me, Gregg. But seriously, the neocons and the military-industrial complex both want war with the Muslins, though for different reasons and I don't know if I can contain them."

"Let's hope young Dr. Conway comes up empty handed," Barton said.

The door opened once again and another man entered.

"Come on in, Brad." the President said. "You're just in time to help us save the world."

CHAPTER SIX

At the Camp Lamar refugee reception center where Roy and Mary found themselves, there was a separate self-service coffee setup in the dining hall with a large coffee maker and all the fixings. It obviously was a popular feature, and the mess hall was obviously the center of activity for the refugees. Roy and Mary were there once more, too early for the evening meal. After walking around the center, peering into all the rooms, they returned to the mess hall and to the coffee pot. They fixed themselves coffees and headed for a large round table in the far corner of the hall where it was quieter. "I'll bet this place is as noisy as the belly of a B-29 at regular meal time," Roy quipped

The large round table seated eight to ten people more or less comfortably, depending on how friendly they were. Three men were sitting there, their meal finished, engrossed in conversation. Mary turned away toward a nearby smaller table, but Roy whispered, "No, let's sit here with these fellows; I want to hear what they're talking about."

Mary smiled at him. "Why?"

Roy smiled slyly as they sat down, "It's my job, it's what I do," he whispered, then more loudly, "Do you gentlemen mind if we join you?"

The man who was talking stopped-mid sentence and he and his companions turned to face the two new arrivals. The man who had been speaking said, "Help yourself, friends," and turned back and picked up his discourse where he had left off, saying, "Sure, I believe it's a conspiracy. Conspiracies are as common as house-flies, contrary to what the media and the uppity-ups of our society would have you think. It's not about duck hunting and skeet shoot-ing. You got to ask yourselves who the hell are these people who want to take away our guns, huh? Tell me that, and what's their real motive?"

Roy smiled, and looked at Mary. "See what I mean?" he whispered.

Roy had a technique he used at those times when he could not conveniently take notes or record the conversation with a small portable pocket recorder, which he sometimes used. To help him remember the talkers, he invented caricatures for them, and the less flattering the better, so long as they had an element of authen-ticity to them.

The current speaker was a man whom Roy pegged as a pomp-ous, loud-mouthed, fat man, perhaps in his late thirties, of the type of semi-literate tradesman, whose union wages squeezed him just barely into the now dwindling middle class. He would be "Fat Man." The second man was tall, skinny and frail in appearance, and kept nodding and bobbing as the first man pontificated. Probably queer, thought Roy; but, of course, he made a mental note to keep that opinion to himself, because queers were now a protected class. He would be "Skinny." The third man was older. He wore a terribly soiled, but well-cut, good quality suit, and a grimy white dress shirt, with no tie. He had thinning salt-and-pep-per hair, and a Certified Public Accountant look.

The CPA answered the Fat Man's question: "I have my own ideas about that—well, not my own ideas exactly; they're other people's ideas, which I accept and embrace wholeheartedly. These people like to make out that the reason they labor endlessly to take our guns away is to end the deaths caused by firearms. I, on the other hand, believe they wish to disarm us so they may subjugate us with impunity. Disarming the public is the first thing that tyrants do when they take over a country. That renders the people impotent, unable to fight back. The tyrants then can work their will on them."

The CPA paused; nobody interrupted him, so he continued.

"You see, when the evil-doers come to rob us of our freedom they don't come to each of us and do battle with use individually. No, what they do is gain control of our government and our institutions, then they send the CIA, or the FBI, or, if necessary, the Armed Forces of the United States to deal with us. That's why the Declaration of Independence is so important to us. 'When in the course of human events—

"Jesus Christ, you're not going to recite the whole goddamn Declaration of Independence are you?" The skinny man asked.

"Of course he isn't," retorted the Fat Man, "he don't know the whole thing by heart."

"Actually, I do know it by heart," said the CPA, but I wasn't going to recite the whole damn thing, I merely wished to call your attention to the fact that the document says it is okay to overthrow the government if it becomes corrupt, and no longer serves the interests of the people."

"You mean overthrow the government by force?" Skinny said.

"Yes, that's exactly what I mean," the CPA answered.

"But, isn't that against the law?"

"Of course it is," the CPA said, grimacing, the veins in his neck bulging. He leaped up suddenly and began walking away from the table."

"Where you going, pal?" Fat Man asked. "Come on back. We'll try to follow you; to understand what you wish to teach us." He turned and winked at Skinny.

"Ignorant bastards," CPA mumbled.

"No, no, come back. We're interested in what you're saying."

The CPA stopped, wheeled around, returned to the table and sat down with them again. "Of course, it's against the law, god-damn it. Do you expect a corrupt government to say to its dis-sidents, 'come on, folks, overthrow us, we know we are evil and corrupt, and we deserve it?' Of course, not, they will not say that. They will say 'if you try it we will rip out your hearts! If you even talk about it, we'll get you for conspiracy.' How could it be other-wise? It follows that the government will do everything in its power to maintain itself, not the least of which is to pass laws prohibiting its overthrow."

The Fat Man guffawed, and took his shot at Skinny. "Well, tell me then, friend, what are you going to do if we don't overthrow them, talk them into surrendering? I'm beginning to understand what our friend, here, is saying and it's pissing me off just to think about it."

"I see your point all right, it's just—

"Thank you," interrupted the CPA."

"Besides," the Fat Man interjected excitedly, "it's all lies they're spreading about guns, in the first place. They've done these stud-ies, see, and where law-abiding citizens got guns the crime is lower."

"That is precisely correct," said CPA, looking quizzically askance at his accidental, temporary companion, "extensive objective stud-ies and evaluations of the impact of an armed citizenry on crime have demonstrated consistently that when the law-abiding citizens have guns, the crime rates in all categories go down. In fact, I have a book, an excellent book on the subject."

"You do? Where is this book?" asked Skinny.

Roy, sighed, and glanced over at the serving line. "Say, Mary, want to get a bite, now?"

"Okay."

⊶⊷

After their meal, Roy and Mary found the housing office and received a small room with two army cots on the second floor of one of the barracks. The latrines, one for each sex, were at the center of the barracks on each of the floors—a very frugal and functional arrangement. The day had been so stressful and tiring that they went to bed immediately and slept soundly.

Late the following morning, Roy awoke refreshed, wondering what to do next. He had no reason to call anyone; there was no one to call. Mary did not know who she was, so she could not call anyone. They had to decide what to do. Roy had showered, shaved, and donned his clean set of clothes, which he did because of Mary, though he might not have admitted it. There was also his unexpected encounter with Doctor Freund, whose enthusiastic appreciation of Roy's textbook authorship had given a boost to Roy's ego. When Mary awakened and readied herself, they walked to the mess hall together for breakfast. He still wore his backpack. They went through the line and found a table.

"What are we going to do today, Mary, got any ideas? Too bad we can't stay here for a while and rest up."

"Let's head south," she replied without hesitation.

"Oh, Mary, be serious, will you?"

Just then, Roy heard his name announced over the PA system. "Professor Roy Hostetler, please report to Dr. Freund's office."

The message was repeated twice more, and Mary said, "Roy, that's you. What do they want with you? Why are they calling you Professor?"

"They are obviously confused." Roy said. "I'm sure it's nothing to worry about." He glanced at the clock on the wall. It was almost nine. "Go on with your breakfast. I will go see what he wants. I won't be long. You wait right here for me."

Roy found Freund at his desk reading a book, his half-circle reading glasses perched on the end of his nose. He glanced up as Roy came in and said, "Ah, good morning, Professor Hofstadter, how were you sleeping accommodations? Was everything to your liking?"

"It's everything I always dreamed a barracks should be," Roy replied.

"That bad, eh?" Freund said, absently, as he took one more glance at the book, inserted a marker, and set it aside. "Please sit down, Professor. There's something I need to discuss with you."

Roy sat down in the proffered chair. "Call me Roy, please, Doctor; I'm no longer an active professor. I don't want to confuse anybody."

"All right, Roy, if you insist. Then I suppose you'll want to call me Leonard."

"I wouldn't dream of it, Leonard; I know how you medical doctors are."

"Have it your own way, Roy. Now, tell me about this wife of yours."

"Tell you about Mary? What do you want to know?"

"I saw her shortly after I saw you yesterday, and she told me, among other things, that you were a stockbroker."

"A stockbroker? Oh, me!"

"I take it then that you are not a stockbroker, in addition to being a field researching ex-Sociology Professor."

"I was afraid of this, Doctor. Mary has been acting very strangely since the disaster, and frankly, I have been worried about her. She has a serious lapse of memory, and she says some of the most outlandish things, with no apparent knowledge that she's doing it."

"Hm, I see. That explains it then." The doctor scratched his chin, as he considered Mary. "This could be very serious, Roy. Why didn't you mention it to me before? It sounds like Post Traumatic Stress Disorder to me."

"I wanted to, but she's terrified of doctors. She made me promise not to give her away because she is convinced she will be fine soon. But, frankly, I'm surprised her examination went as well as it did."

"The exams here are perfunctory at best," Doctor Freund said. "In light of what you say, I'm afraid Mary needs a more thorough examination and evaluation. Then, depending on what we find, she may need medication, or therapy. She should not put this off and hope for the best."

"That sounds like good advice to me, Doctor, but what can I do? She made me promise, and I've already broken my promise to her by telling you. She'll be furious with me if she finds out. By the way, what did she say when you told her you had already spoken to me? Neither of us expected to be talking to a psychiatrist, you see."

"I didn't mention it to her. I wanted to talk to you first."

"Thanks, Doc, I appreciate that. What do you want me to do?"

Freund thought. "I don't want to alarm her, certainly. I suppose we could try to trick her into allowing me to examine her more thoroughly. However, I don't think that would be such a good idea. It would be better to level with her. After all, there is nothing for her to fear. The danger is in neglecting a potentially serious condition. However, I'll leave it up to the two of you to decide; it's a free country. But if you want my advice, you'll get her here tomorrow morning at ten and I'll do the rest."

"All right, doctor, whatever you say. I'll have her here at ten."

Roy smiled to himself as he departed. A plan was already forming in his mind as to how he could get the woman cured of her amnesia, and then he could go on his way south before the weather turned cold. The doctor came to the door and said, "One other thing, Roy. The base has a few efficiency apartments left. Considering Mary's potential condition, I'm going to assign the two of you one of these units for a few days. It may take that long to give her a thorough going over. I'll give the housing office a call for you. You and Mary go on by there; they'll be expecting you."

"That's very considerate of you, Doctor Freund." Roy said, genuinely pleased. "How long can we stay?"

"That depends. Let me give Mary her checkup and we'll see what I find."

"All right, see you tomorrow."

Roy knew Mary would be upset about this new development. He would need to approach her carefully. He found her still sitting dutifully at the table in the mess hall where he had left her.

"What did the Doctor want?"

"My food has gotten cold," Roy said, "Let me get some fresh bacon and eggs and then I'll fill you in."

When he returned, he said, "Freund mentioned how you had said that I was a stockbroker, and he is worried about you. He wants to check you over more thoroughly before we go on our way to parts unknown; isn't that considerate of him?"

"I was afraid this would happen. What did you tell him?"

"What could I tell him? I told him you had been acting a little strange since the disaster, problems with your memory, and all that."

"You didn't!"

"Don't get sore. I had to explain it somehow since we gave him different stories, but listen to what he said, he wants you to come in for a little chat in the morning; he thinks you may be suffering from post-traumatic stress. See, you and I only have to get our stories straight this time, not too much detail, just general information. Oh, and he got us an efficiency apartment for a few days; we're set for a while."

"An apartment?"

"Yes, and all you have to do is go in and talk to him again. A smart gal like you can do that standing on your head."

"I want to see this fancy apartment."

"Don't believe me, huh? All right, you relax and let me have my breakfast in peace and we'll go check it out."

Later, as they walked to the housing office, Mary was quiet. Roy noticed and said, "Now, what's wrong?"

"I don't know, I'm… afraid."

He put his arm around her shoulder. "What are you afraid of?"

"I don't know, exactly. It's the whole thing. Who am I? Where do I belong? I want to know…and I'm afraid to find out."

Roy did not answer immediately. The same thought had occurred to him, and he was not sure what to say. At least she realized her dilemma and that was a positive development. "We have to make the best of it," he said. "We can't let it get us down. Go along with the doctor as much as you can. He might be able to help you after all. He thinks you are my wife, so no one is going to lock you up in a hospital, I'll see to that. I promised you didn't I? So try to relax and don't get in a sweat over it. Take another of your nerve pills."

"That's easy for you to say."

Roy ignored her comment. "I told him a story, too," he said. "Guess what I told him."

"I couldn't begin to guess."

"I told him I was a Sociology Professor on sabbatical, doing field research. That's why they called me 'professor' over the intercom."

"Did you really?"

"Yeah, do you believe it? He calls me Professor Hofstadter, and I call him Doctor Freund. I told him to call me Roy, though. If you hear him refer to me as Professor tomorrow, you will know what is going on. Whatever you hear just go along with it, okay?"

"Whatever you say, Roy."

Presently, they arrived at the housing office. The young corporeal at the desk was expecting them, and gave them the keys to the apartment, along with sheets, blankets, towels, and toiletries, and directed them to their new quarters also on the second floor of the building at the far end.

When they entered, Mary said, "Why, this is nice, Roy, tiny but nice."

It was one medium-sized room, with a small kitchen area and the bathroom off to the side.

"Uh, oh," he said.

"What?"

"Only one bed."

Mary smiled mischievously.

"But there's the couch for me," Roy added.

They threw the blankets and other things on the bed and sat down on the couch.

"Now, first things first," Roy said. "Let's get our story straight."

Roy went over again precisely what he had told the doctor, and had Mary repeat it; and filled in a little more background material. When Roy was satisfied, he said, "That's that. Can I do anything else to make you feel secure about tomorrow?"

"She snuggled close to him, put her arms around his neck and placed her head on his shoulder. "Just hold me," she said.

Roy felt a moment of panic. He put his arms around her clumsily, and hugged her to him. He had hugged her many times before to comfort her, but it had been natural and spontaneous, and paternalistic. Now it was...different; he sensed a stirring in the woman, in her movement, and the way she snuggled to him. The feel and scent of her brought back memories, long suppressed. He must stop this now, he thought. However, he did nothing as she stretched out on the couch with her head on his lap. He stroked her short-cropped hair, her neck, and her shoulders.

"Hmm, that feels wonderful," she murmured, "don't stop." Presently, she took his hand and placed it on a breast, and squeezed his fingers to encourage his exploration. She slipped his hand inside her dress. Her breathing came faster; he felt moistness to her skin.

"He abruptly pulled his hand away. I-I haven't been with a woman in years, he said, awkwardly." I can't perform anymore, I'm sorry."

"Will you tell me about it?"

"No, I can't. Not now."

She continued lying stretched out on the couch, with her head in his lap. He continued rubbing her gently, since it pleased her. She began to squirm under his skillful manipulation. She pulled her legs up, and allowed them to open, revealing her panties, and the smooth curvature of her legs and thighs, and her taut flat belly. They looked more appealing to him now. He felt his pulse quicken, and a mild surge of excitement flow through him, but still no erection. He leaned over her and kissed her breast, while he worked his hand underneath her panties. She was very wet and firm. He manipulated her until she climaxed; it did not take long. Then she lay quiet again. Her skin was hot and damp, and he could smell her. It was a wild primitive smell, which thrilled him. He felt very close to her emotionally. Perhaps he had been hasty in his determination to rid himself of her. She became quiet and still and her breathing became even and regular. He realized she had fallen asleep.

Eventually she awoke and opened her eyes. He still cradled her head in his lap, with his head reclining on the back of the couch, but he was not asleep. Her breasts were still exposed, and her dress was up around her waist. He was admiring her, caressing her with his eyes while she slept. She made no effort to cover herself; she merely looked into his eyes, kindly.

"Did you have a good nap?" he asked.

"Yes." She sat up beside him and took his hand in hers as he continued to recline his head on the back of the couch, his eyes were mere slits staring into hers.

"Now I want a shower," she said, standing, slipping out of her dress. "Come and shower with me." She saw his hesitation, and reached out her hand to him. He took it, she tugged gently, and he rose and stood awkwardly while she removed his clothing, a garment at a time. She hummed the appropriate music, as she swung each garment over her head and tossed it across the room, emulating the bump and grind of the burlesque stage.

"You are a real naughty girl!" he said, as they walked naked to the shower.

Their first shower together was uneventful except for mutual lathering and scrubbing. Afterwards they dressed and Mary said,

"All right Professor Hofstadter, let's get our little apartment ship-shape."

⊷⊷ ⊷⊷

They went early to the cafeteria for breakfast the following morning, and afterwards they reviewed their strategy for the ten o'clock meeting with Freund.

"Now, remember, Mary, you are to say as little as possible and volunteer nothing. Say you remember nothing before the disaster."

"That won't be difficult for me because it's true." "Yes, I know, Mary. I have told him already that you came from a farm in central Illinois, and that you attended the University of Illinois, where we met, and that you have traveled around some with me. However, you won't remember any of that, right?"

"That's right, Roy, I don't"

"There are several different kinds of amnesia," Roy said, thoughtfully, pedantically, "but I don't remember their names."

"Very amusing, Roy."

"Actually," he continued, "there really are different kinds of amnesia. Retrograde is the name of the type that results from trauma, such as a blow to the head. I figure that is what you have. Although, I found no bumps or bruises on your head when I cleaned you up and examined you. However, as I recall, the trauma does not have to be physical, but can be a psychological trauma. Have you had any good psychological traumas lately, madam? A good scare perhaps?"

Mary chuckled.

Roy continued, warming up to the subject, and obviously pleased that Mary's mood was rather light under the circumstances, for he knew she did not want to visit with Doctor Freund again.

"Tell me, my dear, do you remember clearly everything that has happened since I found you and took you to my lair in the Empire State Building?"

"I remember what you told me about it, and I remember waking up with you washing me, then I guess I must have passed out again. I was very sick and weak, you know, and very, very terrified. I am sure I had no food and water for a long time before you found me. Then later I woke up in the middle of the night. I was frightened, and I tried to open a window, I think. I guess my answer to you is, yes, I remember the last two or three weeks well, but nothing before that. I don't want to think about it."

"Okay, that's enough. You have it down pat. We have time to kill until our appointment with Dr. Freund at ten. What do you want to do now? Want to go for a walk?"

"Okay."

Later, when they met with Dr. Freund, he seemed to be in a good mood. After a few minutes of polite conversation, he got down to business: "All right Mary, Roy explained to me you've been having some problems with your memory since the disaster. Now, I'm sure it's nothing to worry about, just the shock and trauma of what you have been through, but just to be on the safe side, I think we ought to delve into it a little, don't you?"

119

"If you say so doctor."

"Good. I want to ask you a few general questions to see if I can understand the nature of your malady better, if you don't mind."

"That's all right doctor. Thank you for your concern."

"Not at all, not at all," Freund paused briefly, and cleared his throat. "Now, Mary, you told me yesterday that Roy was a stockbroker, are you aware of that?"

"Yes, I am now."

"And in reality, according to Roy, he is a sociologist, engaged in field research." Freund turned aside to Roy. "I really do smell another book in the works, Roy."

"Stranger things have happened, Doctor," Roy said again, as he had the last time Dr. Freund had said it.

"Can you explain to me, Mary," Freund said, after his little digression, "what you were thinking when you told me that?"

"I-I was confused, Doctor."

"You actually thought it was true at the time?"

"Uh, I'm not sure, yes, I think I did."

"But you don't any more, you don't now, right?"

"No."

"And that's because you're no longer confused?"

"Oh, I don't know about that."

"Hmm, well, tell me, have you had episodes like this before."

"I don't know, because I can't remember a thing—before waking up and Roy was washing me. I had horrible goo all over me. The smell was terrible, and I was frightened and I wanted to run, to scream. That's the first thing, that's the only thing I remember—nothing before that."

How about your apartment in Manhattan, do you remember that?"

"No."

"How about your childhood in Illinois?"

"Nothing."

Freund leafed through Mary's physical examination report. "No evidence of head injury from the examination. Did I test your reflexes before, Mary?"

"I don't know. What do you mean?"

"Did I tap your knees with a little rubber hammer?"

Mary glanced at Roy, for support. He gave no indication. "No, I don't think so," she said.

The doctor opened a drawer and extracted a small toma-hawk-looking device with a shiny metal handle and a triangular shaped hard-rubber head. "Come here, Mary, and sit down in this chair. Now, cross your legs, and relax." He sat on a stool in front of her.

Mary did as he requested. The doctor took the little hammer and tapped gently on her knees, each in turn. Each time her leg jumped forward, exposing her legs a little above the knees. The Doctor could not have helped but take notice how shapely they were. Mary certainly was a handsome specimen. Dr. Freund seemed to linger there, testing with his little rubber hammer, positioning her legs first one way then the other. Finally, Roy cleared his throat, and Freund ceased abruptly. "Nothing wrong with your reflexes," he said, as he stood up and walked around her slowly, examining her head, feeling her neck, ostensibly looking for evidence of physical trauma. Roy thought he saw Freund looking down Mary's blouse, but he dismissed the idea as preposterous.

Freund returned to his desk, shuffled a paper or two; he seemed rather flustered all of a sudden. He said, "There's no evidence of physical injury, Mary, but I'm not satisfied. I think we need to keep an eye on you for a few days." He shifted his gaze from Mary to Roy. "I would like to do a brain scan, as a precaution. If we find nothing in the scan, then I expect psychotherapy might be called for. How are you doing with the medication I gave you, Mary? You seem to be more relaxed today."

"Yes, I feel much better today."

"And, your cuts and bruises, you are taking the pills, and using the ointment I gave you."

"I am, Doctor Freund."

"Good, good, and I want you to get plenty of rest and relaxation, and exercise and sunshine—go for a walk each day, take it easy, and take a nap. You like to take naps, Mary?"

"Gee, I don't know, Doctor—

"Oh, of course…well, then, come in tomorrow again at ten, and we'll take it from there. How is that?" He looked from her to Roy and back at her again. She looked from him to Roy and back at him again.

"That sounds good, Doctor," Roy said. "Don't you agree, Mary?"

"Uh, why yes, thank you, Doctor Freund."

"Not at all, see you in the morning at ten, Mary. Mary would you mind waiting outside while I discuss something with Roy?"

"Ok."

Freund opened the door for Mary, and she went out and he closed the door again and took his chair. "I don't know, Roy," he said, "she certainly seems confused, but I don't want to worry you, and I certainly don't want to worry Mary. I will see about scheduling a CAT scan at the local hospital if you have no objections. It may take a few days. In the meantime, I will schedule daily thirty minute sessions with her. Oh, and Roy, you need not come with her to the sessions. It's better if I see the patient alone."

"All right, Doctor."

Roy's initial reaction to the last statement was sudden and unexpected resentment, but instantly he saw the value in it; it would help to break Mary's emotional dependency on him, and get her on her feet quicker. Since he had rescued her, they had never been apart for more than an hour.

They slept late the following morning, and, as usual, had a leisurely breakfast at the center.

"While you are seeing the doctor," Roy said casually, "I'm going to hang around the center here, maybe even watch a little TV, and catch up on the news. We should make the center our base of operations, since everything is here, our food, our entertainment, our sources of information. Don't you agree, Darling?"

"You're not coming with me?"

"No. These kinds of sessions are between the doctor and his patient. No spectators are allowed."

"How long do you think the doctor will want to see me?"

"Who can say? Two or three visits, maybe; at least until he schedules the scan. Who knows, he might cure you of your amnesia. Wouldn't that be great? We should leave it up to the good doctor. We got it made, Darling, our own apartment, everything provided—just like the Catskills. People lay out a lot of money for a set-up like this."

"What about going south?"

"There's plenty of time for that."

Roy glanced at the wall clock. "When you get back we'll take the bus into town. I need to find a bank; after that, we will buy us some new clothes. Would you like that?"

"Yes, I would like that very much." She leaned over and kissed him on the cheek, and hurried out.

A week went by, and each morning Mary and Roy had breakfast together and, while she went with her sessions with Dr. Freund, Roy hung around the mess hall at or near the big round table, waiting for her return. He spent his time, enjoyably for a sociologist, of watching and listening to the steady flow of strangers, and some regulars, who for one reason or another, needed to stay over, as he and Mary did. When she returned, she always briefed him on what the doctor had said and done, usually followed by a light lunch.

Afternoons they walked and roamed the base, and gradually they acquired a tan on their faces and necks, and hands and lower arms, and built up their strength, whether they planned to or not.

It was late summer, and occasionally Mary would raise the subject of going south, and each time Roy would brush it off with, "plenty of time for that, plenty of time."

The last time Roy tried to brush her off Mary did not let him get away with it. They were relaxing at the big table before lunch. "Aren't there preparations to be made, Roy?" She asked. "Shouldn't you be explaining things to me? I believe you are humoring me, just putting me off."

"Well, Dear, it's true I still have difficulty seeing you in that role and I'm kind of hoping you will come to your senses. Are you prepared to live by your wits, and sleep under the stars? Of course not. You are a classy woman, a product of an urbane, sophisticated society. Any day now, you will get your memory back, and this idea of going on the road with me will seem like utter nonsense to you."

"Oh, so you *are* humoring me. I resent that."

"You could be hurt or killed out there."

"You'll look out for me, and I'll learn fast, you'll see. I promise you I'll hold up my end. I'll even carry your pack for you, and you can do the leading and all the heavy thinking."

"That's very generous of you, but if you went with me you would have your own pack and bedroll to carry."

"I didn't think of that—that's even better. Where do you suppose we can get my equipment, then, a sporting goods store?"

"No, no, that commercial stuff is too flimsy and fancy, and you'd be too visible and appear too prosperous to the rabble. The people out there on the road would take it away from you the minute you showed your face. Besides, as I said, Army surplus stuff is better because it is sturdier, and the price is right, too. The first thing you have to learn is how to economize, how to live off the land if necessary, and how to blend into the background."

"Army surplus it is, then."

Roy chuckled; the wench was tricking him and backing him into a corner again, right before his eyes and in broad daylight.

It amused him. "It is time for you to go for your session with Dr. Freund. We will talk about it when you get back."

After Mary left, Roy took out his yellow notebook and made a halfhearted effort to clean up his notes from his last session at the round table. A commotion caused him to look up, to see a new group of survivors making their way into the mess hall. He took a moment to look them over. As Freund had pointed out, the center processed most of them expeditiously and sent them on their way. However, there were those among them for whom the base might be their home for a longer period, perhaps weeks, or longer. There were people coming through who had lived all their lives in the devastated areas, and perhaps their parents before them, who had no friends or family elsewhere. Many arrived with nothing but the clothes on their backs, lucky to be alive, and with no prospects.

There were people who had been wealthy. If their bank records existed outside the devastated area, it might take only a few days to track down, and reconstruct their accounts, and restore their ability to access their funds. However, many people would not be so lucky; they would wait, grim faced and trembling with dread as they realized their fate.

Roy did not fit into any of these categories. He was not a native New Yorker; he had no friends or relatives there; he had no property in the ruined city. In fact, Roy had bragged to Mary that his standard of living had improved. He had quite a wad of cash and jewelry of unknown value, which he had taken off the bodies of the rapists after he killed them, just before he threw them out of the ten-story window. He did not regret what he had done; they deserved killing, and he had no choice, anyway. The jewelry, along with most of the cash, now resided in a safety deposit box at the local Merchant's Bank where he had opened an account. Its existence was comforting and liberating.

Mary came back from her session, and sat down beside him. There she was—what a sweetheart she was. He was growing fonder of her with each passing day. She caught him studying her and smiled. He had given her his word, and he gave his word so rarely these days. He was actually enjoying keeping his word. It reminded him of the old days, where there was more honor and decency. Additionally, on top of everything else, he figured he was associating with a better class of people than had been his lot over the past seven years. He glanced around at the people in the cafeteria for confirmation of this sentiment. Hmm, well maybe, maybe not. In any event, the rescue center was a gold mine of human disasters, of subjects to study, to observe, in his quest to determine—

"Hi, Roy. Did you notice that I'm back?"

"Oh, sorry. How did the session go?"

"Fine."

His thoughts turned to Dr. Freund, the strange little Psychiatrist. Who would have anticipated that Freund would have recognized him? It was a heady feeling to hear himself addressed as Professor again, or Doctor Hofstadter. In his seven years of wanderings, no one had ever recognized him before. No one had ever made an overture to him, sought his company, or spoken sympathetically and interestedly to him, unless he had initiated the interaction. In fact, in a moment of nostalgic retrospection, he had once gone into a bookstore and asked for a copy of his Sociology textbook, *Man and the Crowd,* and the clerk had looked it up in the Directory of Publications. She found it. He asked her to read the bio of the author, and she did. He smiled a satisfied smile, thanked her and left the store.

As Roy observed the new arrivals, he realized that he felt little connection with them, little empathy. Given his circumstances, and what he had been through, it was not easy for him to empathize. They were the raw material of his accommodation to his reality for seven years, but the fabric of that life was beginning to fray. It was the woman…it was Mary. He had not bothered to explain his eccentricities to her, to justify himself, as it were. He did not do that sort of thing anymore. He no longer required the approval of others. For seven years, he had cut himself loose from society, from friends and family until, even though he existed constantly in their midst, there was nobody "there" for him. He had become acclimated to his state. In the early days, after the ordeal, he resented even the slightest attempt on the part of others to intervene to "save him"—it was too late—where were they when he needed them. Nobody tried anymore. Nobody paid any attention to him at all anymore. Nobody gave a damn anymore—except Mary.

"That's fine with me!" he blurted out, startling Mary.

He looked around at the people at the table. Had he said that, or had he merely thought it? Nobody responded to him; nobody looked at him. They were doing their own thing—except Mary.

"What?" she asked.

"I'm sorry. I was thinking out loud."

He realized he had been drifting in the fog. At times, in unpredictable moments, his mind still faded in and out of the fog. Sometimes it happened and he was not aware of it. He would become aware only that others were behaving strangely toward him, and he would wonder why they were behaving so strangely toward him. He would wonder what was wrong with them. Most times, he never figured it out. Other times, later on, and with more frequency of late, he would realize that they were behaving strangely toward him because he was behaving strangely toward them. The incidences were briefer and less frequent now—since Mary.

They people at the table had finished their meal and were now talking animatedly. He flipped out his little notebook and extracted the yellow stub of a pencil from the wire binding, and unobtrusively began writing.

Mary glanced at him as he scribbling in his notebook.

"What are you doing?" she asked.

"Taking notes."

"What about?"

"What those gentlemen are discussing," he whispered, nodded his head toward the other occupants of the table.

"Why?"

"I'll explain later."

However, after a few minutes of listening to the chatter of the new arrivals Roy said with a sigh, disappointed at the lack of drama in the conversations, "I suppose we should leave these fine people to their miseries, and have some lunch."

As they walked to the cafeteria line, Mary said, "Oh, I forgot to mention to you, Dr. Freund invited us to his house for dinner sometime, and to meet his wife. He didn't set a date; he said to let him know when it was convenient for us."

"Really? That is unexpected. What do you make of it?"

"I don't know, just being friendly, I suppose."

"Do you want to go?"

"I wouldn't mind going sometime, but I don't have anything appropriate to wear."

"What's wrong with that new red dress?"

"It doesn't fit very well. It needs adjustment. If I had a sewing kit, I could probably fix it."

"Well, we can buy you a proper dress. On the other hand, the PX will have sewing kits; all soldiers need sewing kits. Tell you what, we will go into town tomorrow and buy you a new dress, and I will go by the PX later today and pick up a sewing kit, so we have all the bases covered. How's that?"

"Outstanding."

After they finished their meal, Roy asked Mary what she wanted to do.

"I want to go back to the apartment and do nothing—rest or read. Do you mind?"

"Not at all. I'll be along in a little while."

He walked Mary to the door, then went to the men's room, then refilled his coffee cup, not because he wanted more coffee, but to use as a prop, and returned to the table to see how his survivors were coming along. Another man came up with a tray of food and sat down. He nodded to Roy, and swept his eyes around the table and nodded to the others.

"Good morning, gentlemen," he said, haltingly. For a few moments, the new arrival was busy removing the dishes from his tray and arranging them, just so, on the table before him. It immediately struck Roy as odd that he was so meticulous about it; it was the way the man's hands fluttered above the dishes of food as if in mid-motion he had thought of some deep, distracting thought. The man hesitated, fork in hand, and seemed to whimper; he shook his head in a strange way, and then lit in on the food, eating ravenously as if he had not eaten in days.

This behavior escaped the notice of the others who had turned back to their own affairs: one was smoking a cigarette, another was absently stacking his dishes onto his tray, and one who looked like a lawyer was leaning back in his chair, his head tilted back, his eyes closed. A fourth man took up his tray and left the table. Roy mentally assigned nicknames to the four remaining: the smoker, the arranger, the lawyer, and the new arrival.

Suddenly the new arrival pushed his food away rather violently, plopped his elbows on the table, rested his face in his hands, and moaned, loudly and pathetically.

The abruptness of his action startled the arranger, who turned quickly toward him and said, "Damn, man, what's going on? What's the matter with you?"

The lawyer opened his eyes, brought his head forward, and stared at the man. "What's the matter with him," he asked.

The new man raised his face from his hands; tears streamed down his face creating muddy rivulets through the grime. Roy was accustomed to dirty, disheveled people, being one much of the time himself. It meant little or nothing by way of providing useful information about the poor man's condition, to see him weeping and lamenting. So many people were doing it. Roy waited for the man to blurt out what pained him.

"It's all gone," the new arrival lamented, "Everything! Everything!"

"Is that your problem?" the smoker barked. "You got a lot of nerve! Don't you understand, we are all in the same boat here? We've all lost everything."

The new arrival glared at him, hatred in his eyes. His clothing was soiled, and ripped and torn, but they were obviously of high quality, and expensive. "What did you lose, sir? What did you have to lose? Me? I lost a fortune, my family, my work, my everything."

The arranger, apparently sensing the man's desperate need to talk, said, "go ahead and tell us about it, Mister."

"Yeah," the lawyer said, "go ahead and tell us your story."

The newcomer studied their faces, perhaps expecting to see mockery in them; apparently seeing none, he began speaking:

"My name is Henry Armitage. I am native to New York City, and five generations before me. Everything I had, everything I was, there in the city. ..."

Roy eased the spiral notebook back out from his shirt pocket, inconspicuously, so as not to impact the scene, thinking that at any moment he just might hear something a little different, something worth his time. What emotion was he observing? Was it self-pity, or was it Despair, or Remorse? What? He could not tell yet. He had taken note of the fact that the man, in listing his losses, had put his fortune first and his family second. Hmm, Mary's sewing kit would have to wait.

The man continued: "Why, I spent more to house and service my Rolls Royce than 99.3 percent of the people of the entire world make in a year. I once had an accountant figure it up for me, using all the proper government statistics. I enjoyed thinking that way. I liked to say it at parties and at gatherings of those of my class and station. Sometimes it amused them; sometimes it pissed them off;

I didn't care." I had an estate in the Hamptons, a penthouse in my own building in Manhattan. I hangered my private jet at my own private airstrip on my estate. He paused, thinking, reflecting. "I am—*was* a capitalist in the purest sense. However, I no longer concerned myself with acquiring material wealth beyond my own individual needs—which were considerable, I must confess. They expected it of me, you see—conspicuous consumption, and all that.

"My point is that I no longer had that Midas-like need and compulsion to acquire more tangible wealth, buildings and factories and land, and so forth. After a while, the advantage is so much on the side of the wealthy that we can practically make money at will. I know that sounds strange to you. I can see by looking at the bunch of you that you are not of my—not one of us." He looked squarely into the eyes of the smoker as he spoke. You see, my investments, my holdings, had long ceased to be tangible things, and had been transformed, transmogrified, if you will, into abstractions, into pure money. I dealt in neither bill nor coin, but electrons, which zipped over wires and circuits on the international monetary exchanges. As a matter of pride, and in honor of my progenitors, I headquartered myself, and my elusive assets in New York, in Manhattan and Long Island. I brought them to a screeching halt there." He laughed a strange, hysterical laugh. "I parked my electrons there.

"I am a man of the world; I could live wherever I pleased. However, I favored America, land of freedom and democracy. However, do not be confused, I was not, am not, a democrat; I did not believe in democracy; I only believed in capitalism. The unaware masses, when they think at all, think that the two are the same, but of course, they are wrong, they are entirely different concepts, realities. Yes, I was, indeed, a wealthy man, beyond your comprehension, I am sure, but, as of two weeks ago, I can no longer prove it. I have no identity. I have been unable to contact anyone who knows me. I am totally in a state of exasperation, frustration and despair. The entire infrastructure, within which my electrons resided, is a shambles! My estate, my private jet, my building with my penthouse, gone, and my real fortune, my electrons...where are they? Yet I keep trying, waiting, and hoping. In the meantime, I am stuck in this horrid place, no better off than the rabble, facing up to my predicament as well as I can, while others attempt to locate my identity and my assets, or so they say. I have my doubts … I am, as you can see, as poor and humble as any church-mouse ever was.

"No, in fairness I cannot say that I am the least bit humble, even in my present circumstances, I have no humility. This is true; I swear it!" His voice became loud, shrill. "I am, more an alley rat, rather than a humble church mouse; I am now, for the moment, poor—but humble? No sir! Never!"

"Hey, take it easy fellow," said arranger. Everything will work out, you'll see. Calm down and finish your food."

"Yeah," said the lawyer, "then you should go see a doctor."

Roy got up to go to the PX to buy Mary a sewing kit. No one seemed to notice him leave.

CHAPTER SEVEN

At the conclusion of Conway's meeting with the President, Smithers took him to the office of the Chief of Staff, William Forester, who had just gotten off the phone with the President, and was waiting for Conway when he entered. He stood in the center of the well-appointed office, poised, immaculate, and vibrating at a high frequency. He thrust out his hand and presented a wide, toothy smile, as if the two motions worked in unison by a pulley and lever mechanism, so that if one happened, the other always followed. Forester was a holdover from the Williams administration, and was reputed to be a man of cool competency and efficiency—just the kind of man Conway needed right now. Conway had heard that Forester insisted that everyone call him Willie. "Hi, I'm Willie Forester, he said, as he grasped Conway's hand. He whisked Conway across the room to a lounge area where there were two facing white brocade couches, where the two men could sit face to face. "It's a pleasure to meet you, Doctor Conway." The President has instructed me to lend you every assistance in your forthcoming mission.

"Thank you, sir."

"Call me Willie," said Forester. "The President also tells me that you lost your home and possessions in the disaster."

"Yes, that's true. Fortunately, I was traveling or I would be dead now, like many of my friends and associates."

Forester's demeanor became briefly solemn. "Yes, we all lost someone." He immediately resumed his friendly but professional persona. "I hope you don't mind. I have made living arrangements for you here in Philadelphia at the Ben Franklin Hotel, only a block from here. Their rooms are in great demand now and hard to come by. Many high-ranking officials are living there because of the convenience. I hope you like the accommodations."

"You've done that already? But I've just left the President ..."

Willie smiled.

"Willie, I admit that I am impressed, and I'm sure I will like the accommodations."

"Very kind of you, Doctor Conway, you may move in immediately; you need only stop at the hotel desk for your key. Secure telephone, computer, and other communications facilities are on their way to your new quarters as we speak."

"Willie, who says the Federal Government can't move when it wants to."

"Certainly not I," said Willie, without missing a beat. "I've also arranged transportation for you. There is a car available to you in the hotel's basement garage whenever you need it; just inform the parking attendant. You may also avail yourself of chauffeured limousine service if you prefer. Let the desk know your wishes. There will be certain papers and documents delivered to your room this evening by six, including a letter of authorization from the President, which you may show, but not give, to any governmental official or military person who might question your authority—anyone. You should expect total and complete cooperation within the United States government, including the Armed Forces.

Contact me immediately should anyone balk. Now, Dr. Conway, what else specifically do you need from me?"

"I need to know the name and location of the nuclear submarine nearest to Gibraltar. Assuming there is one nearby, I want it to proceed immediately to the nearest allied port where I may board it, preferably in England. I want the information on the sub, the Captain, and the port by four o'clock this afternoon. I want the sub underway to that port before nightfall. Inform the captain to anticipate an important mission of indefinite duration. I want a fast executive jet standing by at Philadelphia International Airport. As soon as I have the requested information, and am in receipt of the documents, which you say you will deliver to me before six, I will depart for a rendezvous with the sub.

Additionally, I want to know the location and capability of all underwater bathysphere type subs or other underwater exploratory craft capable of attaching directly to the hatch of a submarine for underwater transfer of personnel and equipment. I don't have more specific information on this subject, since it is out of my field."

"Hmm," Forester seemed boggled. "You expect all this to happen today?"

"Yes, sir, by four o'clock. Now, let's talk about communications, and money, and logistics."

⚊⊰⊱⚊

Conway checked into his new hotel suite at the Ben Franklin, and called his motel in Gaithersburg to have his possessions forwarded to his new quarters. He called his MIT professor friend, the Nuclear Physicist, Gregg "Skip" Cooper, with whom he had consulted, to inform him that the mission was on, and to get his equipment ready. Copper didn't answer so he left a message on his answering machine. Then, he went down to the hotel restaurant for lunch. Afterwards, he went for a brief but brisk walk, purchased toiletries in the lobby shops, and then returned to his suite to await Willie Forester's call. He lay on the bed watching an old movie on TBN, and fell asleep. He woke to the jangling of the telephone at five minutes before four. It was Forester.

"Dr. Conway, everything you requested is underway. The sub is driving toward a base in England from its current Location in the North Sea. The details will be in the packet. The jet is standing-by at the airport. I will dispatch a messenger within the next hour with the documents, money, credit cards, secure cell phones, et cetera. Now, is there anything else you require?"

"Outstanding job, Willie, outstanding," Conway said. "No, I can't think of a thing. I'll call you if I do."

"Very good, Dr. Conway, good luck on your mission."

Conway departed the Philadelphia International Airport in the executive jet at 6:55 p.m., local time, during a rainstorm. He looked around the empty cabin; it felt strange being the only passenger. As soon as the plane was in the air, he opened his briefcase in the seat next to him, and began a slow and thorough examination of the packet delivered to him. There was a thick envelope stuffed with hundred-dollar bills, three government credit cards, a secure satellite telephone, by which he could communicate directly with Willie Forester from anywhere in the world, and a second conventional cell phone. His typed itinerary gave the details of his destination, which was an unnamed British submarine base near London. He would land at London's Heathrow Airport, and take waiting ground transportation to the base. There, he would rendezvous with the nuclear submarine U. S. S. Swordfish, commanded by Captain William S. Wingate. The Executive Officer was Commander Barnard Jones.

Willie Forester had indeed done an outstanding job putting everything in place on extraordinarily short notice, and Conway made a mental note to call this to the attention of the President. As the plane leveled off at altitude, the Stewart greeted Conway, and handed him a menu of food and refreshments available to him. Conway ordered a double martini, and a filet mignon dinner. While he waited for his dinner, Conway sipped the martini and read the files on Captain Wingate and Jones, and leafed through the remaining documents. "So far so good."

On board the U.S. S. Swordfish, Captain William S. Wingate received his orders by coded radio message while in the North Sea off the coast of Norway. The orders directed him to proceed with all speed to the (designated) British Royal Navy Submarine Base to take on a passenger for a top-secret mission.

"Barry, what the hell are those yoyo's up to now?" he growled rhetorically to Commander Barnard Jones, his executive officer. "You'd think after all these years in this man's navy those numb-nuts would trust a fellow enough to tell him what his mission is."

"You certainly would think so, sir," agreed Jones.

Captain Wingate was near retirement, and had not yet achieved his first star. The prospect that he might not receive that last big promotion haunted him. His disappointment caused him to grumble some, but only to his close confidants. Nevertheless, he leaned on the throttle anyway, figuratively speaking, and hauled ass—he was a navy man, and a damn good one.

The jet carrying Conway, flying a near great-circle route, passed over Boston and the Cape Cod area. The rainstorm, which had obscured visibility upon their departure from Philadelphia, was far behind them now, and a brilliant moon, reflecting off the ocean below, perfectly etched out the outline of the cape. Where brilliant lighting once illuminated the entire northeastern coastal area of the United States like a holiday display, now a strip of the coastal area, as far as the eye could see, was dark, save for a few patches of light here and there, where, no doubt, men worked on some particularly important restorative effort. The sight saddened Conway, and he put his papers aside to marvel at the spectacle.

Skip Cooper was down there somewhere on the outskirts of what had been Boston, preparing for the mission. Cooper had been busy since the tsunami occurred salvaging what he could of his house and possessions. His property, twenty country acres, had not felt the full force of the ocean, but the house and outbuildings had suffered flooding damage from backwater.

Conway had spoken with him several times by phone after the disaster, not only to discuss the La Palma landslide, but because Cooper was an old friend. Cooper had moved a trailer onto the farm, and was using a generator for his electrical needs, expecting it to be weeks if not months until electric service resumed.

Conway took out his cell phone and dialed Cooper's number. The phone rang several times.

"Hello," Cooper said, rather gruffly, as if the call had interrupted something important.

"Hello, Skip, this is Joe. I am on an insecure phone, so be cool. Guess where I am right now."

"I wouldn't hazard a guess, Joe, where are you?"

Go outside and look straight up. That's me you see up there zooming overhead."

"I just got in and heard your phone message that the mission was approved. That's terrific."

"Yes. I am on my way to Heathrow; when can you join me?

"I have most everything I need together. I could be there late tomorrow, or the following morning at the latest. I need to check the flight schedules."

"Good. I will check back with you later for your arrival time, and meet you myself, or have a car waiting.

"Make that a van instead of a car. My baggage is bulky."

"You got it."

Conway ate his excellent dinner, his mind still on Gregg Cooper, whom he had met four years earlier at a nuclear disarmament meeting in Geneva, Switzerland. He was a tall, fit, robust man in his late thirties with red, close-cropped hair. A gregarious type, they had hit it off, and had kept in contact thereafter. Because Cooper's research work at MIT had earned him a top-secret clearance, Conway had felt justified in discussing the tsunami with him and his suspicions that it might have been manmade. He had expected Cooper to laugh at the idea, but Cooper had not laughed. In fact, Cooper had quickly researched the idea of reactor heating, and had done calculations, which seemed to demonstrate the feasibility of it. He even predicted the size of reactor required to accomplish the feat. Cooper was a civilian, and the mission could be dangerous; but then, Conway reflected, these are dangerous times just to be alive.

Upon his arrival in the middle of the night at the London Heathrow Airport, and a swift ride to the submarine base, the driver took him to the visiting officer's quarters to bed down for the night. The submarine was still three hours out of port. He had a snack in the officer's mess, and retired early.

The driver arrived for him after breakfast the following morning and took him directly to the submarine, where he met with Captain Wingate and Commander Jones. Wingate was an aging man with gray, thinning hair, a good tan, and a general air of good health. His face registered more than surprised when he met the person who had summoned him from his regular duties in the North Sea, and sent him and his vessel hurling through the night. His mysterious passenger turned out to be a very young, (he would only learn later that Conway was twenty-seven.) However, things cleared up quickly for the Captain when the young civilian showed him his credentials—the letter from the President of the United States, which he read, and which Wingate listened to with a level of incredulity that brought a crease to his brow.

After the introductions, the men seated themselves around a table and Conway spoke: "Captain, I will get right to the point. I am here on a top-secret mission for the President of the United States. Notice that I said the President of the United States, and not the Department of State, nor the Department of Defense, not the Navy nor any other agency or branch of Government. I now take the two of you, and only you—not the crew, the crew must be given a plausible cover story—into my confidence. Do you understand? Conway paused to allow his somewhat dramatic words to sink in, and to allow the two men a moment of reconciliation—not that they really had any choice. Their faces registered this strange question as they glanced at each other and Wingate answered, "Yes sir, of course."

Conway began: "There have been rumblings emanating from the Middle-East and elsewhere concerning the collapse of La Palma Island into the sea, which we know has resulted in the worst disaster in our nation's history. These rumblings suggest that the collapse of the island was no accident of nature, but was the work of men—enemies of the United States. So far, these rumblings are within the Foreign Services and the intelligence community, and no responsible official of any foreign government, to our knowledge, currently gives credence to them. However, there are powerful forces who would likely rejoice if these rumblings were true. In their eyes, it would provide justification for war, perhaps a war such as the world has never seen. Even if the rumors were not true, these powerful forces would stop at nothing to convince the people of the United States and our allies that they were true. To them, the pretext is as good as the reality. The President needs to know the truth of the matter, the facts, in order to prepare for any eventuality, to be able to counteract and contain these people, if that should be his decision. He has dispatched me to try to get some answers, with your help.

"Shades of nine-eleven!" Wingate exclaimed, his eyes suddenly bright with insight. "Imagine the mood of the American people if they learned that this awful tragedy was done *to* them by somebody—I assume you are thinking about the Muslims."

"Yes, the Muslims would be blamed, of course, or possibly the Russians or the Chinese, even—who knows—whether they did it or not, but it doesn't have to be true to wreak havoc with the world; it can be a complete lie. We know from nine-eleven how readily a corrupt administration and a controlled media can fabricate lies. All the people have to do is b*elieve* it, or simply be confused enough for long enough so that the perpetrators can carry out their plot—the *fait accompli.*"

"I understand," Wingate said. "What is your mission, then, and what is our role in it," he asked pointedly.

"I'm looking for evidence of causation." Conway said. "Scientists under my direction have already inspected the slide area on La Palma Island searching for any evidence of causation, such as volcanic activity, or explosions, anything which might have triggered unstable conditions within the mountain to cause it to break away. They found nothing, so far, but they and others are continuing their efforts. We want to do the same on the ocean floor. We want to examine the debris field of the slide area at close quarters and take photographs, measurements, and instrument readings, and look for anything out of the ordinary. I have a physicist who is working with me, Professor Gregg Cooper, of MIT, who will be joining me here soon—later today perhaps, or tomorrow. He has the expertise and the instrumentation to take measurements and photographs. I intend to use a small, two-man submarine, of the type used for sea exploration, which has the capability to connect to the hatch of the Swordfish so that we can transfer submerged. I learned while in route that such a sub has been located within our Mediterranean Fleet, in Naples harbor. An experienced mini-sub pilot comes with the sub. He and I will conduct the inspections of the debris field. Your sub, Captain, will provide the logistical support, the home base, if you will, from which we will go out until the mission is completed."

"Why a nuclear submarine; why not a surface vessel?" said Wingate.

"We will be working in the territorial waters of Spain and, while our purpose is peaceful and non-threatening to Spain or anyone else, we cannot afford to be denied access to anything we wish to examine, or to arouse curiosity or speculation from anyone as to why we are there and what we are doing. The world is on a hair trigger right now, so it is absolutely essential that secrecy be maintained."

"Of course," the Captain said, "I understand."

"I intend that we should remain submerged during the entire exercise. We will take delivery of the mini-sub out to sea, and approach La Palma submerged, and remain submerged until we are finished. Conway paused to allow the men time to consider what he said. "Are there any other questions?"

"Yes." Wingate rubbed his chin in contemplation. "Back to your inspection of the island, you say you found nothing?"

"That right."

"What were you looking for, exactly?" the Exec asked, seemingly bothered by some part of Conway's narrative which did not quite make sense to him.

"As I said before, evidence of volcanic activity or explosions that might have triggered movements of unstable rock formations within the volcanoes."

Up to this point, Conway had been careful not to mention anything to do with nuclear energy, remembering the admonition of the President to keep all participants on a "need to know" basis.

The Captain and the Exec glanced at each other then back at Conway. "I don't understand," Jones said. "An explosion makes a hell of a racket, and throws rock everywhere. I should think 'evidence' of an explosion of a magnitude sufficient to tear off half of an island would be self-evident and obvious in the extreme."

"Yeah, Doctor Conway, I have to agree with that; what about that?" The Exec. Added.

Conway saw the skepticism creeping over their faces. He wanted them in full support of the mission, so he decided to go further. "That's correct, Captain, a large conventional explosion certainly wouldn't be too difficult to confirm, but there are other types of explosions, low level blasts such as are sometimes used in quarrying and mining operations which don't have that characteristic. My point is that we found no evidence of any sort of explosion, and ruled it out. But, you might ask, in the absence of such an explosion, how else might one dislodge a volcanic mountain, and bring it down?"

The two men looked at each other again and shrugged. "I don't have the foggiest," Wingate said, and Jones nodded in agreement."

"Then let me give you a short lecture on the geology of volcanic islands, and the remarkable heating power of small-scale nuclear reactors, like, for example, the one you have on board this sub."

Conway talked for an hour, answering all questions posed, recounting the story of past volcanic eruptions on the islands, the heating of trapped water, which had caused geologic slippage in 1971. When finished, he said, "I've told you everything; there are now six people who know what we're doing and why. Is there anything else?"

"No," Wingate said, "I think we've got it, and frankly, Dr. Conway, I'm looking forward to the mission."

"Thank you, sir. Now, if you would show me my quarters, then I need to go on deck and communicate with my satellite phone."

⋙+ +⋘

The following day Conway rode in a chauffeured Royal Navy van to Heathrow to meet Cooper's flight. On the return trip to the base, they stopped off at a roadside restaurant for lunch. The driver had no objection to eating alone so that Conway and Cooper could discuss matters privately; he had his steak and kidney pie at a table close to the window where he could keep an eye on the van.

"The best evidence, of course," Cooper said, as they waited for their food, "would be to find, and visually verify the reactor on the ocean floor, or at least pieces of it. Lacking that, we will measure the radiation levels. If we do find readings significantly higher than background readings, we can synchronize the timers on the cameras and the radiation detectors. Then, we will only have to examine the photographic footage in areas of high radiation readings. Do you follow me?"

"I think so." You're talking about focusing in on the physical location."

"Yes. Now, if we have a cluster of high readings, but find no reactor components, that would most likely mean the radioactive materials are there, but buried under the rocks. Then the sub pilot can creep along over the boulders and physically look through the portholes. If you find nothing at all, it proves nothing, because one cannot prove a negative."

"Okay," Conway said, "how difficult is it to achieve that synchronization you spoke of?"

"Not difficult."

"Good. You must make me an expert on the operation of those instruments in a short time, Gregg."

"I have a problem with that, Joe, because things could go wrong that you wouldn't necessarily recognize right away. If that happens you could lose a whole day. What I am saying is that you should let me make the runs with the pilot. No offense or criticism intended, but it would be better if I were the one down there with the pilot instead of you."

"There's no question about that, but that's out of the question, Gregg, orders of the President."

"What do you mean? Did he say don't let Gregg do it?"

Conway laughed. "No, Gregg, he didn't say that. No one but me must know the results of the investigation, until I give the results to the President."

"Cooper shrugged, and changed the subject. "So, tell me about these new quarters of yours in that fancy hotel in Philadelphia."

"Nothing to tell; I've spent a grand total of about four hours there. I don't even remember the color of the wallpaper."

Their food arrived and the two men dug in. Over coffee and desert, Cooper asked, "Have you ever been in one of these mini-subs, Joe?"

"Me? Heavens no; I've never even seen one—only pictures."

"May the saints preserve us!" Cooper said. You are going to be in a mini-sub you've never seen before, and operating instruments you are unfamiliar with, with the fate of the world hanging in the balance!"

"Piece of cake, man," Conway said.

Both men had a good laugh. They spent the afternoon transferring the instrumentation to the Swordfish, and developing procedures. Later in the evening, they met for dinner with the Captain and the Exec. Conway asked the Captain, "Once we rendezvous with the destroyer which is delivering the minisub, and we transfer it, how long before you can have us submerged over the rubble field?"

"A few hours I should think, after we have checked out the integrity of the seal between the subs. How long do you expect your survey will take?

"I'm estimating about a week. We'll know more after the first run."

Conway slept well that night, and woke the next morning greatly refreshed. It was as if he had passed some mile-marker in this delicate mission for the President. He left Cooper still sleeping in his adjacent quarters, and went on deck to call Willie Forester on the satellite phone to work out the time and place for rendezvous with the destroyer. They came up with mid-afternoon of the following day, at a location north and well over the horizon from La Palma. Conway relayed the information to the captain. His preparations were complete, and they left port within the hour. The submarine was running on the surface, and he and Cooper accompanied the Executive Officer to the conning tower, and experienced the fabulous sensation of riding the huge, sleek, fighting machine as it sliced through the water, creating a smooth-flowing bow wave, which washed the foredeck. Mid-morning, Conway used his satellite phone once again to report the mission underway. In the evening, he and Cooper enjoyed a delicious meal alone in the mess, and then they retired to their respective quarters. After reading for half an hour, Conway dropped off into another restful sleep.

Morning once more and Conway shuffled sleepily into the mess for his first cup of coffee. Again, he had not disturbed Cooper. Two young officers sat talking. He sat down at the long table and the three men said good morning to each other. The two officers picked up their conversation, and Conway caught a few words, something about a woman on board the sub.

"Excuse me," Conway said, "Did you say there is a woman on board the submarine?"

"Yes, sir, that's correct, a young woman from the wreckage of a sailing yacht. She's in sick-bay; she was unconscious and in a bad way."

Conway leaped up, and hurriedly made his way thought the sub to the Control Room. The captain was still in his quarters; Conway spoke to the Officer on Duty. "I just heard that a woman was taken on board the sub last night."

"Yes, sir, that's correct."

"What happened?"

"We were running on the surface around midnight. The lookout said he saw something pass close on the starboard side. It looked like the wreckage of a small vessel. They stopped the sub, and swept the area with searchlights. They were lucky to spot the wreckage, since there was not much of it still above the surface. They found the woman unconscious, lashed to the rigging.

"Has she come around yet?"

"No, sir, not last I heard. Here comes the Captain, now. He'll be able to tell you more about it."

"One of the corpsmen called out, "Captain on deck." and everyone came to attention. The Captain said, "At ease, men. Dr. Conway, I'm surprised to see you here this early."

"I'm an early riser, Captain. I was in the galley and heard about your new passenger."

"I filled him in, sir," the OD said, "except for her current status. I haven't heard anything this morning."

"Neither have I," the captain replied. "Shall we check on her right now, Dr. Conway? She's in sickbay." The corpsmen are keeping close tabs on her."

"Yes. I'm curious to know if her misfortune had to do with the tsunami."

"I'm curious too. We'll find out,"

"If so," Conway continued, "that would mean she's been adrift for over three weeks!"

They found the woman still unconscious, her head on a pillow, her arms, face, and neck, red, swollen, and pealing."

"How is she, corpsman?" the captain asked.

"We have her on glucose and antibiotics, Captain. She stirred some the last few hours, so I think she is sleeping now. Her vitals are ok, surprisingly. I expect her to come out of it."

"Good, keep me advised."

"Yes, sir," the corpsman said, snapping to attention.

When they were beyond earshot, Conway said, "Captain, I don't wish to appear callous or insensitive, but I can't allow the mission to be delayed, nor call attention to it. You understand?"

"I don't think there is any cause for alarm, yet, Dr. Conway. We can attend to her right where she is. If complications develop, and I see no reason why they should, we will deal with it then. Possibly we could hand her off to the destroyer."

CHAPTER EIGHT

Freund had seen Mary every day for over a week and a half, except for the weekend. Roy stopped in to chat with him once, to inquire about her progress, and Freund was very optimistic. "She seems happy," he said. "Her mood is good. The brain scan was negative for brain trauma and pathology, so I think her amnesia is strictly psychological, and I am treating her according."

"So what is your prognosis, Doctor?"

"She could pop out of it at any time. There is no way to tell. Then it could be months, I just cannot say."

Technically, Roy and Mary should have already surrendered their little apartment and moved on, and sought treatment for her elsewhere. They were leaving it up to Freund, who seemed reluctant to let her go. For the last three days, while Mary was with the doctor, Roy had taken runs into town on the shuttle bus. He bought luggage, clothes and little gifts for her. He thought it remarkable how well he felt, how chipper, and energetic he had become.

The matter puzzled him; he gave it a lot of thought. The first thing that came to mind was that he had not refilled his prescriptions, and had therefore been off his medication for weeks, which only confirmed what he had long believed, i.e., that he didn't need that damn medicine. Probably never did. In addition, he had come into a satisfying sum of money, by way of the loot that he took from the looters/rapists that he had killed. That surely was a positive contributor to his mood. Then, the mere fact that he had killed the three sons-of-bitches instead of them killing him and Mary was a real plus in itself in uplifting his spirits. Then there was the epiphany he experienced there on the observation deck of the Empire State Building, when he realized that he really wanted to live, rather than to die. Lastly, Roy had grown right fond of Mary. In fact, when she was not with him, he missed her, he actually longed for her. In light of that, Roy made a big decision, a decision to buy a car. He had been looking at them, and he found a two-year-old Buick that he liked very much. He put a sum down on it, and was in process of obtaining a driver's license. He had not driven in nearly ten years. He was studying the material they gave him for his written and his driving tests. Then the next time Mary brought up the idea of going south with him, he would say, "Hey, Babe, get in the car and let's go!"

⊷⊱ ⊰⊶

The Captain made an announcement over the intercom, informing the crew of the mission. He described the two guests on board the submarine as government scientists looking into the effects of the tsunami. They were taking pictures of the ocean floor and making measurements of the gravitational field. He said they were conducting the tests in secret so as not to alarm anyone. The crew hardly commented. They didn't care. They were accustomed to military secrecy.

In the meantime, as they steamed along, Conway was considering what the captain had said about transferring the woman to the destroyer. He was coming down against that idea, since it might jeopardize the secrecy of the mission, and additionally, he wanted to talk to her about her experience once she recovered well enough. That would not likely be possible for another day or two. To confirm his assessment, he personally inquired of her at sickbay.

"She's coming along well, sir." The corpsman said. "She responded to the intravenous feeding and the antibiotics, and took some liquid food this morning."

"Has she spoken yet?"

"Well, sort of, she mumbled the name 'Carlos' several times. Someone from the Yacht, I suppose?"

"So you still don't know who she is, or where she is from?"

"That's correct, sir, although I was told they got the name of the boat she was on when they brought her aboard. They will check the marine registry."

"Do you expect she's well enough so that I could talk to her?"

"I'll see if she's awake."

The corpsman moved back to a screened off portion of the bay. He returned. She's awake, sir; you can go on back."

"Thank you."

Conway was thinking that if he kept her on board—it could be as long as two weeks—she would have to agree to it. He was no expert on international maritime law and treaties, and so forth, but he knew she had certain rights. However, Conway had no time to sort through all of that now.

"Corpsman, do you see any reason why it would be detrimental to her recovery to remain on board the sub so that we don't have to turn back to port?"

"Not health-wise, sir. We can take care of her here."

"That's good, thank you, very much." He walked back to her bed and pulled back the curtain and stuck his face inside, and said, "Good morning, miss, how are you today?"

"Better," she moaned hoarsely.

"Is there anything I can get you?"

"Carlos ... is Carlos on board?"

"You are the only passenger."

She was silent.

"My name is Conway. May I ask you your name?"

"Linda Noriega. I am from Rio de Janeiro. Carlos is my fiancé. We are to marry soon." She groaned with the effort of speaking. She was weak, and still in considerable discomfort.

"Rest now, Miss Noriega. I'll ask about Carlos and if I learn anything I will let you know."

"Thank you."

Conway made the decision that she was in no danger and was better off right where she was.

The rendezvous with the destroyer occurred at the appointed hour. However, the sea was too choppy for the sub to come alongside the destroyer for a direct transfer of the mini-sub to the deck of the Swordfish. The swordfish stood off two hundred meters and waited for better conditions. Finally, at dawn when the situation still had not improved, the minisub was off-loaded into the sea, and it and the swordfish accomplished the coupling submerged, going no deeper than necessary to get below the rough surface to smoother water below. The pilot opened the hatches between the two vessels, transferred to the Swordfish, which then descended to a greater depth to test the seals between them. Then the Swordfish resurfaced so that Cooper could mount his measuring equipment to the Minisub. They threw a camouflage tarp over it while working in case a spy satellite chanced to be overhead. The process consumed a half day.

"So much for my plan to make the transfer under cover of darkness," Conway muttered.

The lookout maintained a constant scan for other vessels, and saw none, however, Conway figured, there were probably several satellites overhead observing the entire process.

Eventually, everything was ready for the Swordfish to proceed to the rubble field. The Captain ran under eight knots so as not to overstress the coupling and risk damaging the seal between the two vessels. It took another five hours to reach the desired position at the northern tip of the rubble field. The plan was to start there, sweep a swath of the field up and back, and repeat the process with a fifty percent overlap on each pass, until the entire field was covered. After giving Conway an indoctrination in the operation of the mini-sub controls, he and the pilot, a Navy Lieutenant named Wilfred Swenson, climbed aboard, and made their first sweep. It was a learning experience to determine how long a run would take, to test the ocean currents through which they must maneuver, and to determine how close they could come to the rocks without excessive danger.

They returned to the Swordfish after four hours, quite exhausted from fighting the currents, and holding their track over the irregular rubble. The following day was a repeat of the first except they stayed out five hours, until one of the two radiation detectors malfunctioned. Once they returned to the Swordfish, a navy diver went out through another hatch to remove the malfunctioning instrument and bring it in for repairs. Captain Wingate provided a secure workroom for Copper to work on the equipment.

The next day, prompted by the malfunctioning equipment, Cooper, once again made the argument that he should make the runs in the mini-sub with the pilot, instead of Conway, because of his familiarity with the equipment. Conway finally agreed, in as much as the President was aware of Cooper's collaboration in the project and had not objected to his participation. For six more days, Cooper went out in the minisub with the pilot and operated the equipment, and Conway reviewed and evaluated the acquired data

Still no news came in concerning Carlos. The crew had encouraged surface vessels to continue searching for him. The woman had given them their position relative to La Palma when the wave struck. Search and rescue vessels determined the currents in that region of the ocean, and searched the probable path of drift of the yacht wreckage from the time of the disaster until the Swordfish rescued the woman. They found nothing. When Conway looked in on the woman briefly during the week, he made no mention of their conclusion, not wishing to dash her hopes. He spoke only of ongoing efforts. He noted that she was up walking around sickbay, first aided by a corpsman, then by the aid of a walker.

She had told the crew about herself and her family, and about Carlos. Carlos Mendoza was twenty-five, she told them, from Lisbon, Portugal, and she, Linda Noriega, was twenty-three, and from Rio De Janeiro. They had sailed from Brazil, destination Lisbon and his parent's hacienda, to marry in the Mendoza family church. Her parents had planned to fly from Rio to Lisbon for the wedding.

Once Conway had this information, along with names and addresses, he transmitted it to Philadelphia, and the State Department notified their families in Brazil and Portugal. Essentially, the message to her family said only that a United States naval vessel had rescued her at sea, that she remained aboard the vessel, that she was well and recovering from exposure to the elements, and that she would contact them soon. To the family of Carlos, the news was, unfortunately, not so pleasant. They reported only that the search for him continued. Conway deliberately did not mention this to her, nor give her the opportunity to communicate directly with family members for reasons of security.

With each passing day, as her body healed and recovered, her natural beauty emerged. She was out of bed more each day and walking unaided for longer periods around sickbay. All the men were curious about her, and wanted to meet her, but they stayed away and allowed her privacy while she healed from her ordeal.

Conway finally had time to sit down with her and have a long conversation. Linda was somewhat shy with him at first, but Conway was open and friendly with her. She sat across form him at a table in the galley, her hands clasped before her on the table, smiling slightly and expectantly. On her face, hands, and forearms, most of the sunburned skin had peeled away, and most of the raw, red appearance had transitioned to an uneven, mottled tan; her hair was shiny with brushing and washing and had resumed somewhat its natural texture. She wore no makeup, since there was none available aboard the submarine. Still, she was striking in the white navy casual attire which some lucky crewmember had donated to her.

"I'm glad to see you doing so well, Miss Noriega. At last, I have a chance to talk with you about your experience. Are you comfortable? Would you like something to drink?"

"No, I am fine, thank you."

"Miss Noriega, I want to thank you for not objecting to remaining on board the Swordfish while we continued our mission.

"To remain on board is a privilege, sir."

"I suppose I should explain to you who I am, and what we are doing here. My name, as I said before, is Conway, Joe Conway. Formally, people call me Doctor Conway, or Mister Conway, but my friends call me Joe. It would honor me if you would call me Joe. I am a civilian representative of the United States Government. My associate and I, Skip Cooper, are here making observations and taking measurements of the ocean floor in connection with the landslide on La Palma Island, which created the tsunami wave which wrecked your yacht. We have not spoken to you about this matter before, we wanted to wait until you were stronger, and I assume that since you were isolated on the wreckage of your yacht all this time, you have no knowledge of what happened to you."

"Yes that's true. I didn't know what caused it."

"Well, it was a huge landslide on the island of La Palma. It was just your bad luck to have been where you were when it occurred. Because of the orientation of the island, the wave moved westward across the Atlantic, and did enormous damage to the

Americas, particularly the United States. It destroyed cities and killed millions."

"Rio?"

"Rio was spared; hardly any impact there."

Her eyes misted. "That's where my parents live."

"Yes, I know. We notified them that you were safe. I won't bore you with the details of our efforts here on the submarine, and shouldn't anyway, since the mission is secret." He smiled. "Besides, I am more interested in hearing from you, since you actually experienced the event."

"There is not much to tell. It happened so fast. There was no warning. It was a beautiful, clear moonlit night; I saw the island as a speck of light before Carlos saw it. I pointed it out to him. We sailed another hour. Suddenly we heard this terrible noise, this awesome roar, like a thousand cannons going off in the distance. We had only moments to abandon ship. We swept up the face of this enormous, mountain-like wave. It was breathtaking, like a wild roller coaster. We were separated from each other and from the yacht in the darkness."

She continued talking, explaining how in the morning light she had seen Carlos, bobbing in the water. She swam to him and saw that he was still alive, but unconscious, his life vest keeping him from drowning, and she saw the wreckage of the yacht, and had managed to tow Carlos to the yacht and get him on board.

Over the course of the next hour, Conway asked more and more specific questions until he knew it all, right down to the moment she awoke on the tilted, partially submerged deck, and found herself alone. Conway knew at the end of the interview that there was little if any chance that Carlos would be returning to her; he also realized that he was very much attracted to her.

"I am sorry, Miss Noriega, I wish there was something I could say to ease you pain. Your Carlos seems to be an excellent man;

someone I would be proud to know. When he is found I hope you will introduce me to him."

She smiled sadly, "Thank you, sir. I will continue to hope."

A moment of silence passed between them, and then she said, "Should he not survive I will return home to Brazil. I cannot go on to Lisbon, to Carlo's parents, not yet, maybe never. I hope they will understand. I will write them and explain. Frankly, I am in no hurry, now, I will wait as long as there is hope. I feel I am living a great tragic adventure, a simple girl from Rio, from Ipanema, aboard a United States of America nuclear submarine!" She smiled, now, a real smile, for the first time in his presence, and for the first time in his life, Conway was in love.

In the days that followed, at free moments between the missions, Conway found some reason, some pretext, to meet with the girl. At first, it was to debrief her, he told himself. Then it was to explore some detail or other of her story of how she and Carlos had survived their time on the wreaked yacht. The girl must have begun to see through his pretexts. If so, she only smiled coyly at him, and went along with his deceptions. She now called him Joe, as he had requested, and he called her Linda. Once, as he took his leave from her, he boldly took her hand and kissed her lightly on the cheek. She did not protest.

When they had all the measurements, readings, pictures and observations they desired, Cooper removed the instruments from the minisub and they both removed all the data modules from the instruments, which they packed in a case so that Conway could carry them with him at all times to maintain their security.

"All we need when we get to Philly," Cooper said, "is a computer with a lot of memory and a good laser printer."

"I have a computer in my suite at the hotel. It was installed as part of my communications and security equipment," Conway responded. "How long do you think it will take to run the data?"

"I'd say four or five hours if everything goes smoothly. If it doesn't go well, then I have no idea how long it might take."

"I'll speak to Willie about a room for you in the hotel, if you like. If there is none available, you can bunk with me and sleep on the couch."

"What about Linda?"

"What about her?"

"You're sweet on her, and I don't blame you, she's a doll. If you aren't interested, I am. I think it only fair that I warn you."

"I consider myself warned. Yes, I want her to come back with us to Philly. You've read my intentions."

"That wasn't hard to do. Have you asked her, yet?"

"No, I've hesitated to ask her. I am afraid she might take it the wrong way. She is devoted to Carlos, and seems unwilling to accept the reality that he is gone. It is a very delicate time for her. On the other hand, I have to be practical. I don't want her talking to anyone about the mission, or the sub, so I hesitate to just cut her loose. I don't know if I could legally hold her if she insisted on being let go."

"You've got it bad, but I know you won't let it cloud your judgment. You better get on it, though, time is running out."

"Yeah, I know, you're right. I will ask her. If she agrees to come, I will request that an ambulance meet us at the airport to take her directly to Bethany Hospital."

The destroyer returned to retrieve the minisub and the pilot for return to Naples, and to transport Conway and his entourage to a friendly nearby port with had an airport that could accommodate their jet, so it could pick them up there and transport them back to America. After some checking and communicating with Philadelphia, they chose Gibraltar.

The crews of the sub and the destroyer spent several hours making the transfers of the mini-sub and the gear, while Conway, Cooper and Linda prepared, and said their goodbyes to Captain Wingate, and the crew. Then they boarded the Destroyer. Before making port at Gibraltar, Conway picked his moment, and said to Linda, "I would like for you to come to America with me. I want you to meet the President, and to tell him your story first hand."

"Is that the only reason you want me to come?"

"We have excellent medical facilities there. They will give you a good going over. We want to make sure that you are okay."

"Is there any other reason you want me to come with you?"

"I think you know the answer to that question."

"You know that I'm in love with Carlos, and will marry him as soon as he is rescued."

"Yes. Nevertheless, I want you to come. I will see that you are well cared for, personally. When we arrive, you will check into one of our excellent medical facilities. Then, when you are fully recovered and rested, I will take you to the White House to meet the President."

"I am happy to go with you, Joe, so long as we understand each other."

"Thank you. You don't know how pleased I am with your decision."

At Gibraltar, a launch transported them and the instruments to the dock, where a van met them for the ride to the airport. When the plane took off, Linda sat beside Conway, still in her sailor's attire. Once airborne, the steward presented her with several colorfully wrapped packages. She was surprised, and her eyes lit up like a child's as she opened them, to find beautiful clothing and accessories.

"We thought you could use these. They came on the jet from America" He and Cooper were very pleased with themselves, grinning like a pair of Cheshire Cats.

"Oh, they are wonderful," she said, misty eyed, "Thank you so much. Where may I try them on?"

The steward took her to the rear of the cabin and closed a curtain, providing privacy, and access to the restrooms. When she returned to her seat a half hour later, her face was done up lightly, and she wore an off-white summer suit, with a pale blue ruffled blouse.

"Wow, what a doll."

"Gorgeous."

"Thank you, gentlemen," she gushed. "They are wonderful." She kissed them both on the cheek. "I think I will survive now."

━┼- -┼━

"I am relieved that my sessions with the doctor are finally over," Mary said to Roy, when she returned from what was intended to be her last session with Dr. Freund. "He says I am fit as a fiddle and my memory could pop back at any time."

"Wonderful, that is good news."

"Yes. I'm eager to leave this place and get on the road with you in that new Buick."

"It was nice of Dr. Freund and his wife to invite us to their house tonight for, I assume, a going-away party, but I still have to pass my driver's test, you know. It might be bad luck to call it a going-away party until I pass the test."

"Then, we won't call it that," Mary said, as she finished dressing in her new blue party dress, and took the matching jacket from the closet.

"You look ravishing," he whispered."

"Thank you, sir, so do you."

Roy glanced at his wristwatch, a new one. "We better get going. Freund will be here in a couple of minutes to pick us up. I told him we would be out front."

Freund arrived, and drove them in his station wagon to his home. Which was a nice Tudor-style, upscale, middle-class house; a

160

woman came running out the door. Roy thought her a surprisingly stunning figure, not what he had expected at all. She was younger than Freund by a good bit.

"Roy, Mary, I would like for you to meet my wife Blanch."

"Welcome to our home," she said, "I feel like I know the both of you already from listening to Leonard speak of you." She hugged both of them, and gave each a kiss on the cheek. "Come on in, we have time to relax and have drinks and get acquainted before dinner."

Blanche showed them into a large pleasantly appointed living room, with couches and chairs and tables and so forth. Across the room, by French doors, which looked out upon a terrace and beyond that a garden, was a grand piano. Mary's eyes swept the room, and then settled on the piano. She walked to it, ran her fingers over its smooth, shiny surface, slowly and appraisingly, then smiled and said to Blanche, "*Sie haben ein schones Klavier!*"

The mouths of the other three people dropped open. They looked from one to the other.

"What did you say, Dear?" Blanche asked.

"I said you have a beautiful piano."

"No, um—

"Wait, Blanche," Dr. Freund admonished his wife. He glanced around at everybody, frowned slightly, and barely perceptively shook his head 'no' to them.

"Mary seems to speak German," Dr. Freund whispered to Roy.

"Yes," Roy answered, unable to conceal his own surprise, which Freund noticed.

"You knew she spoke German, didn't you?"

"Of course," Roy said, haltingly, also confused.

Across the room Mrs. Freund said to Mary, "It is beautiful, isn't it, Mary? Leonard bought it for me on out third wedding university. Do you play, Mary?"

"Oh, no, I—I—

"Go ahead, dear; sit down," Blanch said.

They all watched as Mary sat on the bench seat for a few moments, and then pulled it up toward the piano so that her feet rested comfortably on the pedals. Without touching the keys, she moved her fingers delicately back and forth over the keyboard, her head elevated and thrown back, her eyes closed. Suddenly she began playing, her eyes still closed. The room erupted in glorious music. Her fingers moved nimbly and boldly back and forth across the keyboard with total familiarity and ease. The others stood in shocked silence.

Abruptly, Mary ceased playing, opened her eyes, and stood up, while staring down at the keys, a look of shock and amazement on her face. Suddenly, she clasped her hands to her face, let out a shriek, and crumpling to the floor. They all ran to her.

Roy sat down on the floor beside her, scooped her up, and cradled her head in his arms. Her skin was damp and hot.

"Bring her here to the couch please, Roy," Dr. Freund said.

Roy obliged. Freund checked her pulse and then placed the back of his hand to her forehead. "She's a little feverish," he said.

"Oh, dear, oh dear," Mrs. Freund lamented.

"Get me a cold compress, Blanche," Freund commanded.

Blanch ran to the bathroom and returned with a damp towel which she handed to Freund, who used it to wipe Mary's face and neck, then he folded it and placed it on her forehead. He kept his eyes on Mary. It seemed to Roy, with an expression of fascination. "Your beautiful young wife is a concert pianist, too, Roy?" Freund muttered.

"She plays very well," Roy answered, slowly, quietly.

Mary began to stir, stimulated by the cool cloth.

"I think she's coming around," Blanche said. Mary opened her eyes. "What happened?" She said weakly, her eyes searching from one to the other of the faces standing over her.

"You're with us, Mary," Dr. Freund said, "Blanche, Roy, and me. You were playing the piano for us and you fainted. How do you feel now?"

"Weak. What did you say? …playing the piano…?"

"Take it easy, now, Mary. Somebody get Mary a glass of water. What happened to you; do you know? Do you know why you fainted? Did something frighten you?"

"No—I—I don't feel well."

"Hm, I don't wonder," Freund said. He turned to the others. "There is something causing her distress which I am clearly missing. We should take her to the hospital in Harriman right away."

"No! We are leaving tomorrow, going south to Florida. Isn't that so, Roy?"

"Oh, I wouldn't advise that, now." Freund interrupted, frowning, turning to Roy again. "Mary obviously isn't well enough to travel, quite yet."

Roy's concern was growing, too. "Can't you tell what's wrong with her?"

"I'm afraid not. We need to get her to the hospital."

"Tell me what to do," Roy said. Where is this hospital?"

"I'll take care of it. Give her a few minutes to come around. Sit down and try to relax, Roy."

Roy sat beside Mary on the edge of the couch and held her hand and used the corner of the damp towel to dab her face and neck. Mary recovered rather quickly and looked into his eyes plaintively. "We are going south, aren't we Roy?"

"Shush. Of course we are."

"I want to go to the bath room," she said. Blanche helped her to her feet and led her rather unsteadily to the bathroom.

"Say, Roy, you've been holding out on me, you didn't tell me what an accomplished wife you had. Where did you say she was educated?"

"The University of Illinois."

"Did she major in music? I'm just curious."

"Look, Doctor, maybe we should get going to the hospital."

Freund jumped up from his chair, "Right."

When Mary returned Roy took her hand and patted it gently. "We're taking you to the hospital, Mary, so they can check you over, just to be safe."

"All right, Roy, if you think I should."

The four of them loaded into Freund's station wagon and drove ten minutes to the Hospital in Harriman. Freund led them into the emergency room waiting area. It was wall to wall with people, many of them conversing in Spanish.

"Oh, my God, look at this crowd," Blanche exclaimed.

There was no place to sit. Freund left them standing against the wall, and crossed to the receiving nurse at the counter and spoke to her. He returned and said, "Come along, they're taking us to an examination room."

A nurse appeared and led them to a large room with lots of medical equipment and several beds, each with a ceiling-tracked curtain for privacy. The nurse pulled the curtain most of the way around, and Mary sat on the edge of a bed. Roy sat beside her and put his arm around her. She leaned her head on his shoulder. "Everything is going to be all right," he whispered. "Remember to keep our stories straight."

Mary nodded.

Presently the doctor came and asked questions about Mary's symptoms. Then everyone stepped outside the curtain while he and a nurse examined Mary. He concluded his examination, and said, "I found nothing obvious. We should keep her here overnight for observation and tests." He turned to the nurse. "Get her checked into a private room, nurse. I'll prescribe a sedative for her and schedule lab tests and x-rays for first thing in the morning."

They discussed it with Mary, and she agreed that she should stay the night. The nurse took her to a room, with everyone tagging along. After she settled in, they said good night to her, and departed. On the drive, back to the Freund house, Blanche said, "this is all so exciting."

Roy gave her a stern look.

"Roy, what is this about you and Mary going to Florida?" Freund asked.

"Florida was essentially wiped out by the tsunami, Roy? Don't you know?" Blanche intoned, glancing at him askance.

"I've heard that, but I want to see for myself. It is too absurd a proposition to pass up, don't you agree? —the idea that Florida is wiped out. Don't you think it's absurd that Florida is gone, Blanche?"

"I don't know, absurd is not the word that comes to mind. I tend to think more of the word 'tragic' or 'disastrous.'"

"Well, it's obvious you lack my sensitivity. You have not had the advantage of my years of dealing with absurdities. What do you say, Doctor? Is it absurd or not?"

"Why, uh…certainly Roy. Tragic, unprecedented…and certainly absurd."

Roy felt that he was suddenly talking inappropriately for the situation, but he was powerless to stop. It was the way it was with him. Under stress, he could not go long in the real world without lapsing into a state of ludicrousness, or inanity. Life was too painfully to endure, and too silly, and too absurd. The weeks without medicine … He had thought he was okay now, that he was over it. Yet events were crowding in on him. Pressures were starting to—

"I wish I could go to Florida with you," Freund said wistfully. "I'm due a vacation. I have been working at that receiving center sixteen hours a day since the disaster, and neglecting my regular practice in the process. I left it in the hands of a colleague. I am not full-time military, Roy; I am in the reserves—got my butt called right up. Last thing in the world I expected. Oh, it was exciting the first few weeks, but I am tired of it now."

Roy put forth a mighty effort: "To answer your question," He said, "Mary and I are going to Florida, but not tomorrow. Tomorrow, I am taking the examination for my driver's license. She is confused. I bought a car, but I have not taken delivery yet, because I don't have a driver's license. Mine expired years ago. Living in New York, what does one need with a car?"

"So, when you get there," Blanche asked, leaving Mary out of it for the moment, "then what? There's nothing there but sand and rubble."

"I guess we'll go to a high place, where we can see the sweep and scope of the devastation."

"There are no high places in Florida, Roy," Blanche said.

"Hey, I have a terrific idea," Freund said. "We can all go in our motor home."

"We?" Roy said, startled.

"Yeah; sure; why not? I can get someone to cover for me and we can drive down together, the four of us. What do you think of that? You could help drive the motor home when you get your license. We could even pull your car if you wanted to. Wouldn't that be fun?"

Roy began to perspire around the collar, and to suspect that his hosts had been hitting the bottle before he and Mary arrived. "So, you have a motor home, huh?" He said, suddenly interested.

"You bet, and it's a nice one, too. I'm a doctor, remember?"

"And a psychiatrist, at that." Roy added with subtle sarcasm.

Everyone seemed to have forgotten Mary for the moment—her piano playing and her speaking German, and her fainting—what with Freund and Blanche gurgling and babbling with each other about a trip down south to Florida to verify that it was not there anymore. The concept seemed as important to them, now, as the trip itself. They even neglected Roy during this time and communicated energetically with each other, and by the time they got to

166

their house, they had made the decision to drive Roy and Mary to where Florida used to be in their motor home.

"Roy," Doctor Freund said with authority, and it was clear from his tone that he would brook no argument, "you must stay with us tonight. We have a very nice guest room where you will be comfortable, and we can go first thing in the morning to be with Mary during her tests."

"That sound like a good idea," Roy said, "I accept the invitation." He was happy to have company, given his current emerging emotional state.

"It's settled then. By the way, I have another wonderful idea; we will swing by the storage lot in the morning and drive the motor home to the hospital so you can look it over and see how well it handles."

They arrived at the Freund house. "I'm famished," Blanche said. "You guys realize we had no supper? I'll warm up the food."

Roy and Freund got comfortable in the study, Freund downed a martini and poured another, while Roy held an Irish whiskey, from which he took an occasional sip. It had been years since Roy had tasted whiskey. Even during his prior life, he had been only an occasional social drinker, who tended to nurse the same drink all the way through a party, periodically replenishing the ice cubes. When he drank at all, he drank Irish whiskey. He was playing a role now for Mary's sake. He had accepted Freund's invitation because he thought the socializing might be good for her, even though it put considerable strain on him. However, he had not anticipated her sudden distress. Now, he felt silly and vulnerable, sitting there, clean shaver, hair trimmed, dressed in fancy clothing, with a drink in his hand—all the trappings of his previous disastrous existence. My, God, how little it takes to corrupt a man, he thought.

Suddenly his backpack came to mind. A wave of anxiety swept over him. Was it safe? He had scooted it under the bed, hadn't he? What if someone broke in and stole his cache of money and jewels?

167

No, wait! He remembered that he put them in the bank, in a safety deposit box.

Come on Roy fight it. He sipped his drink awkwardly, anxiously, as he listened to Freund chatter. What was wrong with that man? What is he chattering about, anyway? It occurred to Roy that the behavior of his newfound friends was bizarre. Roy was an expert on the bizarre.

He felt himself slipping, slipping. The scene, the ambiance, the environment were becoming surreal. He struggled against it, but felt himself rising from his seat, floating off into the mist. He grasped the arm of the couch and held on, as a whimper escaped his lips. In front of him, within his line of vision, Freund babbled on, now grinning like an idiot, gesticulating, and flailing his arms about. Roy was beginning to become angry. Wait! Was it really happening, or was he imagining it?

There was a time not long ago when he would not have asked himself such a question; he would have assumed it was real, he would not have thought to question, it.

Blanche, who had been in the kitchen warming up the food, came into the room, leaned over Roy, and gave him a slobbering tongue-to-the tonsils kiss. Then she whispered, as he gazed deeply into her cleavage, and saw the dark ring around a nipple, "Are you a swinger, honey?"

Roy really floated up this time, drifted helpless into the fog. His eyeballs flickered and rolled upward into their sockets.

Suddenly a powerful hand jerked Roy up by the nape of the neck, and a booted foot kicked his ass, hard.

"Wake up Roy, wake up, now; we have to get ready to go to the hospital."

Roy stirred. "What? What's going on?" He looked around, confused, unable to focus. "How long have I been here, nurse?" He asked.

"Wake up, Roy, you're dreaming. Blanche, get him some coffee; that will start his engine."

Roy opened his eyes a tiny bit, reluctantly, lest he not like what he would see. Then he smelled the coffee. He looked around, now. He was on the couch. Freund and Blanche were standing over him grinning; Blanche held the cup of steaming coffee out toward him."

"Here you go, Professor. Take a shot of this."

"Oh, my God, what happened to me?"

"You dropped off on the couch last night, Freud said, while Blanch was warming up supper. I had no idea you were so tired. You missed your supper again. We decided to let you sleep. Blanche threw a blanket over you. How are you feeling this morning?"

"Good, very good."

"Well, by the time you have your shave and shower, breakfast will be ready. What would you like?"

"Surprise me, I'm famished—whatever you're having."

After a breakfast of eggs, sausage, toast and grits, and a quick glance through the newspaper, the three of them set out for the RV lot where Freund had his motor home parked. "No use getting to the hospital too early," Freund explained.

They signed in at the gate, and drove back to their RV.

"An awesome looking machine," proclaimed Roy, "big as a Greyhound bus."

"Yes, isn't it?" And comfortable as a hotel suite," the doctor said. He dug a ring of keys from his pocket and unlocked the RV door. "We've had some really good times in the old bus."

"Get some windows open and air this thing out, Blanche. Sit down there Roy, while I do a few chores. Blanche, you keep Roy entertained. Don't let him get bored. Just give him a hug, or sit on his lap or something. He can't get it up, you know, so you'll be safe."

Roy could not believe what he had just heard! Talk about a breach of medical ethics

"Oh?" Blanche exclaimed, "No, I didn't know. Roy, is this true? Poor Mary, no wonder she's lost her memory." Blanche pranced over to where Roy had just sat down on the futon fold-out-to-make-a-bed couch, sat down on his lap, put her arm around his neck, and pulled his head over onto her bosom, recalling for Roy his recent dream. Her skirts rode up significantly, which did not escape Roy's notice, either, as he wondered if this was real or if he was hallucinating again. She ran her fingers through his hair, and gently massaged his neck, scalp, and face. "I was a physical therapist, Roy," she said, "before I met Leonard. Do you like that, Roy? Does it feel good?"

"Yes it does, Blanche. Say, I don't think the good doctor meant it literally when he said for you to sit on my lap," Roy whispered in her ear.

"Oh, yes he did, Roy. Don't you worry about *that*."

Initially, Roy was too shocked and startled to say anything further, or to object; in fact, he quickly realized that he liked what Blanche was doing very much and he did not want her to stop. It had been a long time since he had had such intimate human contact as this (other than his and Mary's sleeping and showering together—but enough about that). His very skin tingled under Blanche's expert touch. Her being the wife of another, added an extra layer of titillation to the experience.

"I've never had better, Blanche, as far as it goes," he whispered, "if you want to know the truth."

Freund boarded the RV and plopped down in the driver's seat. Roy eyed him clandestinely, to see what he would say about Blanche's attention. "Uh, you sure this is all right, Doctor?" he asked.

"Oh, don't mind him," Blanche whispered. Freund started up the diesel engine, seeming not to hear

Roy pulled his face away from the embrace of Blanche's ample, supple breasts, and raised her arm a bit to peer through her armpit, and said. "I'm ready whenever you are, doctor."

Freund pulled out with a lurch.

"Oops! Blanche cried, as she toppled off Roy's lap, and over on her back on the sofa, her legs up in the air. She laughed hysterically, and it seemed like an eternity while Roy studied the contours of her inner thighs. She seemed to be in no big hurry to right herself, either, or maybe it was a warp in time-space. In any event, Roy helped her back to a sitting position beside him, and glanced at her sheepishly as she smiled coyly, as if to say, It's all right, Roy, enjoy. Freund attended to his driving, seemingly unconcerned at his wife's bawdy antics.

Blanche leaned over and whispered in Roy's ear, "On our trip to Florida, we're going to have to do something about that condition of yours."

They parked the RV in the hospital lot and hurried inside and up to the third floor to Mary's room. She was not there. They checked at the nurses' station.

"She's gone for tests," the nurse said, glancing up at the clock… shouldn't be much longer." You can wait in her room, if you like."

There were not enough chairs in Mary's room, so Freund and Blanche sat on the bed and Roy took a molded plastic chair.

Presently Mary returned with a nurse. "The Doctor said to tell you that the testing turned up no physical problem, and that her memory problem is most likely psychological. As to her fainting, she should get plenty of rest and sleep, and avoid stress. She could come out of her amnesia on her own at any moment. Dr. Garfield wrote two prescriptions for her. He'll check with you in a few days, Doctor Freund." The nurse handed him the two prescriptions.

"That's it, then? Is she free to go?" asked Roy

"Yes, she is free to go." The nurse seemed bored with it all now.

"Is the doctor here? Can I speak with him?" Roy asked.

"He isn't available now; we have a heavy load because of the disaster. The doctor will mail the lab results to Dr. Freund in a few days."

"It's all right, Roy, don't worry about a thing," Freund chimed in. "I'll take care of all that. Mary, get dressed and let's get out of here."

The men left the room and Blanche helped Mary dress.

They drove Roy and Mary to their apartment on the base in the motor home. Roy called and rescheduled his driving test.

Mary did much better during the following week. Freund resumed counseling her each morning. What he was doing exactly, and whether it was doing Mary any good was a great mystery to Roy. He suspected that maybe Freund was doing it to justify their remaining in the efficiency apartment on the base. He didn't probe Mary about it. If she wanted to comment he left it up to her, and she didn't say much.

In the afternoons, she and Roy shopping at the Post Exchange, walked about the base, or relaxed in the game or TV rooms. The pallor left her face, and each day she grew stronger. Walks in the fresh air and sunshine brought color quickly back to her cheeks and a sparkle to her eyes. And Roy insisted that she have a long nap each afternoon after their walks. Even her raven black hair was growing out nicely. She had no further incidences of fainting, speaking German, or played the piano. She still had amnesia, but with a twist—she still did not remember her previous life, but now, neither did she remember the episode with the piano.

Roy was improving, too. He passed his written and practical driver's license tests, and received his license, and he and Mary went out driving some evening. The days were getting shorter, the evenings were cooler, and they wore jackets, now, whenever they went out. They slept late, had leisurely breakfasts, and while Mary went for her visit with Doctor Freund, Roy hung around the mess hall after breakfast, on the lookout for interesting people to watch and listen to. All the survivors had a story, often tragic, even horrific.

The daily arrivals of survivors had not disappointed Roy. His best trolling spot was still the large round table in the far corner behind the column, where there always seemed to be some sort of spirited discussion. People gravitated to it, no doubt because of its relative isolation and screening from the clatter and noise of the cafeteria line. It was noticeably quieter back there, and people could talk without screaming.

On the next Saturday morning, Roy surprised Mary with a trip to the town of Elkin, fifty some miles away, where according to the yellow pages, there was a sizeable and well-stocked army surplus/sporting goods store. Old habits die hard, and even though Roy now owned a car, he still had got it in his mind that Mary should become acquainted with the techniques of independent living and survival, which had served him so well for so long; that she should eventually be equipped and ready for any contingency. Mary was elated at the idea. They outfitted her with a backpack and basic camping gear, and the best, most expensive walking shoes they could find.

"Shoes are the most important purchase," he said in his most serious and pedantic tone. "Cheap shoes cause blisters."

"Thank you for watching out for me, Roy, you're a dear."

He also bought her a marvelously illustrated survival manual.

When they had finished with their shopping, they had lunch in a nice little nondescript restaurant. They put their packages on the floor beside their table. Roy glanced about the restaurant then leaned over and whispered, "When you have your pack with you, Mary, always ask for a table against the wall, so you can keep an eye on it. They will steal it, even run and grab it and be gone before you know it."

"Yes, Roy," Mary said, "thank you for teaching me."

"Are you having fun?" he asked.

"Oh, yes. I can't wait to try out all my great new gear. Let's go camping tomorrow."

"Suits me."

They spent the following day, Sunday, in a nearby campground, like two kids in a sandbox, assembling and disassembling, learning to do everything, from setting up a pup tent, to starting fires, to cooking.

On Monday morning during Mary's visit to Dr. Freund, Roy made a quick run into town to the bank. When he got back to their usual table in the mess hall, Mary was not there. Immediately filled with foreboding, Roy made a quick turn through the center without finding her, then hurried to their apartment, his heart pounding, his face and neck hot and flushed, and his mouth dry. Everything was in order in the apartment, but she was not there. Her clothes and new camping gear were in the closet and the bureau drawers. "Freund must have kept her late!" He ran all the way to the hospital, burst panting and breathless into Dr. Freund's office, and blurted out, "Where's Mary?"

"Mary? She left here thirty minutes ago. What's wrong?"

"I can't find her," he gasped. "We have to find her."

"Calm down, Roy. Did you check the center?"

"Of course I checked the center. I went all through it."

"I'm sure there is nothing to worry about. She was perfectly fine when she left here. In fact, she asked me if I thought she was well enough for the two of you to go south, and I assured her that I thought she was. She seemed very happy about that."

"Well, where could she have gone?"

"My guess is she's at the Base Exchange...some last minute items...."

"Of course, why didn't I think of that? I will go meet her."

"Keep me advised."

"I will."

Roy ran back to the parking lot for the car, and drove off toward the cluster of low military buildings that served as the Base Exchange, including the laundry and the post office. Mary was not there. In a panic, now, Roy drove all over the base. Then he hurried back to Freund's office. "I didn't find her. I want to drive around town and look for her. Will you help me, Doctor? She may be wandering the street. She may be hurt, out of her mind. She may have had a relapse."

"Calm down, Roy. Let me make a call first; let my people know where I will be. Go outside, sit down, and wait for me."

It was not a large town. They drove up and down every street and alleyway; they checked taxi stands, the bus station, and the railroad station. They parked in the downtown area, and walked through stores, until it was night, and they were exhausted.

"It's time to check with the police, Roy. You see that, don't you? She may be there right now, at the police station."

"She's back at the apartment," Roy said firmly, feverishly. "Of course! She is going to have a good laugh at our concern. Why didn't I realize it? She is getting ready for our departure. I have been telling her we could leave as soon as you released her. She is…Planning to surprise me…that's what she's up to…give it to me good." He laughed nervously, if not hysterically. "That's what it is, Doc. She's there, I tell you. I know it."

They covered the distance back to the base quickly, and Roy ran upstairs with Freund following. Roy flung open the door and rushed in. The apartment was deathly quiet and empty. Roy slumped on the couch.

"Now," Freund said, "we must go to the police."

"No!" Roy shouted angrily."

"Why don't you want to go to the police, Roy? This is their business. This is what they do. What are you afraid of?"

"I'm afraid of nothing." Roy snapped at him angrily, and just as quickly, choked up, and tears filled his eyes.

"Why don't you want to go to the police, Roy?"

Roy raised his face from his hands, but faltered as he attempted to speak.

"She isn't your wife, is she?" Freund said.

Roy shook his head.

"I suspected as much—your different stories, the look on your face the night she spoke German and played the piano like a pro. You want to tell me what's going on?"

"I found her in the muck in Manhattan nearly dead days after the tsunami. She was naked and covered with filth. God only knows what she had endured. I cleaned her up, and I cared for her, brought her back far enough so that we could make a run for it, so that we could avoid the gangs of pillagers and murderers and get out of New York City."

"I see."

"On top of everything else, she had amnesia; that part is true. She does not remember a thing prior to the day I found her. She made me promise not to leave her until she could remember who she was. I agreed, I swore I wouldn't leave her, until...and I figured it would be simpler if we were man and wife until we got clear."

"Well, you may have been right about that, up to now, anyway."

"What do you mean?"

"First things first, we need to go right now and see if she is at the police station. If she is, if they picked her up wandering the streets, I can get her released to me as her doctor. Since you are unrelated to her by blood or marriage, you have no legal standing. What would you tell them? You have no documentation. I will bet you don't even have a photograph of her, do you? You don't even know her name?"

"Her name is Mary—Mary Hofstadter. We decided ..."

"Look, I'll go, and you stay here. You are in no condition. If she is there, I will tell them I am her doctor and that she wandered away from her room here at the base. Just cross your fingers and pray that she is there."

"I'm not going to stay here. I'll stay in the car while you go inside the station."

Freund drove to the police station. Roy was flushed and nervous, his heart pounding. He waited in the car while Freund went inside. He felt like he was about to float off into the fog, but he resisted furiously. "No more!" he screamed, "No more!" Freund returned with the bad news: Mary was not there.

"They will keep an eye out for her," Freund said, but he was not convincing. We still have some places to check, the charities in town, and the churches, but we have to wait until tomorrow. We'll find her, Roy; try not to worry."

A sad resignation gripped Roy. "What happens to her if someone else finds her, if she can't tell them anything?"

"A hospital until her memory is restored, I suspect."

"But, if it isn't restored?"

"Well—

"That's what she was afraid of—being locked away. I promised her I would not let that happen to her. She depended on me."

"Ease up, Roy, you'll make yourself sick."

CHAPTER NINE

Roy vacated the room at the base and found a sleeping room downtown over a drug store. He called the base every day, or went there and sat in the mess hall and listened to the talk, like before. His interest had waned considerably, but he needed the distraction now while he waited for Mary's return. New arrivals were still coming in, though in lesser numbers, some skeletal, cadaverous, grimy, filthy, and some nearly dead. He was not so eager to hear their horror stories anymore.

The weather was turning cooler and he began to take long walks after supper. He showered and shaving daily; he was not going to be a bum anymore; he would make her proud of him. She had saved him, given his life meaning. He bought additional clothing of good quality, and began introduced himself to people he encountered as Doctor Royal Hofstadter, or Professor Royal Hofstadter, and people took him seriously. He did it all for Mary.

Regrets nagged at him: He had not treated her with sufficient respect. He had become accustomed to her, had taken her for granted. He had not realized what a rare, lost creature had fallen into his insensitive hands. His self-recriminations were painful, and with the pain, he sensed that he had made that final step back—he was a human being, once again.

Technically Roy had no business being on base anymore, but with the aid of Dr. Freund, he had obtained special dispensation from the operations people. He continued to eat some of his meals there, paying for them with cash, since he no longer had a meal ticket. He knew that Mary would look for him there first when she returned.

He was sitting forlornly at the round table, when a scraggly bunch of new arrivals came over with their food and sat down. One said to another, as if in continuation of a conversation. "Did you see the television last night?"

"You mean the fighting on the Mexican border?"

"No, about the tsunami, they're saying the Arabs caused it."

"Caused it how?"

"They're saying they blew up that island. Did anyone see that program on television?"

"Oh, that. Yeah, I saw it. That is the stupidest thing I ever heard of in my life. Only a fool would believe something like that."

"I believe it. I believe them A-rabs is behind the whole thing, and I hope you ain't calling me no fool?"

"My statement stands."

Roy's attention perked up, as the two men glared at each for some seconds, neither of them saying anything else.

An older man spoke: "Why so sensitive, friend?" I'm sure he wasn't directing his comment at you, personally, were you, sir?"

"Well, not him personally, I don't know him. However—

"See there, fellow? He wasn't directing his comment at you personally."

"People ought to think before they open their yaps, that's all I'm saying."

The old man continued: "Don't we have enough troubles?" We should be on our knees in a prayer of thanksgiving to Almighty

God for sparing us from this terrible tribulation, rather than look-ing to blame someone for it. Why can't we just live in peace with one another? Do we have to blame some other race or creed for every act of God, for every *force majeure?*"

"But, do you really believe it's true, that the Arabs did that?" the lone woman in the group asked.

"It must be true, or it wouldn't a' been on the news."

A ripple of laughter circled the table, at the absurdity of that observation.

"It's not in our nature to get along," said a man in a soiled gray suit. "All life forms have always competed for food, shelter, sex, power. The winner gets the prize, and the loser gets the shaft."

"Are you a schoolteacher, mister?

The man continued, disregarding the questioner. "In order to win, people will do anything: lie, cheat, steal, kill."

The woman spoke up again "I heard there is a man who rode the big wave all the way across the Atlantic Ocean on a surf board."

"Don't be silly; that's impossible."

"I don't think it's impossible. Moreover, I am not being silly, I heard some people talking about it. I think it's heroic, ranks up there with the Lindbergh flight."

"You can't be serious. How is this fellow supposed to have done this feat anyway? You say he rode a surfboard?"

"A surfboard is what I heard. I want to meet this man. I want to see him. I need a hero."

"I actually think she's serious."

"I am serious."

"How can you think about silly thing like that, when our coun-try is in trouble, when there are people who hate us so much that they are blowing up islands in order to kill us. They are streaming across our borders everywhere, engaged in acts of terrorism and sabotage."

"Listen to him. You don't know any of that is true. That's a conspiracy theory."

"No, I tell you, it's true. Government agents have started lifting suspects off the streets; they're using torture to get information out of them."

"Torture is against the law."

"Don't be naïve; it's only against the law in wartime; and it's the Geneva Convention it's against, not the law."

"The Geneva convention *is* the law."

"I never understood that Geneva Convention thing. What does that mean?"

"Will you shut up with your stupid questions? "They're torturing these guys, see, the towel-heads especially, and the kinky-haired blacks—sure would like to see that."

"What is it they're trying to find out from them?"

"They want to find out who blowed up that island and caused that sunamy."

"What if these people they are torturing don't know anything about it?"

"Well, they'd best confess, anyhow, if they know what's good for them, if they want to get out of there alive."

"You mean make a false confession?"

"That's exactly what I mean; happens all the time. Innocent people even confess to murder, and some get executed. Didn't you know that?"

"Me? No. I never heard of that happening. Why would anybody do something that stupid?"

"I could try to explain it to you … but just take my word for it."

"No, come on man, you said it, now I want to know how you know it. Either prove it or take it back."

"Tomorrow, I'll prove it to you, then."

"How you intend to do that?"

"You'll see. Meet me here for breakfast at eight o'clock and I'll show you something that will prove it to you."

"I don't want to wait. Just tell us how you gonna prove it."

"Okay. I have a newspaper story, a clipping, a long one, tells about a case of false confession. A year and a half after a man confessed to the murder of two campers in the desert outside of Phoenix he was on death row awaiting execution. Then he was released from prison, a free man, because they caught the real killer."

"Why did he confess, then, if he didn't do it?"

"Because when the police got through with him, he believed he was guilty. He was a man in the fog."

Roy perked up. He understood that. He could identify with that.

After a few quiet moments, someone said, "About this fighting at the border, it's a queer thing."

"What is?"

"That a bunch of drug smugglers could stand off the U. S. Army this long."

"How long has it been?"

"Four weeks now, at least."

"I haven't paid much attention to it."

"Has it been on the news a lot? I only saw it that one time."

"They are carrying it right regular, now; seen a mention on the evening news yesterday. You know how it is, though, twenty-four seven on the disaster, with hardly anything else on. They hardly even take the time to give even the weather report, these days."

"The major news outlets are playing it down, but the 'fringe crazies' on the Net are coming out with all sorts of conspiracy theories. They say it ain't drug smugglers at all."

"Who do they say it is?"

"They say it's an invasion."

"An invasion? By whom?"

"Some say the Mexicans. Others, they say it's everybody—everybody in the whole fucking world that hates us, come together."

"That's ridiculous."

'Well, I didn't say it, they said it, and that's not all they say."

"This 'they' is the fringe crazies from the internet?"

"They're on the internet, that's true, but I don't know that I would agree they're crazy. They've been right before."

"Ok, now what was it you were going to tell us 'they' were saying?"

"They say there are civil disorders springing up all over the country. The government won't let the TV show it, and the internet is so censored when it comes to this sort of thing that it is useless. Only people that know about it are the locals, and they don't know what's happening at other places, see, because they're isolated from each other."

"That's the most ridiculous thing I've ever heard. What about travelers? What about telephones? You don't really think you could keep something like that from the general public do you?"

"Don't get mad at me, I didn't say it, they said it." They control everything, don't they? That's what I hear."

A quiet man spoke up for the first time. "Your illiterate friend is quite right in a twisted and distorted sort of way. Things are happening out there and the press is not reporting it. What else is new? They do that all the time. There is big trouble out there, friends, big trouble. To my way of thinking, America is finished, just another experiment in government that went awry, that did not work out. The American government is hopelessly corrupt as are too many of your private institutions. Frankly, it will be a great pleasure for me to see it go, and a source of satisfaction to me to have had a small part in it."

"Who are you?"

"An old man who's seen quite a lot, thank you."

"Well, old man, what 'small part' have you played in bringing about the demise of 'corrupt America?'"

Among other things, I am a historian, a book-writing historian. We book-writing historians make it difficult for people to conceal their sins on a permanent basis."

"What kind of accent is that you got there mister? You're not from here are you?"

"A little bit of everything in my accent, actually; English originally, influenced by the Scottish, Irish, and American versions of the same tongue, and with a little spice added from faraway lands. Spent quite a few years here in America, in fact; picked up a few idioms and inflections here. But I was born in London."

"Well, Mr. Historian, it would be a mistake to count us Americans out too soon. We are an energetic and resilient people, who have shown time after time an amazing capacity to learn, to adapt and to prevail."

"In olden days, against indigenous aborigines, perhaps, but America has lost its soul and its will. It is Sodom and Gomorrah today. It is irretrievably lost, fit only for God's holy purifying fires."

"That's treason, sir, to speak like that, and while we have troops in harm's way. American boys are dying, right now, in many places around the world, as we sit here enjoying our coffee. They're dying for our freedom and democracy, and for the freedom and democracy of others around the globe, such as your England."

"Freedom and democracy, huh? How long has *this* war been going on, now? About thirty years, isn't it."

"The fight for freedom and democracy is never ending. And while it continues, we got to support the troops!"

"Of course," grunted the English historian.

"If you don't like America, why don't you get the hell out?"

"Precisely what I intend to do, just as soon as my transportation arrives," the Englishman said, glancing at his watch. "I say, there's my driver now," he nodded toward the doorway." You gents and lady," he tipped a finger to his forehead, "have a good day and a good life," and he was gone.

All at the table glanced up to see a large influx of new arrivals as they entered the dining hall from the reception area. A young soldier led them through the food line.

"I'm surprised to see so many people after so much time. Where have they been? How have they survived?"

Maybe they are moving people from other centers, consolidating or something."

"Could be."

"Notice how most of them are young and middle aged? Hardly any old people at all."

"The old and the slow always die first in disasters," interjected the 'schoolteacher.' "Perhaps that is as it should be, if there is any meaning to the concept of 'should'. Should is a judgment word, like the word, purpose. It implies something. It is like the natural science teacher describing the form or behavior of some living thing. He makes statements like, 'the shape of the bird's bill is for the purpose of cracking seeds.' Or, Maybe, he says, 'the Galapagos iguana, ordinarily a land animal, developed the ability to swim and dive under water so that it could eat the algae on the submerged rocks at the bottom of the bay.' Or, he says, 'The purpose of the prehensile tail is to enable the monkey to use it to hold onto branches.' These sorts of statement are incorrect and misleading, because they imply fore-planning, which implies that the bird actually decided that it wanted someday to crack nuts, so it consciously and deliberately developed this bill to do so; or the monkey said, 'boy, I sure hate it when I fall out of those trees. I think I'll develop me a long tail, a prehensile tail, so that I can wind it around those branches, and it will be just like I have another hand.'"

"Say, mister, what does 'prehensile' mean?"

"None of it happened that way," the teacher said, ignoring the question once again and continuing unperturbed by the little ripples of laughter. There was no purpose there, you see, and there was no pre-planning. Genetic changes and mutations occur all the time, in all living things. Sometimes a change will give some advantage to one individual over another to survive and reproduce, and if there should be a limited food supply, for example, the one with the advantage will survive and reproduce. Sometimes it is by pure, sheer chance that one survives and reproduces and that another dies. This process may occur slowly by small increments over a very long period, or it may happen abruptly. In any event, at the end of the process, the species will be different. Species change will have occurred."

"What are you saying this means?"

"It argues against a plan, or a planner. It argues against volition, against a rational mind at work. It argues in favor of an existentialist view of the universe, and an absence of God, in the religious sense."

"Whew! Heavy duty! All of that comes out of the monkey having a long tail!"

"It's not just a long tail; it's a prehensile tail."

"Well, come on, now, pal. What does all this prove, though?"

"It proves, my dense friend, that in the land of the blind the one-eyed man would be stoned and driven from the village."

Roy's coffee was cold, but he did not want to go to the free coffee pot and warm it up. He pretended to sip his coffee, quietly and inconspicuously and didn't say a word. Nobody noticed that he didn't say a word. If fact, if you had asked them about it later, they would all have said that he had participated in the conversation, so stealthily did Roy go about his "field research," of "seeing what the fools will do next." Listening to these fools was the only thing could take his mind off Mary.

Eight people now occupied the round table. It was the most that Roy had seen at any one time. Only one man was eating, a latecomer. Others lingered, like Roy, seemingly reluctant to leave, as if the community at the round table constituted a source of comfort in the midst of chaos, confusion, and despair.

There was another lull, while the old man who was eating took his last bite of eggs, wiped his mouth on a paper napkin, and looked around at the people at the table. "I was a home builder back in Kansas," he said, pausing a moment to sweep their faces as if to determine the level of interest. "I built a real fine home for seventy-nine, five, and, I mean it when I say it was a nice home, with walnut paneling, nice kitchen, real nice amenities. Then I went to Hawaii. Are any of you familiar with Hawaii? Costs sure were different there. It was because of the Japanese. They would buy anything—drive the prices through the roof. I was a builder there, too. I adjusted to the price structure. I made out fine; had a nice house on a river. I was associated with this real estate woman, see—she has got it made now, worth millions—she sent me out to look at a house for her, to see if she wanted to buy it. It was an old house— shanty, really—and it was for sale, but it sat on leased land, so one had to buy the house and assumed the lease on the land. Well, I went back and told her I didn't think it was worth buying, and she said, 'Hell, Charlie, they only wanted 48 thousand for it.' However, I couldn't see it. Nevertheless, she went ahead and bought it anyway. 'You know what that lease is worth today? Don't ask.'"

"So you made out all right there, though, huh? You adapted to the new price structure and everything?"

"No I didn't. I went broke. It was the Japanese again. They started coming in droves, and, as usual, they were buying everything in sight, and I am doing okay, you know, making a living, putting a few dollars away. Then I put everything I had into building a million-dollar house in the swankiest section of the city, high on a hill with an awesome view of the ocean. I used my own money, my own savings, instead of borrowing all the construction money, to save on the construction interest. That construction interest will eat you up. Each day when I drove to the lot to work on my house, I passed through the Japanese neighborhood down the hill a way. I would see their big shiny Mercedes sitting on their circular drives, in front of their three car garages, and my mouth watered with the expectations of the profits I was going to make on that house.

"One morning the Mercedes were not there, and the next morning they still weren't there, and the next. I asked a man further down the hill, what was going on. He said the goddamn Japanese were gone; just like that. You know what happened, it was during that oil embargo and the resulting energy crisis, and the Japanese government began restricting the amount of money those people could take out of their country, and they just started pulling up and leaving Hawaii, and suddenly the bottom fell out of the demand for expensive houses. My million-dollar house was not worth a million dollars anymore, nowhere near it, and the house was not even finished yet. I would have more in it when I finished it than I could possibly get out of it. I was ruined. I was broke."

Roy closed his notebook, stuck the yellow pencil stub in the metal coil, and placed the notebook it in his shirt pocket. He had had enough for today—and maybe forever. He made his way to his room. A small, dreary room over a drug store in a seedy part of town, which was all he could find. He sat at the rickety dinette table, with the spindly legs; and on one of the two equally rickety chairs, with three different paint color evidenced at the chipped places. The last coat was a dusty blue over green, and a pretty shade of yellow underneath.

Leaning forward, his hands clasped before him on the table, his shoulders hunched, and his expression gloomy, he took up a pencil from the table, and began doodling on a yellow pad, his eyes glazed over, unseeing. He drew squiggly lines parallel to each other, and stars, and figures made by circling dots without lifting the pencil point from the page. He had a pint bottle of whiskey on the table, but he had not opened it. He glanced at it from time to time, but he never made a move toward it. He wrote a sentence on the pad. Seven times, he wrote it: "*Shall I, wasting in despair, die because a woman's fair?*" *And make pale my cheeks with care, cause another's rosy are?*"

"Ah, Mary…"

He dropped his head down on his forearms on the table, and wept. He could remember no more of the poem, or the author. It was just as well; he did not want to try. Mary was gone, and he could do nothing about it. Suddenly he needed to get out of that room. He rose from the table, snatched his windbreaker from the bed, and left the room. He walked dejectedly down the dimly lit hallway and down the stairs, which opened onto the sidewalk beside the drugstore. He glanced up and down the street, as if uncertain what to do. There were few people about. Half way up the block on his side of the street was a pool hall. He went there, peered in through the glass. He went inside, stood for a few moments watching a game of sixty-one, considering playing a game by himself. Instead, he turned and left, walking aimlessly on down the street. It was a commercial neighborhood, with typical dirty streets. He had not paid much attention to it before. Now, he took notice of the oily and grimy pavement with globs of chewing gum flattened paper-thin, and black with dirt, and the gutter littered with crumpled cigarette packs or chewing gum wrappers.

He saw his reflection in the plate glass window of a liquor store, his gaunt, weary, and sad face in the flickering colored lights of the neon beer signs. He went inside, then turned around and left, and hurried back the way he had come, back to his room. The bottle of whiskey still sat on the table; he searched stupidly, incompetently, for a glass, and caught his reflection, once again, this time in the little, cracked decrepit mirror over the sink, which he used for shaving. He stared long and hard at his reflection. He opened the whiskey bottle, poured the contents down the drain. He grabbed up his pack and dumped the contents on the bed. Out tumbled old clothing, his radio, his sterno stove, his first-aid kit, and his notebooks. His eyes fell on the notebooks. He sat on the bed and flipped through each of them. How many hours had he pored over them? How many years had their scribbled contents motivated him, kept him moving? The handwriting varied greatly from book to book and place to place—he had not noticed that before. He had changed over time. Whole sections were unreadable scribbling, mere gibberish. He gathered them up and tossed them in the garbage can. He took his radio from the pile on the bed, and the cashmere scarf, which had held his pirate's loot, which he had removed from the bank's safety deposit box the day before, and threw the rest, sleeping bag, the pack itself, and the miscellany, into the garbage can. He emptied the closet, stuffed his clothes and remaining possessions into a plastic garbage bag, threw the room key on the table, and left the room. Out on the street, his two-year green Buick, parked at an expired meter, had a ticket under the wiper blade. He wadded it up and tossed it away, threw the bag in the back seat, and started the engine.

He followed the main drag out of town and headed toward the interstate. Eventually, he would find his way back home, but for now, all he wanted to do was drive.

The lines and creases of his face began to relax as the car picked up speed, as one last fleeting thought assailed him—he would not see where Florida used to be—not this trip.

CHAPTER TEN

Linda's comprehensive examination at Philadelphia's Bethany Hospital confirmed that she had no internal injuries or serious conditions, only rough treatment from the elements and deprivation of food and water, the effects of which were fading rapidly. Still, the doctor thought it wise for her to stay a few days to rest and continue building up her strength and energy under medical supervision. Everybody agreed, and Conway and Cooper left her there and returned to the hotel room to begin their work.

Conway placed a call to Willie Forester. "Hi Willie, calling to let you know I'm back, and that the woman we rescued is at Bethany Hospital for a check-up."

"Wonderful, Dr. Conway. I trust everything went well?"

"Yes. I expect to have my report ready the day after tomorrow if everything goes well. I would like to have an appointment to see the President then."

"That's Wednesday. Let me check his calendar," After a short pause, Willie said, "I can work you in at nine, Dr. Conway, how's that?"

"Fine. Thanks, Willie."

Conway placed a call to Admiral Stanfield at the NSA as a matter of courtesy to let him know that he was back from the mission, although he was not at liberty to discuss the particulars of the mission with him. Nor did Admiral Stanfield inquire about it. He also called his secretary, Jasmine, to let her know he was back in town because she worried about him so much when he was on foreign assignments.

Early the next morning after breakfast in the hotel dining room, he and Cooper cranked up the computer, loaded the first program, and settled in for a long session of data processing. They had measurements from the radiation detectors, magnetometers, gravimeters, and photographs from the digital cameras to process. Each type of data had its own program and produced its own finished product in the form of tables, charts, or diagrams, which they would print out in their individual forms and append to a written report, along with selected photographs. The most informative printout would be a map of the entire debris field showing contour lines of equal radiation readings, much like a weather map depicts contour lines of equal barometric pressure. Anomalies would leap right out. Photographs of the area of an anomaly might then show wreckage of machinery. They worked all day, except for a lunch break with food sent up, and by early evening Conway combined the generated graphs and data sheets with his finalized written report and the job was complete.

"We are in agreement then, Skip, that there is absolutely no evidence of human causation."

"Yes, that's correct."

"Well, I certainly am relieved, as I'm sure the President will be, also. I could not have done it without you, Skip. He slumped in his chair, and allowed the stress of days to drain from his face. He sat for several moments, and then leaped to his feet again and walked around the room, stretching his arm and back.

"A job well done," Cooper said.

Conway smiled broadly. "How about a cool one; I'll call room service."

"Sound great. Might as well order dinner too while you're at it, I'm too tired to go out."

Conway called room service, and they sat down to wait. Cooper pushed the button on the TV remote and the TV leaped to life. While they were on their mission, Conway and Cooper were too busy to pay much attention to the news of the day. They heard bits and snippets, and some of what they heard was puzzling, for example, border clashes with drug dealers. However, they also noticed a marked increase in the rhetoric for war. Of course, talk of war in itself was nothing new, not in the age of 'terror;' there was always talk of war. In fact, the United States had been at war, at some level of intensity, somewhere with someone, for the last forty years. It had become part of the fabric of society, hardly noticed, except for the reports of victory here or there around the globe. However, there was something new and frightening in the current rhetoric. Phrases like, "...deal with them once and for all," or, "the only good Islamist is a dead Islamist."

Speculation that the Islamist had somehow caused the tsunami had begun to filter out into the mainstream while they were away on their mission, though it had not yet gained traction with the public. Conway had seen it mentioned publicly for the first time on a television newscast on the jet coming home. Things change fast in the modern age. He also saw a few reports of civil disorders in several cities, primarily, but not exclusively, in the west, such as Phoenix, San Diego, Los Angeles, and Denver. Now, as Conway and Cooper relaxed before the TV, waiting for their beer and supper, they noticed that the rhetoric in the coverage given by media to border conflicts and civil disturbances had intensified, and concern was evident in the voices and manners of the talking heads.

"Very disturbing, Skip, what do you make of it all?"

"It's part of some master plan, Joe, not for us to know—out of our pay grade."

"It's getting worse, Skip. Our enemies are taking advantage of the confusion and chaos in this country."

"It looks that way, doesn't it? It depresses me. Turn it off, please; I don't want to think about it right now."

Conway shrugged, pointed the remote toward the set to comply with Cooper's request, when the scene abruptly changed to a newsroom with a stern-faced man sitting at a desk. Conway paused, his arm still elevated, the remote still pointed threateningly at the screen. He knew bad news was on the way. It had become all too common.

"We interrupt this program to bring you a Special News Bulletin: Moments ago, a Central Airlines Jet with two-hundred and thirty-seven people aboard exploded in mid-air as it departed Chicago's O'Hara International Airport. We take you now to the scene with Jim Fishbind of station WJAD, Chicago. Can you hear me, Jim?"

The scene switches to a vantage point on the roof of a tall building. A man stands in shirtsleeves, holding a mike staring into the camera, while behind him a plume of smoke wafts skyward. The man says nothing; he raises his left hand to his earpiece, and his eyes dart to some unseen person behind the camera. The sound comes on.

"Yes, Dan, I can hear you, now. Behind me, you can see what remains of flight 408, which departing Chicago, bound for Los Angeles. Moments after takeoff, the aircraft erupted into a ball of fire. Emergency personnel are continuing to converge on the scene, and the first word is that there are no survivors. Burning wreckage rained down over a relatively small area, causing several house fires, since the aircraft had not attained much altitude. We have been unable at this early stage to talk to anyone as to the possible cause.

The reporter paused; once more, his hand went to his earpiece. "One moment, Dan," he said, something is coming through. Dan, we have just received an unconfirmed report that a missile brought down the airliner. An eyewitness stated that he saw the missile rise up from the ground and strike the aircraft.

"My God," said Cooper. "What next?"

They continued watching, even after their food and beer came.

Conway woke the following morning to a knocking at the door. On the couch, Cooper slept on. It was the hotel waiter with breakfast and a newspaper, which they had ordered the night before. The waiter set up the table, and by the time he finished, Copper was on his feet, and splashing water in his face. They ate breakfast and read about the airliner. Authorities confirmed a stinger-type missile brought it down. Numerous witnesses had verified the account. They also read of developments in the western cities: a riot in Denver, street fighting in Phoenix. Most disturbing of all, saber rattling by the Neocon crowd. They and the Controlled Media blamed everything on "Islamofascists," and called for what they termed a "decisive response" from the President.

"Something sinister is afoot," Conway said.

"Yes, it does seem suspicious. You had better be careful, boy. You are in a precarious position, my way of thinking."

"Yes, I agree, this is a time to be very cautious."

"Say, Joe, if you don't need me anymore, I think I'll pick up the instruments at the airport, and get back up to my place and check on things. I can take a shuttle flight and be home in no time. What do you say?"

"That's fine with me. My appointment with the President is set for nine tomorrow morning. He has a lot on his plate right now.

After I get cleaned up I'm going to visit Linda, and spend some time with her."

"What about your report? You're not going to leave it lying around in the suite, are you?"

"No, I'll take it and the data modules down to the hotel safe after I clean up, or on the way out. By the way, that reminds me, I have to erase the files on the computer. Don't let me forget that. I'm going to shower while you're still here to keep an eye on everything."

When the shower started up, Cooper ran off a copy of the report and the data files onto a DVD disc, which he placed in his bag.

After Cooper departed, Conway put the report and a backup disc in a manila envelope, erased the files on the computer, took the envelope and the case with discs and the data modules to the lobby and watched as the desk clerk put them in the safe. He noticed that the desk clerk seemed edgy and preoccupied as he carried out the task and presented Conway with a receipt. There was excitement in the lobby, people running in and out noisily, others clustered around a television.

"What's going on?" he asked the clerk.

"Haven't you heard? Just minutes ago, there was an attempt on the Presidents life."

"What?"

"Yes, an explosion in the parking garage as the President was preparing to leave the new White House. I'm surprised you didn't hear the explosion."

"Just minutes ago, you say? I was watching the TV earlier. I must have missed it by only minutes."

The explosion killed several people, they say. The President planned to depart the building at the precise time of the explosion, but he had delayed leaving his office by a few minutes. It's on the TV over there." The clerk pointed across the lobby.

Conway hurried across the lobby and edged his way in among the people crowded around the TV. He caught the tell-end of the report."

"…those killed apparently were in the Presidents entourage. For security reasons, the President has been taken to an undisclosed location."

Conway hurried to the elevators and back to his room, and switched on the TV.

"Two talking heads were discussing the assassination attempt. Head number one said, "The assassins obviously knew the President's schedule, right down to the minute. That makes it an inside job in my book."

Conway dialed Willie Forester's office. The line was busy. He waited, and tried twice more, with the same result. He tried to call Admiral Stanfield, but had no luck there either.

He was concerned about Linda, injured and alone in a strange country, and with such goings-on. He hurried to the hospital and made his way to the sixth floor. He found Linda in the lounge area near the nurses' station amidst a cluster of people, some sitting, some standing, presumably patients and staff, watching a TV set. He heard the excited voice of the announcer. He came up beside Linda, touched her arm and said, "Hi." She turned to him, a look of concern on her face. "Someone just tried to kill your president."

"I know," he said. They turned back to the television, which displayed the outside of the temporary White House. Smoke billowed out of the entrance to the underground parking garage. People and vehicles moved around rapidly. A large red and chrome fire pumper was on the scene, and hoses fed into the garage entrance.

The scene switched to the lobby of the hotel, where people were exiting the elevators and the stairways, moving rapidly, but in an orderly fashion. The lobby appeared to be undamaged, and the announcer shortly confirmed this, by saying that the garage sustained the major portion of the damage. He added that the blast destroyed the President's limousine, killing two of his staff, and injuring three more, but that the president was unharmed and had gone to an undisclosed location for security reasons.

"What does this mean?" she asked.

"It's too early to tell. The investigators are still arriving on the scene. He motioned to her to follow him out of the group and asked, "What did your doctor say?"

"He says I am fine, and ready to leave, but he wants me to stay at least another night. They are feeding me very well. I am within a few pounds of my previous weight. I walk around the hallways; I stretch in my room. Actually, I feel good."

"Then I'll come for you tomorrow. Your room at the hotel is ready. I had a meeting with the President scheduled for nine o'clock tomorrow morning, but now I don't know if it's still on; I couldn't get through the switchboard. I can't tell you exactly when I'll be here for you tomorrow."

"Don't worry. I will be here when you come. Do you need to go now?"

"Yes,"

"Be careful. Oh, I should tell you that I talked to Mother and Father on the phone last evening. They had difficulty understanding why I'm in a hospital in Philadelphia, USA."

"Were you able to satisfy their concern?"

"I think so. Mother wanted to fly here immediately, but I persuaded her to wait. I said she must allow her fledgling daughter to learn to fly on her own in the real world. Father agreed with me, and that turned the tide."

"Okay."

"Is there any progress in restoring my passport and my other documents? My parents asked me about that. They could assist with that, I'm sure."

"I called the State Department yesterday, and was told they were in contact with Brazilian authorities. We'll check with them again tomorrow once we get you to the hotel."

"Okay."

"Bye."

"Bye."

She called playfully after him, "May I assume there is no connecting door between our rooms?"

"Well, actually…"

"Then, may I assume the key is on my side?"

"Oh, absolutely, the key is definitely on your side."

"Then, I suppose the arrangement will be satisfactory."

Their eyes met and lingered for an instant, and then he said, "I really must go."

Sam Hanson, a reporter covering the White House for the Daily Star, had been a fixture around Washington for many years. Of course, there was no Daily Star anymore, because there was no Washington anymore, so Hanson had followed the federal government to Philadelphia, when he found employment with a local affiliated newspaper owned by the same Jewish family that owned the Star. The tsunami had not destroyed Hanson's home near Washington since it was inland. His wife, Veronica, and their two teenage children, were still there, while Hanson lived temporarily at the Ben Franklin Hotel in Philadelphia, the same as Conway. He was one of the lucky 'civilians' remaining since the feds had practically commandeered this hotel for government personnel.

Hanson was an unassuming man with a well-established paunch around his middle, and a stoop to his shoulders from long years bent over the keyboard. His brown hair was thinning, and always needed trimming, and he wore horn rim trifocals, which he was forever pushing up on his nose. All of this tended to gain him entry into many places, since he was imminently non-threatening in appearance; however, he could be quite aggressive at times when on the scent of a good story. In fact, he had a reputation for being an exceptional investigative reporter, as his frequent feature stories of corruption and chicanery in government attested. Once, another reported asked him the secret of his success as an investigative reporter, and Sam said: "I tend to go where things are likely to happen and keep my eyes and ears open. After a while I can start to smell bits and pieces of a story, sniff um right out, you see. You get to noticing little things, and you file them away, and often times they start interacting, creating swatches of a fabric, then a tapestry."

"What the hell did he just say?" The other reporter asked, once Hanson had walked away.

Hanson was in the lobby of the hospital standing in front of the bank of elevators, waiting for a car. Impatiently, he watched the lights above the elevator door. The elevator nearest him stopped on the sixth floor. He mentally flipped a coin as to whether, once it moved again, it would travel up or travel down. He won the mental toss; it started down. When it arrived on the ground floor and the door slid open, out stepped Doctor Conway of the NSA. Hanson recognized Conway; he had seen him on occasions at the NSA headquarters. He started to speak to him, but it was obvious that Conway did not recognize him, so he said nothing, and entered the elevation just as the door began to shut. He wondered why Conway was at the hospital.

An hour later, Hanson returned to the Ben Franklin Hotel. Instead of going directly to his room he stopped off in the lobby, found himself a comfortable stuffed chair, took up a section of newspaper from the table, while keeping an eye on the comings and goings in the lobby. At that time of day, the lobby was awash with government bigwigs. Soon, Conway walked through the lobby toward the elevators. Hanson might have paid no attention to him in such abundant company, had he not seen him earlier at the hospital. He rose from his chair, and followed Conway across the lobby, where he entered an elevator, and in half a minute, the floor indicator lights above the door showed it stopped on the tenth floor. Hanson had not seen Conway in the hotel before. Possible he had a room there. Hanson sauntered over to the desk clerk, with whom he was acquainted, and asked, "Wasn't that Doctor Conway of the NSA I saw just now crossing the lobby?"

"Yes, he has a suite here."

"A suite? How does he rate a suite?"

"Beats me. The President's office set it up. Funny thing is, they set it up for him about two weeks ago, and he has spent a total of two nights in it."

"You don't say? Been out of town on a secret mission, no doubt."

"No doubt."

Hanson displayed the appropriate facial expression to demonstrate that he was properly impressed with the clerk's knowledge. "Thanks," he said, and walked back toward his comfortable stuffed chair. Why would the Office of the President be handling Conway's lodging? Why would he rate that kind of attention? What kind of mission might it have been?

Instead of resuming his chair, Hanson left the hotel, jumped in his car, and drove back to the hospital. He rode the elevator to the sixth floor, looked around, saw nothing out of the ordinary. He walked up and down the hallways, glancing into rooms where the doors were open, looking for anything out of the ordinary. The door to room 623 was closed, and a woman sat in a chair outside the closed door. Hanson walked on to the nearest nurses' station and asked the nurse, "Why is there a guard posted at room 623."

"They don't want the lady disturbed."

"Who is she?"

"Who are you?'

"I'm Sam Hanson, reporter with The Philadelphia Press."

"Oh, I know you. I've read some of your stories, Mr. Hanson."

"Thanks. I was here visiting, and I happened to see Doctor Conway, and I was wondering why he wanted a guard on the lady's room."

"Doctor Conway? Oh, he's the nice looking young man that was here earlier."

"Yes, that's him. He *is* a fine looking young man, and smart too, I hear."

"I am not supposed to give out that information." The nurse smiled, as she glanced at her room roster, and spoke low and confidentially. "Her name is Linda Noriega. She is a victim of the tsunami, they say. A US naval vessel rescued her. She is a foreign woman, speaks very good English, though. Do you think there's a story here, Mr. Hanson?"

In his room at the hotel, Conway's phone rang, and he answered it. It was the desk clerk. "Hello, Doctor Conway. A newspaper reporter would like to speak with you. It's Sam Hanson with the Philadelphia Press."

"Put him on."

"All right, sir, one moment."

"Hello, Doctor Conway. I don't know if you remember me."

"Yes, I remember you; we met when I was sworn in at the NSA. How are you?"

"Good, sir, I was wondering if you could spare me a few minutes."

"What for?"

"I would like to interview you."

"Interview me? What about?"

"Your recent mission."

Conway hesitated, puzzled. "What mission might that be, Mr. Hanson?"

"The one you just returned from, sir."

"What do you know about my mission?"

"Very little, that's why I'm calling."

"I'm sorry, I have no comment."

"Could I ask you about something else, then?"

"Go ahead."

"Can you tell me about Linda Noriega in room 623 at Bethany Hospital?"

Conway was stunned silent. Finally, he said, "Do you have time to come up to my room, Mr. Hanson? I'm in 1041."

"I'll be there in three minutes."

Conway put down the receiver in a state of confusion. He had told Linda not to discuss his mission with anyone, or about her being picked up by a submarine, and he did not believe she had violated that request. He had assigned the guard to her while in the hospital because of her traumatic ordeal and because she was in a strange country, not because of any perceived threat to her safety. So how did a reporter get on to her and tie the two of them together? Moreover, how did that reporter know about his mission? He answered the rap on the door. "Come in, Mr. Hanson," he said, extending his hand. Hanson took his hand and pumped it a couple of times. "Thanks for seeing me."

"You asked about Miss Noriega, it's really quite simple. She was aboard a small sailing yacht, which the tsunami destroyed. Her companion, the only other person on the yacht with her, is still missing, and presumed dead. The woman was alone on the wreckage of the yacht for several days without food and water, and when found was unconscious and in a bad way. We have simply placed her in a good hospital to recover. All of her identification papers and personal effects were lost, so she is without passport until her government can replace her credentials. I'm working on that through the State Department."

"She is a citizen of another country? What country is that?"

"Brazil. She is a stranger in a strange land. The lady with her is to protect her from the curious, like you, until she is well enough to go on her way."

"May I interview her?"

"I'm afraid not. She wishes to avoid publicity for family reasons. People from other cultures are not the news hounds many of us are. In fact, I suggest to you there is nothing newsworthy about her, and I ask you not to print this story about her, if you can call it a story. There are many victims of the tsunami, many people who lost loved-ones and whose lives are disrupted if not destroyed, and they deserve some consideration."

"Yes, but they aren't under the care and protection of a high level NSA official, currently conducting highly secret operations out of the President's office."

"Well, I see your point. However, no one said I was conducting highly secret missions, or about the President's office."

"Then you're not working out of the President's office?"

"I didn't say that either. I think our interview is over, Mr. Hanson. May I depend upon you not to cause the lady distress by making a story out of nothing?"

"Just another point or two, where did you say this lady was rescued, and what's the name of the ship, and, uh, oh yes, one more thing, how did you come to be involved with her? Were you on that ship?"

"I'm sorry; I've told you all I intend to. You will have to excuse me."

"All right, Doctor Conway. I apologize for disturbing you. I will consider your request not to see a story in this, but I make no promise. Thank you very much, sir, I'll see myself out."

In a moment, the door lock snapped and he was gone.

The following morning a two-column article appeared at the bottom of page two: "*Mystery Lady, Rescued at Sea.*" Hanson had recited the bare facts, and mentioned that the woman was recuperating at a local hospital. Neither her name nor her room number appeared in the article. It was as if Hanson were taunting Conway, threatening him on some level, if he did not come across with more information. Conway called the guard at the hospital and directed her not to allow anyone other than medical personnel speak to Linda until he arrived. When he hung up the phone, he read the newspaper article once again. "This guy is up to something," he mumbled. "What is it?" He lifted the telephone receiver again and dialed the front desk. "I'm expecting a visit from Sam Hanson, the newspaper reporter; when he arrives, please send him right up."

While he was at it, he tried Willie Forester's number again and to his surprise, the call went through.

"Willie, I've been trying to reach you since yesterday. Is my meeting still on with the president? I'm anxious to meet with him as soon as possible."

"Sorry, the president is still incommunicado. I'm sure you understand."

"Well, Yes. However, he did instruct me to report my findings immediately to him, and in light of what I am reading in the newspapers, and watching on television, I would think those findings would be quite relevant and timely. You did tell him I was back and wanted to report to him, didn't you?"

"Of course I did. In fact, he mentioned on the run, that I should ask you to deliver your report to me, and bring everything, data, and backup materials. Then I can get it to him at a slack moment."

That statement brought Conway to a skidding halt. He was speechless, not knowing how to respond to the president's Chief of Staff. What he had just said was contrary to Conway's explicit instructions from the president—diametrically opposite, in fact. Even given the explosion, which was undoubtedly an assassination attempt on the president, Conway could not believe the president would casually make such a radical departure from his adamant expression of the need for confidentiality.

"That isn't what he told me, Willie. He was very explicit and emphatic about it."

"Well, sure, Doctor Conway, but things have changed rather drastically since you talked to the president. Now I'm extraordinarily busy myself as is everybody in the office so I suggest you get over here right away and bring that report and backup material with you."

"Still Conway hesitated, too long, prompting another angry retort from Forester. "Maybe you would prefer if I sent someone there for it. I can have someone there in fifteen minutes."

"No, no, Willie, it's just that ... are you going to be there all day, and can I get through security?"

"I'll be right here all day and I'll leave word downstairs that you're coming."

"And you don't think I could just pop in for a minute with the President?"

"No, Doctor Conway, and that final. Now get off it will you and do your job. These are troubled times."

"Yeah, tell me about it. All right, I will be there at two. See you then."

"Goodbye, Doctor Conway. Thank you for understanding."

Conway rose and paced around the room. Absentmindedly he took a diet drink from the small refrigeration, popped it open, and sipped at it as he continued to pace around the room. The telephone jangled loudly and startled him. He jerked up the receiver. "Hello!" he said, uncharacteristically abrupt. It was the desk; there was a call from Hanson.

"Put him through."

"Good day to you, Doctor Conway," the voice said pleasantly, "you were expecting me?"

"Yes, Sam, I was, actually. I see you ignored my request not to publish that story. So now what do you want?"

"I'm considering a follow-up story. Do you have anything you would like to add to what you told me yesterday?"

"Like what?"

"Oh, like how the lady was rescued by a nuclear submarine."

"I'll meet you in the lounge in twenty minutes. Have you had breakfast?"

"No."

"Then I'll buy your breakfast, and you can explain to me why I shouldn't have you arrested and thrown in jail for violation of the Espionage Act."

"Don't be so naive Doctor Conway, "Hanson said as he worked on a fork-load of sausage and eggs. How do you think I get my information? Sometimes people want me to know things so they tell me. I am going to pin it down for you a little. I got it from someone in the White House and that's all I'll tell you unless you reciprocate and tell me about the submarine and what it has to do with your secret mission and with the woman."

"Everything I told you about her was true. I told you that a United States Naval vessel rescued her. That vessel happened to be a nuclear submarine. It was running on the surface at the time. What is the big deal about that? From our point of view, we do not want the location of our subs known. So is that your big scoop for tomorrow, your big follow-up story? If so, you are wasting your time and mine. There is simply no story. Furthermore, if you reveal any vital information about that sub or its location you could easily violate the law and find yourself in hot water. You should be writing a follow-up story on the assassination attempt, or writing something to cool down the rhetoric for war."

"Look," Hanson said. "I realize you're upset with me, sorry about that. From what I have been able to glean so far, that submarine was the Swordfish. It was on a mission off the coast of La Palma, Canary Islands, and you were on board that submarine. That's all I know right now, but it's reasonable to assume you were engaged in an investigation regarding the slide which caused the tsunami; am I right about that?"

"It's not for publication, but yes. So what? That is classified information. If you publish it, we are both in trouble. As to the woman, she was traveling with her fiancé from her home in Brazil to his home in Portugal. They were to be married soon. When the wave struck, it was night; they saw the lights of La Palma; they heard the noise of the slide. They saw the wave coming toward them in the moonlight. Do you wonder she does not want to talk to the press? Now, that is enough of that. You have something else on your mind so why don't you stop playing games with me and tell me what it is, lay it out for me. You're not really that interested in the woman."

Hanson hesitated, sipping at his drink, stalling. "That's true," he said, finally, "however, I am interested in the submarine and your mission there at La Palma. I would speculate that your mission had something to do with the clamor for war that you alluded to earlier that seems to swirls all around us these days. People are making book as to when we strike and whom we will strike. If I am right about that, your story could be vastly more important than the tragedy of a young bride-to-be. Am I getting warm, Doctor Conway?"

"You must be nuts if you think I'm going to play that game with you."

"All right, forget it. You are right about me, Doctor Conway. I do have something else on my mind. I remember when you first came to the NSA. I was in the room when Admiral Stanfield presented you to the press. I was impressed and so were some of the others there; we discussed you that evening. I have watched you to the extent that's possible and followed your career. I concluded that you are a man of integrity. If I 'm wrong about you, God help me."

"You're beginning to frighten me, Mr. Hanson, out with it now, what's on your mind?"

"Have you talked to the President since you returned from your mission?"

"No. What has that to do with it?"

Hanson glanced around and lowered his voice. "I believe the President has been kidnapped."

"Kidnapped!"

"Shush, hold it down please. Yes, I was there yesterday in the underground garage at the 'White House' when the explosion occurred. The blast destroyed the President's limousine and killed the two men in it, and injured others. The president came down in his secure private elevator seconds later; he had two men with him whom I assume were staff or Secret Service. He seemed completely confused, surprised, startled. As soon as the elevator doors opened some CIA types who were waiting at the elevator were on top of them hustling them into three waiting black SUVs with dark tinted windows. The president was in the second one. They put his men in the third one. They whisked them away out the exit the sirens going—very dramatic. I was in my car across the garage. Moments later an announcement came over the intercom system to the effect that the president had departed to a secure location and that Forester, the Chief of Staff, was in charge of the office until the President returned. In the meantime, the security in and around the building increased very dramatically and immediately. I had just left a press briefing and was heading back to the Ben Franklin Hotel when the explosion occurred and had just gotten in my car. Fortunately, for me I was far enough away from the blast so that I was uninjured although my ears are still ringing. I drove out the garage exit right after the SUVs carrying the president and his aides."

"Sounds to me like a very efficient response to protect the President."

"If the president had been in the limousine he would have been killed. He was a minute or so late and that saved his life. Having failed to kill him, his would-be assassins did the next best thing, they kidnapped him. I don't believe the President knew what was going on," Hanson continued. "He was forcefully separated from his bodyguards and kidnapped. I do not believe he wanted to go, to get in that SUV. I believe they took him against his will. You know something else I believe?"

"I'm afraid to ask."

"I believe there has been a coup and that we are only days if not hours away from World War Three."

Conway felt an icy stab of fear; a cold, clammy hand clutched his heart, and was squeezing. "Why are you telling me this," he said somberly, with an edge to his voice, "instead of someone who might believe you and who could do something about it if they did?"

"Who do you recommend?"

That caught Conway by surprise. He could not answer the question; he could not think of anyone either … other than his boss, Admiral Stanfield. Had it really gotten that bad? He challenged Hanson. "That seems to me to be a startling conclusion to draw from the events as you describe them. What evidence do you have to back it up? You witnessed a few seconds of drama occurring under extraordinary circumstances and you come to this bizarre conclusion. There are simpler explanations."

"I haven't told you everything yet. I followed the SUVs. I stayed far back just keeping them in sight. When they turned onto the expressway they turned off the flashings lights and the sirens and slowed to the normal traffic flow."

Conway was surprise but said nothing.

Hanson continued. "Have you ever played Three Card Monty, Doctor Conway?"

"Three Card Monty?"

"Yes, a playing card variation of the old game of 'find the pea under the walnut shell.'"

"I know what it is. No, I can't say that I have. However, I know how to play it. I can't wait to hear how Three Card Monty plays into your conspiracy theory."

"That's what I did there on the expressway; they moved the walnut shells, and I tried to find the pea."

"Explain."

"The three vehicles began jockeying around. One would take the lead and then another would take the lead, back and forth several times, while moving in and out of traffic and passing other vehicles. Then one of them peels off at the Newberry exit and suddenly I have to make a decision: am I going to follow the one that peeled off or am I going to follow the two remaining on the interstate?"

"What did you do?"

"I followed the two on the interstate. Then at the next off-ramp, the second one peels off. Same question."

"And?"

"I followed the one remaining on the interstate. Another couple of miles and that one also left the interstate. Now I am a little less cautious because I cannot lie back as far as I was before or I will lose the vehicle in the street traffic. I followed it close as I dared to a complex of buildings in the Brookline Industrial Park area off Beaker Street. That third and last SUV drove into a building with a garage type door which immediately closed behind it."

"And you think the president was in that last SUV?"

"Yes."

"How come you're so sure?"

"I've always been good at Three Card Monty."

"What did you do next?"

"I parked by the curb and watched the building for ten minutes. Nothing happened. Nobody left, nobody came."

"What kind of building was it?"

"It was a typical one story medium sized industrial building with glassed front entrance and with a flag pole out in front, a big box with no windows except in the front, but probably has a lot of skylights and a lot of sliding garage type doors all around."

"You know that the government has leased an awful lot of commercial space in the city to house itself. As for the antics of the vehicles on the interstate that sounds like a typical evasive maneuver that security types would employ routinely in such a situation. It doesn't necessarily mean a thing."

"I realize that is a possibility, maybe even a probability and I was conflicted, didn't know what to do, who to tell my suspicions. I stopped my surveillance of the building and returned to the temporary White House. I could not get in the parking garage. Security had it blocked off with yellow sawhorses and blinking lights. I parked on the street and walked to the entrance. Armed guards denied me entrance to the building. I showed them my press credentials. The guard said, sorry and waved me off. I asked the guard where they took the injured men from the explosion and he said he thought they went to Bethany hospital so I drove there. That is where I saw you get off the elevator."

Hanson stopped talking and they just sat there, looked at each other. After a while Conway said, "That's quite a story. From this, you conclude that the United States of America has experienced a coup, the President was kidnapped, and is being held in an industrial building in the Brookline section of the city, and we are only hours away from World War 3. Have I accurately summarized your position?"

"That's it," he said calmly. "Oh, with one addition, I believe your life is in danger."

Another chill went up Conway's spine. "My life is in danger? Why?"

"I'm making some assumptions here, but if you went for something, answers to questions, and you came back from your mission with the wrong answers, answer the warmongers don't want to hear and don't want anyone else to hear, they may try to prevent you from telling it. Timing is all-important in a venture of this sort, as I see it. They have already taken care of the President who opposes their aims and everything is in motion to achieve their *fait accompli',* after which, what you or anyone else has to say will not matter. Until such time, you could possibly delay them, put a monkey wrench in the gears, and maybe even stop them, so they will do whatever they have to do to stop you. Do you remember post 9-11 and the lead up to the Iraq war? Once they got that war going people could talk, argue, and debate all they wanted too. What difference did it make then? It is the same thing now.

"You know too much, Hanson," Conway snapped. "You know where I have been and what I was after. How do you know all this? Do you know that I found nothing to implicate the Muslims? I found no evidence of human causation, at all. As far as I can see right now it was an act of nature—a predicted act, too, I might add, by scientist, years ago. I have told no one this except you right now. Did your source in the White House tell you that too?"

"No I didn't know that, but I'm not surprised. Look, the president has been abducted all right and not by Islamofascists but by the Neocons and they had to improvise on the spot. They are probably confused and disorientated themselves. Initially, they intended to kill him. However, they failed and had to improvise on the spot. They may have decided he is more valuable to them alive than dead. There might still be time to save him."

"This whole thing sounds like a Hollywood movie script to me."

"I know. Why do you suppose I didn't go to someone in the government right away? There is no one I felt I could trust. And I may be wrong about everything, who knows?"

"All right, suppose I believe you, what do you expect me to do about it?" Conway asked.

"Prove me wrong. Go see the President, see if he is alive and well, and at his desk conducting business as usual. If he is not, get the troops out to that warehouse to rescue him.

"I've already tried to see him. Willie Forester wouldn't let me."

"Maybe he is in on the coup," Hanson said. "If there is anyone left in government whom you trust, and who has any power, I suggest you go to him and tell him what is going on, persuade him to get troops and go and rescue the President."

"Let's get out of here," Conway said abruptly.

They walked out into the lobby.

If you're right about this," Conway continued, "they are probably watching me right now. I have a hunch. I want you to come up to my room with me."

"What for?"

"Because I'm willing to bet someone has been in my room while I've been down here in the restaurant with you."

Moments later, Conway stood outside the door to his room and listened. He heard nothing. He placed his ear against the wood. Still nothing. He turned the key in the lock, eased the door open, and peered inside; all was quiet and still.

"Doesn't seem to be anyone here," Hanson said.

Conway moved about slowly and carefully surveyed the room, pulled out the drawers and checked the bathroom. "Someone has been here, though, and it wasn't the maid." They have done a search. It fits with what you have been saying. That means Willie Forester is in on it. He practically demanded that I give him my report earlier when I asked to see the president. He has sent people here to get the report, as he threatened, the bastard. What would those people have done to me if I had been here? Mr. Hanson, as they say in class-b movies, there is not a moment to lose. There is one man I am certain I can trust. I am going to see him now, and

I want you to come with me. If he buys your story, I will give you that interview. No, I will do better than that, I will give you a copy of the report. It is in the hotel safe. We will get it on the way out."

"Who is this man?"

"Admiral Stanfield, my boss at the NSA. First, I want you to drive by the building where they took the president; I want to see it for myself. I am about to bet my life and my career, and maybe yours too. If he buys it, the report is yours. What do you say?"

"Let's go," Hanson said.

They stopped in the lobby and Conway showed the desk clerk his receipt and received the manila envelope, and the data tapes.

⊷ ⊶

"Good God, it's finally happening," Admiral Stanfield said when Hanson finished his story, and Conway had lent his endorsement. Those bastards are planning a complete takeover of the country, and planning to launch a major war at the same time. We must stop them. First thing is to see if the President is back in the White House. He picked up the red phone. "This is Admiral Stanfield. Get me the president. This is a matter of greatest urgency." What? What do you mean, 'not available?" Where is he, Willie? and who is running the damn government? Well, see that you do."

After the admiral vented his spleen for a few moments, he settled back in his fine leather chair and stared fiercely into space. Then he leaned forward, one hand on the arm of his chair, the other hand on the desk, fiddling with a gold desk pen, which he rolled back and forth under his finger. His face was a mask of concentration.

"Gentlemen" he said, "I'm convinced what you're telling me is the truth. These boys are capable of anything. Leave the president to me. I have to confer with some others. Keep totally quiet about this. As to that report, until they see it spread all over the front

215

page of the newspaper, they're going to do everything in their power to find it and destroy it."

"I believe Willie Forester is in on the conspiracy" Conway said, "but I can't figure out how he knew the report was unfavorable to their position. I haven't told another soul, other than Mr. Hanson a few minutes ago, and he hasn't been out of my sight."

No sooner were the words out of his mouth than a light bulb came on in his head. "Skip," he said, "Skip Cooper."

"Who is that?" Hanson asked.

"The only other person in the world who knew the results of the investigation," he said.

"Forget him for now, Joe, you're in danger." Admiral Stanfield said urgently. "Until this is resolved you must trust no one; you understand? No one. You must go into hiding, get out of town all together, and lay low. You have done your share. Do not tell anyone where you are. Call me, in a week or two, from a pay phone. Leave everything else to me. As for you, Mr. Hanson, you are a brave man and a patriot. You get that report in the paper today and if we manage to get out of this alive, and with our nation intact, you will be remembered."

Admiral Stanfield became thoughtful, shook his head in disbelief. "The nation is shaking itself apart right now" he said, "everybody is afraid; villains have come out and shown their true colors. God willing, we will get through it. Better get going, we've all got our work to do."

As he and Hanson walked toward the elevator Conway said, "I have to stop by my office. Would you mind waiting for me in the lobby? I won't be long."

He got off on the fifth floor and Hanson continued down.

Jasmine, his secretary, was at her desk, and looked surprised to see him. It was the first time she had seen him since he left on the submarine mission. He motioned her to follow him into his office and handed her the data tapes and the envelope which contained his typed report, and the DVD disk, which contained the report and all of the back-up data. "Quickly, make copies of these, two for me and one for the Admiral, then file it away in a safe place until I ask for it. Should you not hear from me, and the need arise, give it to someone you trust."

While she copied the reports, he opened a wall safe in his office. Conway had aliases that he used in his clandestine work, each complete with a full sets of credentials. In addition, without the agency's knowledge, he had created another identity, known only to him. He took these documents from the safe, along with a thick envelope filled with hundred dollar bills—his pin money. He spoke quietly with Jasmine, scribbled on her pad, took the two copies and departed the office.

Hanson drove rapidly toward the center of the city. "What are you planning to do now?" He asked Conway.

"Drop me off at my hotel. I have to grab a few things from my room. I should be okay, since I'm not due to meet with Willie Forester until two o'clock." He glanced at his watch as he spoke. They won't make a move on me until they realize I'm not coming. I will rent a car, pick up Linda, get her settled in her room, then make myself scarce.

"They'll check on car rentals if they're really serious about finding you."

"I'll have to risk it."

"No, you don't have to risk it. You can take my car."

"I couldn't do that."

"Yes you could, and there's no time to argue. It's almost one o'clock. Drop me off at the paper. Use the car as long as you need it. Park it somewhere and let me know when you're through with it, and I will have it picked up and returned to me."

They wheeled up in front of the newspaper office. Conway handed him the report. Hanson removed the car keys from his key ring, gathered his personal effects, and got out of the car. "Good luck," he said.

"Thanks. Be seeing you."

Conway drove rapidly through the midday traffic. It was now five minutes until one. He had an hour and five minutes to pick up Linda at the hospital, get her checked into her room at the hotel, then make himself scarce. After that, Forester would know that he was not coming to their 2:00 p.m. meeting. He held his cell phone in front of his eyes as he drove and hit the programmed button for the woman guarding Linda. When she answered, he said, "This is Conway, I'm on my way to pick up Miss Noriega. I am fifteen minutes away. I don't have time to explain. I want you to get Linda ready and have her outside the front entrance in fifteen minutes. Don't bother to check her out of the hospital now. I'll have someone do that later."

Traffic delayed him and he was late. He wheeled in the drive to the Hospital main entrance at 1:25. Linda and the guard were still there waiting. Linda threw her suitcase in the back seat and hopped in, waved goodbye to the guard, and they took off.

"What's going on?" she asked immediately.

"Problems," he said, "for the country, "and possibly for me. I'm taking you to your hotel to get you situated—

"Hey, slow down, I don't understand what you're saying?"

"Oh, I'm sorry." Conway made a conscious effort to relax and slow down his delivery. He started again with his explanation. "None of this is likely to make a lot of sense to you, but in less than an hour, I'm due to meet with Willie Forester, President McGruder's Chief of Staff, to turn over to him my findings from the submarine mission I was on when we rescued you. I am not going to that meeting, and that is likely to make Willie angry. There is just no time to go into it, to explain it all to you. In fact, the less you know the better, because it is possible someone may ask you about me. You know nothing about the issues or me. You can tell the truth about everything with complete impunity."

"But, you're in trouble. Are you going away?"

"We refer to it as 'laying low for a while.' I have money for you, and you should call your parents right away and ask them to come for you. I will give you my contact's name in the State Department. I am sure between my contact and the urging of you parents, you will be on your way home in no time. I 'm sorry things did not work out the way I thought they would. You won't get to meet the president after all. I've asked my secretary, Jasmine Jones to contact you, also, and keep tabs on you as long as you are here, and help you with whatever you may need."

Linda said nothing. Conway sensed that she was not happy with the arrangement. He saw no fear in her eyes, only a confused disappointment. As he approached the hotel entrance, he saw the cars and the SUVs. They were unmistakably government vehicles, complete with men in dark suits and sunglasses. "Oh, damn, they're here already," he said.

Conway took a quick left turn down a side street, and sped away from the hotel as fast as he dared, unsure if anybody had spotted him. "A slight change of plans," he said. "I'll have to get you a cab to take you back to the hotel. Everything else is the same."

"Where will you go?"

He glanced at her face. Her features were distorted with concern, her eyes wide with compassion and caring. "Somewhere on the edge of the city," he said, "to a motel. I don't know after that. I need time to think it through."

"Then I will go with you. It will seem more normal, a married couple; I even have a suitcase."

"But—

"No buts."

Conway was a pushover on that one. He put up only nominal resistance before he gave in to Linda's wishes. They drove to the outskirts of the city, on the southwestern edge, on the Interstate 476 bypass. They stopped at a shopping mall and he bought a few items of clothing and toiletries, and they had a belated lunch at a food mart in the mall.

After they left the mall, they gassed up the car. It was five o'clock by the time they checked into the Wilburn Motel, under Conway's secure alias, and carried their things into the room. Conway went out to the machine for ice, and prepared drinks for them while Linda freshened up. He flipped on the TV to catch the evening news. Linda joined him, and they watched the usual fare of local, state, and national news, then weather, and sports—nothing to distinguish the news of the day from the news of yesterday, or the day before. The pundits debated the war news from the various areas of conflict throughout the world, reports from the tsunami-devastated region, forest fires in the northwest, clashes along the Mexican border.

"The world is a mess, right now," Linda murmured.

"Yes, it is."

At seven, Conway excused himself and stepped outside to a public telephone. By prior arrangement with Jasmine, he dialed a public phone in a mall near her home. She answered immediately, and gave him some startling news. "The agency is in chaos," she said. "I saw none of this personally, but the word is, that a few minutes before quitting time today, six or seven men came to the agency, went directly to the Director's office, pushed past secretaries and aids, and went into his office. Then, shortly thereafter, they left with the Director in tow."

"What! The director has been arrested?"

"That's what everybody believes."

"Has anybody asked about me?"

"No."

"No call from the White House from Willie Forester?"

"No."

"All right. I'll call again tomorrow evening, same time."

"Be very careful out there, boss. Trust no one."

"Good advice."

"Conway walked to the motel office and bought a copy of the Philadelphia News. He saw no two-inch headlines as promised by Hanson. "Is there a later edition of the Philadelphia News?" He asked the clerk.

"No, sir, that's it."

Back in the room, Conway leafed through the entire newspaper, and found not a word about his report. They must not have had time to get it done for the late edition, he thought. That had to be it—unless something went wrong. He considered calling Hanson, but decided that would be too risky. He would wait until the morning edition before he took any action.

He struggled with the notion of telling Linda what was going on, and decided to tell her. It was not fair to her to keep her in the dark.

"I made a call," he said, "and things have taken a turn for the worst. It's dangerous for you to be with me, now. You must go back to the hotel and contact your parents. They will come for you. It's the best thing."

"Tell me what's going on, and I'll decide what's best for me."

"Can't you see I'm doing what's best for you? Why must you be obstinate?"

"Because I … care for you … and I believe you care for me too, even though we haven't spoken of it; even though we have never kissed. And even though I still wait for news of Carlos."

The sudden acknowledgement of her feelings for him flooded his mind with emotion. He took her in his arms and for the first time kissed her. "Yes, and that's why you must go back."

"No, that's why I must stay."

He relented again. They made love that night, with thoughts of terrorism, conflict, and world domination far from their minds.

CHAPTER ELEVEN

Roy turned south out of Harriman, New York, on the New York State Thruway, then later switched over to the Garden State Parkway near Spring Valley. Remembering and experiencing what it was like to be that free was exhilarating to him, and his soul began its ascent from the pits. Zipping along at seventy miles per hour, he opened the windows and let the chill wind buffet him, and wreak havoc with his hair. It was glorious, for a while, but got old quickly. He closed the windows, and drove on for three hours more. Near Trenton, he switched to Interstate 95 to swing through Philadelphia to get a look at the new National Capitol, but could see little in the darkness, but he did manage to get lost a couple of times and had to stop each time and ask directions. Unimpressed with Philadelphia, he set out once again, and soon found himself on I 476, heading south. Unsure where the road was taking him, he stopped at a restaurant to eat and to study a road map. He had a steak dinner, and apple pie, and got in a right comfortable frame of mind, which helped him decided to check into the adjacent motel for the night after he finished his meal.

The restaurant was not crowded. He looked around the room at his fellow travelers: There was a salesman, he figured, eating alone; a tourist family with fidgety children; and an assortment of nondescript others, hard to categorize, including one striking couple sitting apart, talking quietly. He noticed that the man would gesture to emphasize a point, while the woman nodded, her expression serene but serious.

Roy could not peg those two. They did not seem to fit into his "people watcher" categories. They were of the right age to be young married, or lovers perhaps, but they were two focused and intent on each other to be married, and two serious, even polite, to each other to be lovers. Hmm, strange, he thought.

He studied their behavior until they rose from the table, paid their tab, and left the restaurant. He watched them through the window as they walked across the parking lot shared with the motel. They stopped at a car, opened the trunk and removed something, then walked across the lot to the other side and up a flight of stairs and down the balcony to their room.

Roy stayed up late watching an old Bogart movie on television. Old movies were one of the few things he could tolerate on TV for very long. He eventually dropped off to sleep in his chair, with the TV playing. He slept fitfully, never awake enough to get up from his chair and turn off the TV and go to bed.

Around three, he awoke with a jolt. His body ached from his cramped position in the chair, and his mouth tasted like last week's tuna salad. The TV had awakened him with an abrupt increase in volume. The screen displayed a picture of the man from the restaurant, and beside it, an artist's sketch of a woman, unmistakably the beautiful young woman who accompanied the man in the restaurant. Roy listened: "...Doctor Conway failed to appear at a scheduled meeting with the President to present his findings from an inquiry into the cause of the collapse of the Island of La Palma. Doctor Conway is a high official with the National Security

Agency. Security cameras recorded his departing the parking facility of the NSA as a passenger in a light green late model sedan, license number NY 345-HQS.

"The subject matter of Dr. Conway's report is controversial, and the speculation is that there are those who would wish to quell it for political reasons. Fortunately, Philadelphia News has obtained a copy of the report, and has published it in the early morning edition of the newspaper. The startling finding of Doctor Conway in his report is that human intervention caused the landslide, which resulted in the devastating tsunami wave. Islamic terrorists are suspected. The details are not available at this time. The Cabinet has scheduled an emergency session for today to take up the issue."

"Holly molly!" Roy exclaimed.

"In a possibility related matter, a Brazilian national, Senorita Linda Noriega, of Rio de Janeiro, who was hospitalized after rescue at sea from her damaged yacht by a U.S. naval vessel, who is known to have some relationship with Conway, disappeared from her room at Bethany Hospital at approximately the same time that Dr. Conway disappeared.

Roy had read enough. He leaped up from his chair. "This is heavy duty," he said, as he hurriedly dressed and headed to the restaurant for a copy of the morning newspaper. On the way, he walked by their car, and verified that it was the one described on television, right down to the license number. Strange, he thought, very strange. Don't they know people are hunting for them? Something doesn't add up here.

He stopped, whirled around and hurried back to his room, packed his suitcase, put it in the trunk of his Buick, went to the office and checked out, bought a paper, and then he went to the coffee shop and got a table by the window where he could keep an eye on both their room and their car. He was too excited to eat, so he quickly scanned the newspaper. There it was on the front page in big headlines. "Was Tsunami Deliberately Caused?" Below this story was another: "Prominent Government Official Feared Kidnapped." He read both stories hastily. "Jesus!" he said several times. He threw a bill on the table, folded the newspaper under his arm, and hastily departed. As he exited the restaurant, a black and white police car turned into the far end of the parking lot shared by the restaurant and motel. It cruised along slowly behind a row of cars, a spotlight playing on license plates.

Roy ran across the lot and took the stairs two at a time. He raced down the balcony to the room of the "young lovers" and rapped quietly but persistently on the door. No sound came from inside the room for thirty seconds, and then a voice said, "Who is it?"

"A friend. They are on to you. The police are checking license plates right now. You've got about two minutes to get out of there and come with me before they find your car."

Ten seconds of silence, then the window drape beside the door pulled back a few inches. The lock clicks. The chain rattled. A face peered out at him.

"They know the car you are driving; it was on TV and in the paper. I can take you out of here if you hurry. Grab what you can and let's go. Trust me, quickly now!"

It was one of those moments, exceedingly rare, when a decision was required instantly upon inadequate information. If Conway called it wrong, he and Linda might very well forfeit their lives. "All right," he said. The chain rattled, the door swung open, the man stepped inside the room."

Linda was already dressing. Roy Grabbed their suitcase from the stand, tossed it on the bed, and began to throw everything he could see, personal items, papers, anything, into the suitcase. They were out of the room in under a minute.

"My car is parked there, the green Buick."

As they wheeled out of the parking lot onto the street, the black and white police car turned onto the row of cars where Conway parked his car. By the time it would most likely take them to make their way down the line to Conway's car, Roy would be zipping south on I-476. He glanced in the rearview mirror at his two dazed and confused passengers. "Allow me to introduce myself," he said formally, "I am Professor Roy Hofstadter, Doctor of Sociology. Perhaps you've heard of me." He handed the newspaper over the seat to Conway. "You made the headlines this morning, Doctor Conway."

"Suppose I told you, Professor Hofstadter, that I have a nine millimeter Glock pointed at your neck," Conway said calmly, and I asked you to leave the expressway at the next exit and drop us off in a busy, well-lit commercial area, what would you do?"

"The Glock won't be necessary. I will take you wherever you want to go. However, if I were you, I would want to put a few more miles between my woman and me and those cops back there. Then, on the other hand, I might ask you to show me that Glock—whatever that is. I assume it is a handgun—because I do not believe you have one. I helped you pack, remember. I had a good look around. Of course, I've been wrong before."

"Why are you helping us, Professor Hofstadter," Linda asked, to turn the conversation. "We're complete strangers to you."

"Well, my dear Miss Noriega—am I pronouncing that name correctly? I've only seen it in print."

"Yes, that's very good."

"Thank you. To answer your question, I had dinner across the room from the two of you last evening in the motel restaurant, and I sensed something different about you. I am a people watcher, Miss Noriega. I pride myself on my ability to figure people out, put them in their proper pigeonhole. Well, the two of you were a challenge for me. I kept an eye on you and your car until you went inside for the night. I slept poorly last night, went to sleep in a chair, watching the infernal box—I am ashamed to admit it. I awoke abruptly at three a.m. with your pictures on the screen, and

I listened to the story. Then I went to the coffee shop and bought an early morning paper, and there you were again. I have not read the article all the way through yet, but I read enough, and just from what I have read, I have decided that it is a pack of lies. Simply put, I believe nothing my government says, and I believe nothing the media says, so my course of action was clear. Now, where was it you wanted me to drop you off?"

"I think I'd like to put a little more distance between us and those cops back there, Professor, if you don't mind. What do you say, Linda?"

"I'm with *you*."

"Do you have identification, Professor?" Conway asked.

"Certainly," Roy said, would you like to see it?"

"Yes."

"Roy handed his wallet back."

Conway opened it and turned on the dome light. "Hm," he said, "a brand new driver's license, a library card from the University of Illinois, and an Alumni Association card, both expired ten years ago."

"It's a long story," Roy said.

"Okay, no matter, that's good enough for me." Conway said, giving Linda a smiling sidelong glance. He handed the wallet back to Roy and turned off the dome light. "And where are you bound now Professor, back to Illinois?"

"I thought I was for a while yesterday, but, now…no, I don't think I am, now. See, I was in New York City when the tsunami struck, and I…misplaced someone important to me. I am at loose ends now…I don't care where I go. Where do you want to go?"

"New Orleans," Linda said smartly. "I have been there with my parents. We have friends there. They can get us out of the country— to Brazil."

Only then, after she had spoken so definitively, did she turn and gaze into Conway's eyes.

It was another one of those extraordinary moments, the second in the same night, when Conway and Linda made a quick decision on insufficient information.

"Yes, New Orleans," Conway said.

"I can do that," Roy said enthusiastically.

They decided to drive straight through, stopping only for gas and for food. Mid-morning at a restaurant stop Linda placed a call to her parents in Rio. She told them as little as possible about her situation, so as not to alarm them, only that she was in route to New Orleans, accompanied by government agents and that when they arrived there she planned to check in to a hotel near the International Airport. She asked her parents to find out from the Brazilian government how she could travel from there to Rio, since she had no passport or other identification. "I'll call you again when I check into the hotel. I hope you have some good news for me."

Back on the road, Roy had the car radio tuned to a local music station when abruptly the music stopped mid-tune and an announcer's voice intoned: "We interrupt this program for an important news bulletin. We have received reports describing military operations of some kind in the industrial section of the city of Philadelphia, the temporary capital of the United States. Reports are sketchy. News crews are on their way to the area. Witness have reported hearing brief bursts of heavy arms fire, and of seeing military equipment including personnel carriers. There is speculation that this may relate to the attempt on the life of the president yesterday morning. Please stay tuned for further reports."

Upon hearing the news bulletin, the first thing that popped into Conway's head was that Admiral Stanfield had managed to round up enough support for a rescue of the President. All the members of the Administrative Committee, and especially General Bradford were in the President's camp, and Bradford was still in command of the armed forces. He was the person to whom

Stanfield would logically have gone. He could authorize the troops and order the rescue attempt. That is likely what happened, but it would have been difficult for him to do it secretly, without the conspirators learning of it. That could cause serious difficulties. Conway realized that he needed more information. Should he risk calling Admiral Stanfield's office?

"Professor, I would like to propose a change of plans, in light of what is going on in Philly," Conway said. "I would like for us to stop at a nice motel instead of driving straight through. We have been driving since about four o'clock this morning? It is eleven now; that's seven hours. That is enough driving for one day, ever for dangerous fugitives like us. Besides, I need to get near a TV with cable and 24-hour news coverage and a telephone, so I can find out what is going on in Philly. What do you think? Linda?"

"Fine with me,"

"And me," Roy said. "By the way, my name is Roy."

"Then I am Joe and this is Linda."

"Linda asked, "Does that military activity on the news report mean anything to you, Joe?"

"Yes it does."

"Can you talk about it?"

"Yes, as soon as we find a motel with a good restaurant and cable television."

They had started out from Philadelphia on Interstate 95, but north of Baltimore they detoured over to Interstate 81 to avoid congestion and possible road outages in and around Baltimore, which had suffered considerable damage. Now, they were near Knoxville, still on 81, and found a motel to their liking. They rented adjoining rooms. After settling in they had lunch, bought several newspapers in the lobby, then converged in Conway's room. They looked through the newspapers, turned on the TV to a news channel, and listened to the ongoing coverage of the attempted assassination of President McGruder, and to the mysterious military maneuvers reported on earlier. There was much speculation that the two events were related.

The announcer reported that the President had made no public appearance since the assassination attempt, after which, he had gone to a secure location. His continued absence was causing some concern. A check with the White House Press Secretary had elicited the response that extensive investigations were under way to identify and apprehend the conspirators, and that the President did not wish to detract from these investigations, or attempt to draw conclusions until the fact were in. Once the preliminary investigations were concluded the President would hold a press conference.

It was clear that tensions were high in Philly and that people were afraid. Indeed, people all over the country were concerned and afraid.

Joe switched channels, to see if other stations had any different slant on things. There were talking heads and guest who offered a range of opinions as to who or which group was responsible for the attempt on the life of the President.

As Joe switched through the channels, he heard his name spoken. Two men were discussing his report to the President. He and Linda perked up immediately, and Roy said, "Is that you they are talking about, Joe?

"Yes."

The voices continued: "Nobody knows how they got it wrong, exactly opposite Dr. Conway's actual conclusion. The story broke in the newspaper that human intervention was a factor in the collapse of the island. There was an immediate and strong reaction. People all over expressed outrage and demanded action. They assumed it was the Muslim extremist; some called for war. But the very next morning, this station received, and I assume that other stations and new agencies did as well, an official copy of Dr. Conway's report from the NSA, signed by Admiral Stanfield himself, stating that human intervention was not a factor."

"Do you think it was deliberate, someone wanting to stir up things even worse than they already are?" the guest asked.

"I don't know, but it sure looks that way. We called NSA headquarters and asked to speak to Dr. Conway, to invite him to come on the show to clarify the matter, but were told that he was out of town on assignment."

"Well, I'll be damned!" Conway exclaimed excitedly. "The Admiral took care of me! I was very worried about that report."

"So, a little good news then, huh?" Roy said, "That's great. So does this mean that the bad guys are not looking for you anymore?"

"Could be. It's hard to say, the situation is so volatile. I imagine most of the perpetrators are either rounded up by now by the FBI, or are two worried about their own skin to stay mad at me for long."

"But what about the President?" Linda said.

"Yeah, we still don't know if he is alive or dead. At seven this evening I'll call my secretary. We have an arrangement. She will be awaiting my call at a public telephone. Maybe I will find out then what's going on. Admiral Stanfield told me to lay low for a couple of weeks then call him. But I'm chomping at the bit! I feel like I should be back there."

"What could you do if you were there? They might still try to come after you. It might complicate things. Maybe you should obey you superior, and call him in two weeks. I could show you a lot of Rio in two weeks."

"Joe smiled, "Umm, now that's a thought!"

At seven, Conway called his secretary who reported that Admiral Stanfield was okay, and that the people who were thought to be there to arrest him earlier were really there to help him rescue the President. It had been successful. And the President was going to address the nation the following evening. "But everything is still in an uproar," she said, and rumors are flying. So keep it quiet until the President makes his announcement."

"Will do. This is really a relief. Maybe things will work out okay, after all. Stanfield told me to lay low for a couple of weeks, so that is what I'm going to do."

"Do you want me here at this phone at seven tomorrow?"

"No. If I need to speak with you again, I'll call you at work."

Linda called her parents. They had contacted the Brazilian passport office, and they were preparing a letter for her to use temporarily in lieu of a passport They would email it to her parents, who would forward it to her at her hotel when she got there. "We are in Knoxville, Tennessee, now, Mother. We decided to stop for the night."

"I don't understand why you have to go all the way to New Orleans. Why can't you just get a flight from there, or anywhere else, for that matter."

"Maybe we could, now that you have me cleared with the passport people. I'll ask Dr. Conway."

When she finished the call to her parents, she said to Conway, "Why do we have to go to New Orleans, Joe? Mother asked me, and I didn't know what to tell her. She wanted to know why I couldn't catch a plane here."

"Hmm," he said, "That's a good question. Knoxville has an international airport. We could check if they have direct flights to Rio."

I'll do it," Linda said. "If they do, I'll call mother back and have her email the letter to me here when she receives it."

"Sounds like a plan."

Linda spent much of the afternoon on the phone. Finally, she had her letter, she knew the flight schedules to Rio, and now there was only one issue remaining to be resolved: "Well, Joe, as you North Americans like to say, it's time to fish or cut bait, are you coming with me for that two-week vacation or not?"

"I wouldn't miss it for the world."

"Excellent, I'm very happy. Shall we invite Joe to come along too. Quite possible he saved both of our lives. I am sure he would benefit from a two-week vacation on the beaches of Ipanema."

"Great idea I'll ask him." Conway went out in the hallway and rapped on Roy's door. He was watching a ball game on television.

"Roy, I intend to accompany Linda to Rio, see her home safely. She suggested, and I concur wholeheartedly, that you come with us. Park your car in the hotel garage and come with us for a two-week vacation, on me. Otherwise, I won't know how to thank you for the service and friendship you have given us. What do you say?"

"Joe, that sounds like a whole lot of fun, but I'll have to pass. I'm ready to go home now."

CHAPTER TWELVE

E ven in the midst of the chaos and disorder, which lasted for
thirteen months, and in the subsequent two years after things
cooled down, Roy had rebuilt his life. He no longer took harsh
medications, and he no longer drifted off into the fog, nor endured tyrannical demons.

He had only recently returned from a visit to Rio, to see
Conway and Linda—Conway had decided not to return to his
job in Philly—and to celebrate with them the birthday of little
Royal Conway, whom they called Roy. The family lived in a con-
dominium near her parents, overlooking the beautiful beaches of
Ipanema and Copacabana. Conway was a professor of Languages
at the *Universidad Federal do Rio de Janeiro*, which had necessitated
his learning yet another language: Portuguese. He did not mind;
in fact, he enjoyed it immensely.

Roy came frequently to Chicago from his home in Champaign
to further his research and writing by using the abundant research
facilities of the city, and the University of Chicago, and to search
for his daughter. Upon his return to Champaign, as he was taking

steps to rectify wrongs perpetrated against him, and to reclaim his life and his dignity, he had hired a private investigator to search for his ex-wife and daughter. In due time the investigator learned that his ex-wife had remarried, and had taken the girl and relocated with her new husband to Chicago.

Upon learning of their whereabouts, Roy staked out her modest home on the outskirts of the city and called on her when her husband was away in order to avoid embarrassment and possible hostility. She was not glad to see him. She had changed enormously. She had not taken care of herself. She had not stood by him in his trials and tribulations, and even now, was sullen, resentful, and non-communicative. Though he no longer had love for her, he was saddened beyond measure to find her in this condition, and his halfhearted efforts to achieve a friendly reconciliation faltered and failed. "The girl, my Sally, where is she?" He asked her.

"She no longer lives here. She is on her own. I hardly ever see her anymore."

"What is her address?"

"I don't know her address. It changed so much in the beginning, so many men, sleeping around—

"What are you saying?"

"Your daughter is little more than a street walker, a prostitute. You might as well know."

"Roy was stunned. "You must know her address."

"I tell you, I don't. I have an old address, but she moved, or she is staying with someone. I can give you the old one, if that will do you any good, but she will not see you. She hates you for going off and leaving her, for abandoning her."

"But I didn't—

"Yeah, well, I don't want to hear it. That's all in the past."

Roy began searching for her on his own, but got nowhere. He brought the investigator back, who starting at the old address, then went from lead to lead, until eventually, someone pointed her out to him on the street. It was not quick and easy to find her, because she had changed her name, and had no place of her own, but lived with first one person then another. When told of all this, Roy was beside himself with grief, and was almost afraid to find her, to actually confront her, not knowing what the outcome might be. The investigator drove him to her usual spot on the street where she solicited, and stopped the car at the curb. To Roy's surprise, she sauntered over toward the car, scantily dressed, the miniskirt practically nonexistent. As she came near, Roy studied her features, and her walk. He did not recognize his little twelve-year-old daughter, Sally, whom he had not seen in eleven years. But, as she drew nearer and he saw her eyes, they were Sally's eyes! In a moment, she, his daughter, would rest her arms on the car window frame, on the passenger side of the car where he sat, look in at him and say something like, "looking for a good time, mister?"

It was more than he could endure. He turned to the Investigator, and practically screamed at him, go! Go now! The Investigator put his foot down on the accelerator and sped away.

Roy saw her in the rearview mirror, wave her arm in disgust, turn, and walk back from the curb. He had not expected it to go like that. He had only wanted to see her from a distance. He was not ready, yet.

The investigator dropped him off at his hotel. He was, shaken and despondent. The room confined him, so that he wanted to scream, and tear at his hair. His daughter was a street prostitute and he had run from her! No, he had not run from her, but from fear that she would reject him. It was a supremely stupid idea to see her like that for the first time in eleven years, to confront her, to embarrass her. What had he been thinking? She was only twelve when he saw her last. He would probably only have one chance to get it right. He must give it a great deal of thought, because failure to save her, to win he back, was not an option!

He grabbed up the door key and stormed out of the room, down the elevator, to the outside, and walked briskly up the street. The hotel, he had been told earlier, was on the edge of the theatre district, and popular with out-of-town theatergoers. Since it was within walking distance, he headed that way, seeking diversion, something to ease his troubled mind, to shake him out of his melancholy.

When they were first married, he and his wife had enjoyed the theater; it was part of campus life, and academia. That was all in the past. His writing consumed so much of his time now that he had abandoned the notion of resuming his teaching, which would have been difficult, or of recapturing other aspects of his previous life.

The years following the disaster and his departure from New York had been eventful and fulfilling for him in many ways in spite of everything, the nation's civil strife, the lingering economic recession, the loss of national sovereignty. The country seemed little more than a third world nation now, along with Canada and Mexico, comprising the so-called North American Union. So much had changed, and was still changing.

But, he had realized a small fortune from the sale of the jewelry—his booty from New York City, which, added to the cash he came out with, and his disability payments, and the royalties from his books, together, enabled him to live quite well. He had used much of the bounty to hire lawyers. His enemies had paid, and paid dearly. He suffered no pangs of conscience for his unearned windfall from the bad times.

"It is an ill wind...."

Now, only one thing remained—his daughter—he would find a way.

After walking for a long while he found himself in the midst of theaters, with brilliant lights, and colorful posters on the walls and under the theatre marquees. Suddenly he stopped in his tracks. There on a theatre poster was a picture of Mary, smiling down at him. She was dressed in a shimmering white sequined gown, and was standing with her right hand resting upon a grand piano. Roy stared at the poster, unable to believe his eyes. Was it really Mary? Her hair was long now. She looked healthy and fit, but in her eyes was a hint of sadness.

No, there was no mistaking it, it was Mary! The event was a piano recital. "by "the world famous pianist, Maria Regina. Her first American concert tour in over three years," the poster announced.

Roy's pulse quickened. Mary's was a concert pianist, as he and Freund had suspected. He checked the time schedule, noting that the performance was scheduled for nine p.m., less than two hours away. He rushed to the ticket office, now closed, and banged on the window with his fist. At last someone opened it and said, "What is it? What do you want? Can't you see we're closed?"

"A ticket for tonight's performance," he said, unable to conceal his excitement.

The man laughed. "There are no tickets. We've been sold out for weeks."

"Sold out? But I must have a ticket. It is very important. Please! I'll pay extra—whatever you want!"

"Go away." The man slammed the window closed.

Roy continued to bang on the window, talking loudly. A police officer approached. What's going on here? What's the commotion about?"

"Nothing officer; it's just that I must have a ticked to tonight's performance."

"Oh, yeah, what's the urgency?"

"I know her ... from before. This is my Mary!"

"The cop looked at him suspiciously: "So you know her, so what? You better move along and stop causing a commotion."

Roy slinked away, while the cop stared after him.

He walked on up the street, but he stayed close by. There must be some way to get a ticket to the evening performance. He could hang around the theatre and maybe buy a ticket from somebody. He glanced at his watch. There was still an hour and a half to go until show time. He saw a restaurant; he went inside, and sat near the window where he could see the marquis of the theatre, so that he could tell when the people began to arrive. He ordered coffee and a sandwich. Time passed slowly, but finally, it was time to go; people were there in front of the theatre.

Scalpers usually hung around outside theatres to sell tickets at inflated prices. He looking around for them. He approached several people and asked if they had tickets to sell, but no luck.

Abruptly there was a frenzy of activity, and people were congregating on the sidewalk in front of the theatre. Roy hurried into the gathering crowd. "What's going on," he asked a man next to him. Before the man could respond, the crowd surged toward the curb, as a long black limousine pulled up in front. The doors opened; two men and a woman got out, turned and stood deferentially by the door as a beautiful dark haired woman stepped daintily from the rear seat to the sidewalk and was met with cheers and clapping. She smiled, raised her hand cheek-high, and waved to the crowd.

It was Mary!

"Roy surged through the crowd toward her, screaming, "Mary! It's me, Roy!"

She vaguely glanced his way, and then resumed her smiling and waving, as she walked with her entourage toward a side door of the theatre, as fans and spectators parted to allow her passage.

"Mary, it's me, Roy!" He called out again, loudly, and with urgency in his voice. The sheen joy at seeing her had left his face which now showed consternation, as he realized that very shortly she would be beyond his reach, and that he had not gotten her attention. He had to do something. He charged into the crowd, pushed people aside, and rushed up to her, calling, "Mary, Mary," and clutched at her arm.

Startled, she emitted a little shriek of surprise; and cow eyes looked directly into his, but without recognition. Two men grabbed Roy and pulled him away from her, and dragged him, flailing, and shouting

"You don't understand...!"

The two men held Roy against the wall, and frisked him for weapons. Finding nothing the first man said, "What's your problem, mister? Why were you calling Miss Regina, Mary?"

Roy was shaking uncontrollably. "That's Mary, my Mary. I saved her life. I brought her out of New York. She didn't know her name. I named her Mary." He was babbling now, hysterical. "She disappeared. I couldn't find her. I have not known what happened to her all these years. I must see her! Talk to her!"

"I'm afraid that's impossible."

"What? Why? Why is it impossible? She is just there, inside the theatre, just beyond that door, and I am here. She will know me. She will want to see me!"

"Wait here. Karl, keep him here." The first man went inside the theatre. A few minutes later, he returned. "Come with me he said to Roy. They entered the theater. Roy followed the man around behind the stage to a long hallway, to a row of dressing room. They stopped at one and entered. The dark haired woman sat on a stool facing him, behind her was a dressing table with a light-rimmed mirror. As Roy entered the room, she rose, took a step toward him, and looked closely into his face.

"They tell me you say you know me, sir."

"Mary, don't you remember me? It's me, Roy, Roy Hofstadter. Don't you remember me, Mary, New York, the wave, the Empire State Building?"

Mary looked at him long and carefully. "No. I don't know you, sir, I'm sorry. You have me confused with someone else. I am Maria Regina. Now, if you will excuse me, I must prepare for tonight's concert."

"But, Miss Regina...Mary...?"

"Come along, sir," the man said, "I'll show you out."

In despair, Roy relented. "Good-bye...Miss Regina. I'm sorry—

"This way, Mr. Hofstadter," the man said, curtly.

As they walked toward the door, Roy said, "I couldn't get a ticket to the performance tonight, they're sold out—have been for weeks. Could I please stand in the back, in the wings somewhere, and listen to her play? I have heard her play only that once—

"You have heard her play?"

"Yes."

"In person?"

"Yes, only for a few moments, in New York, when we were at the rescue center. I know little about classical music, but someone said it was a concerto by Chopin. It went something like this." He hummed the tune.

A look of surprise and recognition flashed briefly across the man's face. "What rescue center was that?" he asked.

"It was an old military base near Harriman, New York, named Camp Lamar."

"And you say you met Miss Regina at this camp?"

"No, no, I took her there from New York City. I saved her life. I found her nearly dead amongst the muck and mire. I nursed her. They flew us to Camp Lamar by helicopter. She had amnesia. They treated her there, but she disappeared—over three years ago. Now, she doesn't remember me."

"The man stopped short at the end of the stage. "You may stand here and listen to her play, Mr. Hofstadter?" You'll be able to see her at the piano from this angle."

"Thank you, sir, thank you. Are you her manager?"

"I am that and more; I am her brother. My name is John von Broun. Regina is my sister's stage name."

"Von Broun? That's German, isn't it?"

"Why, yes, my family was originally from Germany."

"She spoke German once."

Von Broun gave him another odd look. "I will stand with you for a while," he said, "before the performance starts. Do you mind?"

"Not at all."

"Where are you from, Mr. Hofstadter, and what do you do?"

"I am a retired Professor of Sociology," he said. "I write books, now."

"You say you were in New York City at the time of the tsunami, and that you saved my sister's life? How did this happen, Mr. Hofstadter?"

"I was in the lower part of the Empire State Building, in the stairwell, when the tsunami struck. The building broke in two and the upper section fell away. It was quite terrible. I stayed inside for days to recover from injuries from being tossed about, and to allow the mud time to dry and harden so I could leave, then I ventured outside, and I came across her, barely alive, covered with mud and filth."

"Do you have identification, Mr. Hofstadter?"

Roy sensed that the man was beginning to believe his story. His hands shook as he extracted his wallet, and showed the man his driver's license, his social security card, and, in his excitement, handed him the entire wallet, as he had done that night in the car with Conway.

"You seem to be who you say you are, Mr. Hofstadter. What is it you want with my sister? Do you merely wish her to remember you for old time's sake, or, to thank you for saving her life?"

"No ... I ... I ... love her. I have been in despair since she left me. I searched for her for months. I am in Chicago on personal business. I stumbled upon the theatre by chance...."

Suddenly, the crowd erupted in applause, the curtain opened, and lights lit up the stage. Miss Maria Regina/Von Braun walked out, bowed to the audience, and took her seat at the piano. The orchestra began to play; she joined in."

"We have been so worried about her, Mr. Hofstadter." Von Broun's voice assumed a hushed and somber quality. "She remembers nothing of her ordeal. It eats at her, constantly. A truck driver found her walking along a road in Pennsylvania. All she would say to him was that she must go to Chicago, which was our home and base of operations then, as it is now. Fortunately, he was a kind and honest man. He took her to a police station. I shudder to think … She was the lone survivor. Her entire entourage, her company, perished in the disaster in New York."

Von Braun paused, thoughtful, then said, "Will you excuse me, Mr. Hofstadter, I must leave you now, but please don't go away, I will return shortly."

"Yes, yes, I will wait," Roy, said, trembling with excitement. "Wild horses couldn't drag me away!"

THE END